Also by Harry Harrison from Gollancz:

The Stainless Steel Rat Omnibus

HARRY HARRISON

GOLLANCZ

LONDON

The right of Harry Harrison to be identified as the author of
this work has been asserted by him in accordance with the
Copyright, Designs and Patents Act 1988.

First published in Great Britain in 2011 by Gollancz
An imprint of the Orion Publishing Group
Orion House, 5 Upper St Martin's Lane,
London WC2H 9EA
An Hachette UK Company

A CIP catalogue record for this book is available
from the British Library

ISBN 978 0 575 10102 9 (Cased)
ISBN 978 0 575 10103 6 (Trade Paperback)

1 3 5 7 9 10 8 6 4 2

Printed in Great Britain by
CPI Group (UK) Ltd, Croydon, CR0 4YY

The Orion Publishing Group's policy is to use papers
that are natural, renewable and recyclable products and
made from wood grown in sustainable forests. The logging
and manufacturing processes are expected to conform
to the environmental regulations of the country of origin.

www.orionbooks.co.uk

To Moira and Todd,
whose loving aid and support made
this book possible

IT WAS THAT TIME OF day that should be inviolate, one of the rare moments in life when everything is going perfectly. I leaned back in the armchair and turned on the room-sized stereo—woofers the size of locomotives, tweeters that vibrated the teeth in your head—and J. S. Bach's toccata and fugue saturated the air with beauty.

In my hand was a glass of just-poured three-hundred-year-old treasured bourbon, chilled with million-year-old ice brought from one of the outer planets. How perfect! I smiled benignly and raised the glass to my lips.

Like a throbbing toothache, or a mosquito's distant whine, something penetrated paradise. A tinkle-tinkle that clashed with mighty Bach. I felt a snarl twist my lips as I touched the volume control and the great organ throbbed unhappily into silence. The front doorbell could be clearly heard again.

Tinkle tinkle . . .

I punched an angry thumb at the button and the view-screen came to life. A smiling, sun-darkened face leered out at me; broken teeth—and was that a straw hanging limply from his lips?

"You in there, Jimmy? Can't see nothing . . ."

A wispy white beard, a battered cap, an accent horribly familiar: I felt the hairs stirring on the back of my neck.

"You . . . you . . . !" I gurgled hoarsely.

"Guess you can see me allrighty! I'm your long-lost Cousin Elmo come all the way from Bit O' Heaven."

It was like waking from a nightmare—and discovering the terrible dream had been true. A name I thought I would never hear again. The planet of my birth that I had fled so many years ago. Unwelcome memories flooded my brain while my teeth grated together with a grinding screech.

"Go away . . ." I muttered through the gnashing.

"Yep—a long way to come. Though I can't see you I can tell yore glad to see me." The imbecilic smile, the bobbing stalk of straw.

Glad! Elmo was as welcome as a plague of boils, a poison chalice, a raging tsunami . . . Why hadn't I installed door-mounted guns? . . . I thumbed the volume control viciously, which only amplified his hoarse breathing, the straw-chomping lips. I hit the weapons detector, which flashed green. If only he had been armed, a reason to destroy . . .

"Let me in, Jimmy, I got some great news for you."

There was a sound now along with his voice—a high-pitched squeal I thought I would never hear again. Trancelike I rose, stumbled to the front door, unlocked it . . .

"Why Little Jimmy—you shore growed . . ."

A sirenlike squeal drowned out his words as a small black body shot between my legs, quills rattling, heading straight for the kitchen.

"A porcuswine!" I gurgled.

"Shore is. Name's Pinky. Brought her along to remind you of the good old days!"

I was reminded all right! Dull, depressing, stupid, stifling, claustrophobic—yes indeed, I did have memories of Bit O' Heaven! A loud crashing and even louder squealing came from the kitchen and I staggered in that direction.

Destruction! Pinky had overturned the garbage can and was rooting in it happily as she pushed it crashing around the kitchen. Elmo stumbled by me holding out a leather leash.

"Come on, Pinky, be a good lil' swine!"

Pinky had other ideas. She drove the bin around the kitchen, crashing into the walls, knocking over the table, squealing like a siren with Elmo in hot pursuit. He eventually cornered her, dragged her out by the hind leg, wrassled her to a fall—at full scream—and finally got the leash on her.

Garbage covered the floor, mixed with broken crockery. As I looked down, horrified, I saw that I was still holding my brimming glass. I drained it and my coughing joined the angry squeals.

"Shore nice to see you, Jim. Mighty fine place you got here . . ."

I stumbled from the room—aiming for the bourbon bottle.

Elmo and companion followed me with grunting companionship. I poured myself a drink with shaking hand, so shocked by this encounter that I actually filled a glass for him. He glugged it down and smacked his lips, then held out his empty glass. I sealed the bottle. That single drink probably cost more than he earned in a year from his porcuswinery. I sipped at my own while his bucolic voice washed over me with stunning boredom.

". . . seems there has been a kind of interplanetary secession out our way, futures in porcuswine shares is drying up . . ."

With good reason, I muttered to myself—and drank deep.

". . . then Lil' Abner diGriz, yore forty-eight cousin on yore papa's side, said he saw you on the TV, he did. We was all talking and Abercrombie diGriz, been to a big school, cousin on your mama's side, he looked it up somehow on the computer and said you was in great shape, a millionaire somehow . . ."

Somehow I would like to throttle Abercrombie slowly and painfully to death.

". . . so we all kind of chipped in and rented this old spacer, loaded her with porcuswine and here we are. Broke but happy, you betcha! We knew once we got here that you would take care of yore own kin!"

I drank deep, thought wildly.

"Yes, ahh . . . some merit in what you say. Porcuswine ranching, fine future. On a suitable planet. Not here of course, this planet, Moolaplenty, being a holiday world. I would hazard a guess that farming isn't even allowed here. But a little research, another agrarian planet, write a check . . ."

"Might I interrupt for a moment—and ask just *what* is going on here?"

Innocent words spoken in a tone of voice of a temperature approaching absolute zero.

My darling Angelina stood in the kitchen door, holding out a broken teacup. I visualized the kitchen—*her* kitchen—from her point of view and my blood temperature dropped by ten degrees.

"I can explain, my love . . ."

"You certainly can. You might also introduce me to the person sitting on my couch."

Elmo may have been a rural idiot but he was no fool. He scrambled to his feet, his battered cap twisting in his hands.

"Name's Elmo, ma'am, I'm Jimmy's kin . . ."

"Indeed . . ." A single word, two syllables, yet spoken in a manner to strike terror into the hearts of men. Elmo swayed, almost collapsed, could only gurgle incoherently.

"And I presume that you brought that . . . creature with you?" The broken teacup pointed at Pinky, who was stretched out and burbling gently in her garbage-stuffed sleep.

"That ain't no critter, Miz diGriz—that's Pinky. She's a porcuswine."

My darling's nose wrinkled slightly. I realized that many years had passed since her last encounter with these animals. Elmo babbled on.

"From my home planet, you understand, a cross between wild pigs and porcupines. Bred there to defend the first settlers against the terrible native animals. But the porcuswine done licked them all! Defended the settlers, good to eat, great friends."

"Indeed they are!" I chortled hollowly. "As I recall during our magical engagement on Cliaand, that you were very taken by a piglet porcuswine named Gloriana . . ."

A single icy glance in my direction shut me up with a

snap of my jaw. "That was different. A civilized beast. Unlike this uncouth creature that is responsible for the wholesale destruction of my kitchen."

"Pinky's sorry, ma'am. Just hungry. I bet she would apologize iffen she knew how." He nudged the guilty porker with his toe.

She opened a serene red eye, clambered to her feet and yawned, shook her spines with a rattling rustle. Looked up at Angelina and squealed a tiny squeal.

I waited for the skies to part and a lightning bolt to strike the swinish miscreant dead on the spot.

Angelina discarded the shard of pottery, dropped to her knees.

"What a darling she is! Such lovely eyes!"

I swear Pinky smiled a beguiling smile. As from a great distance I heard my hoarse whisper. "Remember how porcuswine love to be scratched behind their ear-quills . . ."

Pinky certainly did; she grunted with porcine pleasure. Other than this happy swinish chuckle, silence filled the room. Elmo smiled moronically and nodded. I realized that my mouth was hanging open. I shut it on a slug of bourbon and reached for the bottle.

Swathed in gloom I saw only trouble ahead. All my dreams of swinicide and mass murder vanished with my darling's newfound amour.

"So, Elmo, you must tell me all about your travels with this adorable swinelet."

"Her name's Pinky, Miz diGriz."

"How charming—and of course I'm Angelina to family." A chill look in my direction informed me that all was still not forgiven. "While we're chatting Jim will pick up a bit in the kitchen before he brings in the drinks trolley—so we can join him in celebration . . ."

"Just going, great idea, drinks, munchies, yes!"

I made my escape as Elmo's nasal drone hurried me on my way.

I shoveled all the crockery—broken and unbroken—into the disposal and ordered a new set from Kitchgoods. I could hear its clunking arrival in the cabinet as I stepped out of the kitchen and hit the nuclear unbinder in the floor. The binding energy that held the molecules together lessened just enough so that the spilled garbage sank out of sight; there was a satisfying crunch as it became one with the floor when the binding energy was restored.

A sherry for Angelina, a medium-dry one that she enjoyed. I rooted deep in the drinks closet until I found a bottle of Old Overcoat coal-distilled whiskey—proudly displaying in illiterate lettering, "Aged reely over two hours!" Elmo would love it.

I added a bowl of puffed coconuts and wheeled my chariot of delight into the family room.

". . . and that's how we done ended up here at yore place, Miz Angelina."

The nasal phonemes died away into blessed silence.

"That is quite an adventure, Elmo. I think you are all so brave. Thank you, Jim." She smiled as she took the glass of sherry.

The room temperature rose to normal. The sun emerged from behind the clouds. All had been forgiven! I poured a tumbler of Old Overcoat for Elmo who glugged it—then gasped as his mucous membranes were destroyed on contact. I sipped happily until the voice I loved spoke the words that sealed my doom.

"We must make plans at once to see that your relatives and friends—and their sweet companions—are well taken care of."

A shipload of refugee rubes and their companion swine well taken care of . . .

I could see my bank balance depleting at lightning speed with nothing but zeroes looming on the horizon.

CHAPTER 2

MOST OF MY ATTENTION WAS on my drink when the nasal whine of Elmo's voice cut through the dark thoughts of my coming fiscal failure.

"The captain said *what*?" I broke in.

"Just that we was longer getting here than he thought so we owe him eighteen thousand an' thirteen credits. He ain't letting any more critters—human or swine—offen the ship until we pay up . . ."

"That's called kidnapping—and pignapping—and is against the law," I growled. Cheered to have a target for my growing anger. "The name of this miscreant?"

"Rifuti. His first name is Cap'n. Cap'n Rifuti."

"And the ship is called . . . ?"

"*Rose of Rifuti.*"

I shuddered.

"Don't you think it's past time we paid the captain a

visit?" Angelina said. She smiled down at the snoring Pinky—but the chill of death was in her words as she thought of the crooked captain.

"We shall—but in some style," I said, turning to the viewscreen and punching in a number. The screen instantly lit up with the image of a robot—apparently constructed out of groundcar parts.

"Moolaplenty Motors at your service Sire diGriz—how may we aid you this lovely summer's day?" it said in sultry soprano voice.

"A rental. Your best eight-seat vehicle."

"A Rolls-Sabertooth, gold-plated, satellite-guided with real diamond headlights. It will be in your drive in . . . thirty-six seconds. Your first day's rental has been debited to your account. Have a good one."

"We leave," I announced, leaning over and scratching Pinky under her ear-quills. She grunted happily, stretched, climbed to her trotters and gave herself a good rustling shake.

The groundcar was waiting for us, humming with barely restrained power; the robot chauffeur nodded and smiled mechanically. The albedo was so high, with the sun glinting off the gold plating, that I had to squint against the glare. I handed Angelina into her seat, waited until the porcuswinette curled up at her feet, and joined her. After Elmo clambered aboard I pressed the pearl-studded GO button on the armrest.

"To the spaceport."

"Arrival time three minutes and twelve seconds, Sire Jim and noble passengers." The robot chauffeur had obviously not looked too closely at Elmo. "And welcome as well to their pet dog . . . errr . . . cat . . . pszip . . ." Its voice chuntered to a halt, its computational software undoubtedly unacquainted with porcuswine.

For a few moments I was cheered by the gold-and-diamond luxury; then deeply depressed when I thought of the coming assault on my bank balance.

Moolaplenty was a holiday world and catered to the very rich and even richer. The glint of the diamond headlights drew a salute from the spaceport gate guard as that portal swung wide.

"We're going to the *Rose of Rifuti,*" I said. His nostrils flared at the name; unflared when I slipped a gold cinque coin into his tip pocket.

"You jest, sire."

"Alas, it is our destination."

"If it is, I suggest that you stay upwind. Row nine, pad sixty-nine."

The carputer beeped as the driver heard the location and we surged forward.

While all about me the riders smiled, laughed, grunted porcinely, I was struck down and immersed in the darkness of gloom. I hated the fact that Elmo had ever been born and grown up to invade my happiness. I was cheered that Angelina was cheered, but I had the depressing feeling that all was not going too well.

I was right. Our magic motor stopped, the doors swung open—and we must have been downwind because a certain effluvia crept over us. The eau de barnyard flashed me back to my youth.

"Porcuswine . . ." I muttered darkly.

"Not the most welcome reception," Angelina said, frowning at the spacer.

An understatement if there ever was one. Each of the landing fins of the battered, rusted spaceship was attached to a thick chain, which in turn was bolted to the ground. A heavy chain-link fence circled the pad. There was a single large gate in the fence, that was just closing behind an official-looking vehicle. A dozen armed guards scowled at our arrival while a grizzled sergeant stepped forward and jerked his thumb over his shoulder.

"No visitors. All inquiries at the guardhouse."

"But that car just went in!"

"Officials only. They're an inspection team from Customs and Quarantine."

"Understandable. Now Sergeant, would you be kind enough to do me a favor? See that this donation reaches the Old Sergeants' Rest Home and Bar."

The thousand-credit note vanished as swiftly as it had appeared. It tempered our conversation.

"The ship's quarantined. Just those medical officers allowed inside now."

But it wasn't quite working out that way. A gangway had been run out from the lower spacelock. The officials had just started up it when loud cries and a fearful squealing sounded from the open lock. An instant later there was a thunderous pounding as a black horde of quill-shaking, galloping porcuswine poured out of the ship. The officials dived for safety as the stampede swept by. The thundering herd headed for the gate, which was now closed and locked. The lead boars snorted with porcine rage and turned, leading the pack around the circumference of the fence.

Then, waving shovels and prods, the angry farmers poured down the gangway and ran after them in hot pursuit. Round and round the fenced enclosure they rushed. I leaned back against our groundcar and beamed happily.

"Beautiful!" I said. Angelina frowned at me.

"The swinelets might get hurt . . ."

"Never! The sows are the best mothers in the known universe!"

Eventually the great beasts tired of their circular performance and were herded back aboard the ship. I resisted the urge to clap in appreciation of the performance. The sergeant waited until the clatter of hooves had died away and considered his litany of woe.

"Quarantined with good reason, I would say, sir. In addition to these sanitary problems there are financial ones. Landing fees, rubbish removal and site-rental charges have not been paid. If you wait here I'll send for an officer to give you the gen."

Then he moved like a striking adder. Kicking the gate open, grabbing the yiping Elmo by the collar and hurling him through it, hauling a squealing Pinky by the leash right after him. The gate slammed shut behind him and he dusted off his hands.

"This guy and that thing got out before the quarantine came down. Somebody is in very bad trouble."

I sighed tremulously and suspected that that person would surely turn out to be me. I dug deep into my wallet again. All I could see ahead was my bank balance spiraling downwards,

ever downwards. I also saw that one of the guards was hauling Elmo and the loudly protesting Pinky to the spacer. They
went up the elevator in the access gantry. Their arrival in the
ship provoked almost instant results. Short moments later a
uniformed figure emerged and retraced their footsteps.

As he came towards me I saw the wrinkled uniform, battered cap and even more battered, unshaven face. I turned
away from the sergeant and looked coldly at the approaching
figure. This repellant creature had to be Captain Rifuti.

"I want to talk to you!" he shouted.

"Shut up," I suggested. "I'm the only chance you have of
getting out of this mess. I talk and you answer? Understand?"
My patience was wearing thin.

His face was twisted and dark with anger. He took a deep
breath and, before he could say anything, I made a preemptive strike.

"Sergeant, this officer appears to have violated quarantine
procedures. He is commander of an unsafe ship, has kidnapped
his passengers, as well as committing a number of other crimes.
Can you put him behind bars—at once?"

"Good as done." He reached out then stopped; no moron,
the sergeant and he quickly twigged as to what was going on,
then added in a growling voice, "Unless he shuts his cakehole
and follows your instructions." For punctuation he grabbed
the protesting captain and gave him a quick shake that rattled
the teeth in his head.

Crooked he certainly was, but stupid he was not. His face
darkened and I thought he was going to burst a blood vessel.
"What you want?" he asked, albeit with great reluctance.

"Slightly better. You have told your passengers that they

have additional fees to pay. You will produce records justifying these payments. Only then will I pay these and the spaceport charges that you have incurred. After that we will discuss what is going to be your next port of call, to which you will transport your passengers and their cargo." This last was a feeble attempt to get rid of my friends and neighbors—not to mention their porcine companions.

"No way! I gotta contract that says I bring 'em here and here they stay!"

"We'll see what the quarantine authorities have to say about that." Grasping for straws, aren't you, Jim?

Some time later—and a good deal lighter in the bank account—I sat in the base commander's office sipping a very fair domestic brandy that he had been kind enough to open for us. The mayor's first assistant had joined us. They smiled—as well they might with all my money in their coffers—but they were firm.

Elmo's pilgrims and their quilly creatures were not welcome on the holiday world of Moolaplenty. This was a vacation planet for tourists—as well as home for well-heeled residents like me. And all the food was imported. Not a single farm or tilled field sullied the well-manicured countryside. Dreadfully sorry, but this policy was entrenched in their constitution, pinned down in the law books, inviolate and unchangeable. We are desolated, Sire Jim, but do have another bit of brandy the base commander smarmed. With no reluctance whatsoever I accepted. All I could see was gloom and unhappiness and a prevailing blackness in my future.

Blackness—the color of porcuswine quills . . .

CHAPTER **3**

LIGHTER IN BANK BALANCE AND heavier in heart, I led the way to the gantry elevator and thence into the welcoming airlock of the *Rose of Rifuti*. My Angelina smiled, then laughed aloud when she heard the distant squeals and grunts of a porcuswine herd. My bucolic youth down on the farm flashed before my eye—with concomitant black depression. I had fled the agrarian cesspit of Bit O' Heaven for a successful—and happy—life of crime. Now I felt myself retrogressing through time, returning to a life-choking farming fate that I thought I had left far behind me. I went down the entrance corridor, staggering under a dark cloud of gloom.

I was jarred back to the present by sudden loud squealing that assaulted my ears—accompanied by shouts of pain and picturesque cursing. More crashing and the sound of mighty hoofbeats sounded down the corridor. Then, squealing and grunting, a porcuswine thundered around a bend in the corridor and galloped towards us.

Angelina, no coward, gave a little shriek at the sight. Who could blame her?

One tonne of outraged boar rushed directly at us. Sharp tushes sprayed saliva, tiny red eyes glared.

Sudden death was but meters away.

Salvation rose reluctantly from the dark depths of my memory and I heard my voice, calm and relaxed, gently beguiling in a swinish way.

"Sooo-eee . . . sooo-eee . . . here swine, swine swine!"

With skidding hooves a tonne of outraged pork skidded to a halt before me. Sinister red eyes rolled up to look at me; the razor-sharp teeth chomped and drooled. I reached out, gently lifting the creature's meter-long quills with my left hand, reached under with my right and scratched vigorously behind the beast's ears.

It shivered with pleasure and burbled happily.

Angelina clapped her hands with joy.

"My hero!"

"A humble childhood skill that proved most useful," I said, scratching away to the accompaniment of blissful swinish grunting.

Crisis averted, I became aware of a tumult of shouting—plus some screaming—that grew louder. Then two of the crewmen came into view, running towards us carrying a stretcher with a recumbent figure. Close behind them a galloping crowd of angry farmers, waving pitchforks and clubs—very much like the last scene in a vampire film. Leading them, his face red with rage, was the normally placid Elmo.

"And iffen he comes on this deck again he won't leave it alive!"

The subject of his wrath appeared to be Captain Rifuti himself. He moaned theatrically as he was carried past, clutching an obviously broken arm with his good hand.

"We caught him sneaking into the sty deck!" Elmo stopped and smiled down at the happy boar, then got in a quick quill-scratch of his own. "Gnasher here knocked the cap'n over. Was going to eat him if we hadn't got there in time. Swinenapping, that's what it was—he was after one of our porcuswinelets! And we know *why*!" Even Angelina joined in with the horrified gasps.

"You mean he . . . wanted to . . . ?"

"That's right, Miz Angelina." He nodded grimly and every-one gasped again. Except me; it was a little too hypocritical since I did enjoy my breakfast bacon now and then.

Angelina's horror turned quickly to cold anger. Unhap-pily aimed at me since I was the nearest target.

"Well, former farmer DiGriz—what do you mean to do about this?" Her tone of voice lowered the air temperature by ten degrees. I groped for an answer.

"Well, first I'll turn this fine tonne of porcuswine over to his owners. And then I'll take care of the rapacious Rifuti."

"And what will that cataclysmic action be?"

I looked around, then whispered, "I'll tell you in private since there are other ladies present." Desperately buying some time—since my mind was emphatically empty of any inspi-ration. "Stay with Elmo and I'll find you later. I don't want you to see what happens next, for I am mighty in my wrath!"

I shouted the last, turned and stamped down the corridor after the miscreant.

But what could I possibly do? Rifuti had paid quite a price already for his attempt to supplement the ship's undoubtedly rotten rations. Plus, I had a lot more important things to think about besides his failed swinenapping. This little contretemps had already cost me a small fortune with no end in sight.

I was on the bridge deck now with most official name plates on the doors in some ancient language—from the captain's home world presumably. UFFICIALE, CAPITANO, COMUNICAZIONE and OBITORIO.

I didn't want to see the capitano just yet, but the entrance next to his held more promise—since it sounded very much like the Esperanto *komunikoj*. I knocked and opened the door.

Lights flickered on a U-shaped control board, a speaker crackled with static.

"We're closed," the man at the control console said, not glancing up from the 3D comic he was reading; a tiny scream rose from its pages. "Open at fifteen hundred."

"I want to send a warpdrive interstellargram—and pay cash."

The scream was cut off in mid-gurgle as he slammed the magazine shut and spun about in his chair.

"We're open. What you got?"

The lure of lucre, the call of cash—it never failed. I had been mulling my problem over and the answer seemed obvious. Money means banks and banks means bankers. And my son James was now a most successful banker. I scratched out a brief cry for help.

I soon had my answer and sent a return communication answering his relevant questions. The operator's eyes glowed warmly as the cash-on-the-line pile of credits grew.

"Will the captain see any of this?" I asked.

"You just out of the funny farm?" he sneered. Hard to do when you are biting down on a silver credit; it joined the others in the desk drawer.

My wallet contained just dust when the last communication from Bolivar arrived.

BE THERE SOONEST WITH SINGH.

I was broke, so I would have to wait until soonest to see who or what this was.

"Come back any time!" the operator chuckled. My snarl and the slamming door his only answer. I was now in the right mood to see the captain. I threw open the door of his cabin and was instantly cheered.

He was screaming and writhing on the top of a hard desk while green-clad demons held onto his limbs and tortured him. I did not interrupt. Particularly when I saw that they were medics who were setting his broken bones, reducing his fractures— a most painful procedure.

Once the cast was in place the needles came out and I interrupted.

"Painkillers, yes—but I want him conscious to answer a few questions."

"Why?" the doctor asked, his occupation now revealed by the stethoscope around his neck.

"Because I must find out some most important facts."

As I spoke I groped through all my pockets until, fortuitously, I found a single coin, dredged it out and passed it over.

"A hundred credits donation for the charity of your choice for your assistance in this important matter."

"Thank you. For the Children's Aid Society. Plus I didn't really appreciate some of the curses he laid on us. A pain-killer and a stimulant."

Needles flashed. Then they bundled up their equipment and were gone. The red-eyed Rifuti turned his wrath on me, but I got in a snarled preemptive strike before he could speak.

"You're in big trouble, Rifuti. The police are on their way to charge you with attempted swinicide, assault and battery, kidnapping, grievous bodily harm and barratry." He gurgled incoherently, but I drove on mercilessly.

"But you are lucky that I am here to save you. I will have the police drop the charges. I will pay all the debts of your passengers, both two- and four-legged. I will pay all port charges accrued here. And—wait for it!—I will pay a fair price to buy this decrepit excuse for a spaceship."

He gurgled again and his eyeballs bulged at this last and I nodded and smiled benignly.

"Because if you don't agree you will be dead within twenty-four hours." I husked this in a venom-dripping voice.

His face turned dark with anger and he opened his mouth to speak. Then his eyes bulged even bulgier and he gasped.

A scalpel had appeared in my hand—liberated from the doctor's bag—and was rock-steady just millimeters from his eyes. With a quick flip it neatly punctured the tip of his prominent nose and was still again—with a glistening drop of blood on its tip.

"Say *yes* . . ." I whispered.

I stayed silent, cold, counting upon his undoubtedly dicey history to put the frighteners on him.

"Yes . . ." he whispered back.

The scalpel vanished and I stepped back. "I'll be back to you with my offer. Of course, if you talk to anyone about this you won't live until morning."

I exited. I didn't know if my threat would work or not. If he did complain to the authorities I would see to it that he was sneered at—and a lot of official charges would be dropped on him. At the very least my nebulous threats could only help the financial negotiations to come. I returned happily to face my dear wife. As I strolled I was already embroidering and im-proving on the story of my success.

I tracked Angelina down to the messhall where she was having a bucolic tea with the lady farmers from Bit O' Heaven. The men had been dismissed as redundant and sent back to work. Angelina smiled when I gave her a thumbs-up sign and a big nod. She bit daintily into a wurflecake and slipped a bit to Pinky who, just as daintily, snuffled it down.

"Ladies—" I called out, "if I might have your attention. The forces of evil have been laid low, the captain—very painfully—bandaged and repaired. And made to see the light."

"And which light would that be?' Angelina asked.

I smiled and bowed to my attentive female audience.

"All debts will be paid. These kind people, and their por-cine charges, will find a new home on a sunlit paradise planet. The good guys win!"

I pumped my fist over my head in a victory salute in an-swer to their joyous cries of happiness. Angelina started to speak but I beat her to it.

"Not only that, but our good son, James, is on his way here at this very moment to handle the finances and mechanics of the agreement!"

"Jim, you don't mean it?"

"I do, my love—I most certainly do!"

She leaned over and gave me a most inspiring buss on my cheek, radiant with joy, while the audience applauded. But, happily, she did not lean so far over that she could see that the fingers of both my hands were crossed behind my back.

Oh let it happen, oh powers that rule the odds of seeing that white lies come true.

Oh *please* let it happen—or Slippery Jim diGriz is really in the deep, deep cagle.

Angelina's brow furrowed with thought. With good reasons—my pep talk had more holes in it than a *truo* cheese. I chuckled and turned away, speaking over my shoulder.

"Sorry, no time for tea. James asked me to do an inventory of the ship for him. I'll be back soonest."

If I had a conscience I would be staggering under the weight of all my white lies. But I had happily laid that burden down when I opted for a life of crime.

But I did want to see what shape the ship was in. I started my survey on the bridge deck and worked my way down to the engine room. With each noisome compartment entered, each scuffed door opened, my depression grew. Firstly, no one seemed to be on duty. None of the stations were manned; lights were turned low or burnt out. Filth everywhere. The *Rose of Rifuti* was a spacegoing slum. It was only when I reached the dorm deck that I found any trace of the crew. I pushed open the door labeled TRESPASSERS WILL BE SHOT and fought my way in against a miasma of old food, stale sweat and dope fumes. I kicked my way through the discarded trays and crushed drink containers to reach the bunk where a scruffy man lay smoking a green joint and listening to a scratchy recording of some coal-mining and steel-mill music. I knocked the music player to the deck and crushed it under my boot heel. The unshaven music lover looked up and snarled an oath.

"Ekmortu stultulo!"

Drop dead stupid! My temper, by this time only held in place by a slender thread, cracked. In an instant I dragged him from the bunk by the collar of his soiled jumpsuit, shook him teeth-rattlingly, cursed a mighty oath and—if this wasn't enough—the scalpel appeared—large before his popping eyes.

"Take a breath and you're a dead man," I growled with the voice of doom.

Only when his face began to grow blue with incipient cyanosis did I hurl him, gasping for breath, back onto his bunk.

I glared around at the terrified men who lolled on the other sordid bunks.

"Now hear this! I have just bought this ruin of a spaceship and am the new owner. You will obey my orders or—" My wrist twitched and the scalpel sped the length of the room and thudded into a distant pillow—a scant millimeter from the shocked face of a crewman.

I spun on my heel, dropped into a karate killing position and glared at the now terrorized crewmen. "Anyone disagree with that . . . ?"

Of course none of them did. Nostrils flaring I turned slowly, facing them down one by one. Stalked the length of the bunk-room and retrieved my scalpel.

"My name is James diGriz. You may call me master—
LET'S HEAR IT!"

"Yes . . . Master . . ." the ragged response came.

"Good. I will now inspect the rest of the ship and will return in precisely one hour. By that time you will have cleared
up this swinesty, washed and shaved, be prepared to be loyal
crewmen—or die . . ."

The last words were spoken so coldly that they breathed a
mutual moan and swayed like trees in the wind. On this high
note I exited and continued my depressing inspection of the
specious spacer.

The engine room was last and the unoiled door hinges
squealed like all the others. The shouted voice rattled off my
eardrums.

"You are a mechanical moron! Don't you know which end
of a screwdriver goes into the slot of a screw? Come closer
and I will demonstrate on your—"

There was a pained shriek and a crewman fled by me, followed by a veritable hail of screwdrivers. His pained moans
died away down the corridor; I nodded approval; at least someone was working on this garbage scow.

He was gray-haired and as solidly built as one of his engines, bent over the guts of one of them, probing in the re-
cesses behind an open panel. As I approached I heard him
mutter imprecations.

And I understood them! A language I had learned painfully on a very painful planet. Cliaand.

"Well done, oh mighty engineer, very well done!" I said in
the same tongue. He straightened, spun about, jaw-dropping.

"You are speaking Cliaand . . ." he said.

"I'm glad you noticed."

Then his eyes widened and he pointed a greasy finger at me.

"And I know you—you were the pilot of my ship during the Final War. In fact I even remember your name: Lieutenant Vaska Hulja."

"What a memory! Whereas I have completely forgotten yours."

"Stramm, Lieutenant Hulja."

"Lieutenant Hulja is gone with the war! My name is Jim. It is a pleasure, good Stramm. I was indeed your pilot. And, sadly, your saboteur. Let me apologize at last for blowing up your fine engines."

He waved away the words and smiled broadly. "I should thank you, Jim. Ended the war and got me out of the navy and back to work as a civilian." His smile turned swiftly to a depressed frown. "Not your fault that I signed on to this bucket of rusty bolts."

"Soon to change," I said and shook his oily hand, then wiped my hand on the rag he passed over. "You'll never guess who the new owner is."

"Make my day! It isn't . . . you . . . ?"

I lowered my head and nodded slowly. He chortled with joy and we pumped a greasy handshake again.

"Can I ask you a few questions about this ship?"

His smile vanished and he growled deep in his throat. "Ask, but you won't like the answers."

"I agree in advance."

"The captain's a crook and a smuggler. The crew are alcoholic villains. They were only hired because by interplanetary law a crew this size is required. They do nothing. Their work is done by robotic controls which are slowly deteriorating. I'm surprised we made planetfall at all. I've already quit this job. But I want to adjust the atomic generator before it goes into meltdown. My engines are sound—but nothing else on the ship is. All patched up and jury-rigged and decaying while you watch. I've already quit and I have sabotaged the engines. I'll put them right—when I get my overdue salary. Welcome, Jim, welcome to the *Rose of Rifuti.*"

I sighed a tremulous sigh. "I had a feeling that's what you would say, oh honest engineer Stramm. At least things can't get worse."

Even as I spoke these words aloud my mother's oft-repeated dictum whispered in my ear.

Bite your tongue.

Firmly superstitious, she believed you were tempting fate to say this. Ha-ha—so much for superstition . . .

There was a crash as the door burst open and Elmo staggered in, red-faced and clutching his chest.

"Jim . . ." he gasped. "Come quick! The worst has happened!"

He drew in a tortured breath and spoke in a doom-laden voice.

"They are here now—hundreds maybe!" he shouted aloud, dark with despair.

"Men with guns! They want to kill all the porcuswine!!"

CHAPTER 4

I FORGOT THE ELEVATOR AND bounded up the stairs like a maddened gazelle. Staggered, panting, onto the sty deck, then through the open door and skidded to a stop before a mass of outraged farmers. It was the last reel of the vampire film all over again. Facing the brandished shovels and pitchforks defending their beasts was a small band of armed and terrified soldiers. They had formed a square, facing outwards, guns raised. A frightened bureaucrat—clutching a paper-shedding briefcase—shivered inside the square. It was a disaster in the making.

"Men of Bit O' Heaven, cease and desist!" I shouted. "Lower your weapons—for James diGriz is here! You are saved!"

My words began to have an effect. Shouted cries changed to angry mutters; one by one the agricultural implements were lowered. With half of the problem solved—for the moment—I turned and spoke to the soldiers. I knew they were only used to nonviolence on this peaceful planet. It took only a touch on one trigger . . .

"The revolt is at an end. Don't point those guns at these simple folk who were but defending their livestock! Lower your weapons—and put on your safeties!"

Slowly and reluctantly they obeyed the voice of authority. Conflict was averted. At least for the moment.

Angelina pushed through the farmers and smiled as she took my arm. She spoke slowly and firmly. "All be well now that Jim is here."

There was a murmur of agreement; farm weapons rattled to the deck.

We turned away from them, a united front, and I spoke in a mediatory tone.

"You there, with the briefcase—can you tell me what this is all about?"

He stopped shivering and straightened up.

"I certainly can. I am chief of staff of the Planetary Quarantine Corps. We decontaminate and protect. I received a call from Central Hospital that a crewman of this vessel had come to them in great distress. He said that there was an outbreak of the dreaded tusk and trotter disease among the beasts on this ship. He feared for his own life and those of his shipmates—"

"Just a minute," I interrupted. "I am puzzled. In all my years as an inadvertent timeserving swineherd I never heard of this strange disease. Have you?" I asked, turning to my bucolic audience.

There was a mass movement of head-shaking and a chorus of noes.

"Well, there you are," I said, turning and smiling benignly on the befuddled functionary. "Might I suggest that we all wait patiently while you contact your medical department for details of this dreaded disease?"

"Order arms," the sergeant shouted and the butts of the weapons hit the steel deck. The functionary dug a phone out of his briefcase and muttered into it.

The silence stretched, tension grew. His mutter became a mumble—then a growl as his free hand shook wildly in the air. In the end he slammed the phone back into his briefcase, turned red-faced and angry.

"Fall your men in, Sergeant. Take them back to base. The medics thought I was bonkers—they laughed! No such disease. A prank! Heads will roll . . ."

"Were you told the name of the crewman who reported the disease?" Thoughts of murder, decapitation and worse danced in my head. He shuffled papers again.

"Yes . . . here it is. The disease was reported by one Captain Rifuti."

I could hear my teeth grinding together as he exited, muttering, behind the troops. The audience shouted with joy, porcuswine squealed in the distance, Angelina gave me a warm and loving kiss. We were saved . . .

For the moment. Gloom descended. The powers of evil were united against me. I must act—and at once. I sighed tremulously with the realization that all of this was going to be very, very expensive; visions of zeroes danced in my head.

"What do we do next?" Angelina asked. She listened to the loud squealing. "The porcuswine sound so upset!"

"I'm so upset!" I grated with clenched jaw. Were my teeth

really grinding together? "Finances . . . bank balance . . . I must find out the worse . . . I must use your phone."

I took her phone, entered the bank number, punched in my access code, bulged my eyes . . . let the phone drop to the deck from my vibrating fingers.

"Gone, all gone . . . all our funds . . . and more bills still coming in . . ."

From a distance I heard Angelina's voice warm with reassurance. While I was wondering if suicide was an option.

"Poor Jim. What will you do?"

Do? "Sit down," I gurgled.

Helping hands led me to the messhall and sat me in a chair. I was getting too old for this kind of cagle. "Drink." I breathed and a glass was pressed to my lips. I drank and choked.

"Water!"

"A mistake," Angelina said, turning towards the sea of worried faces. "Would any of you have a drink for Jim that is slightly *stronger* than water?"

There was a muttering among the men and after a few moments a smoked glass bottle with an ominous black cork was thrust forward. It was decorked, tilted, poured—was it steaming in the glass? I glimpsed the label.

PORCUSWINE PAIN-KILLER—NOT FOR CHILDREN OR PREGNANT SOWS

Sounded good. I sipped, drank, glugged, squealed.

"Thank you," I said as I wiped the tears from my eyes and rustled my bristles. "The future is clear. I know what must be done."

The silence was immense, my audience held their breath. "What?" Angelina whispered, speaking for all of them.

"I must . . . see my bank manager."

A moan of sympathy hummed through the air. My mood changed instantly. The Stainless Steel Rat—he who walks alone—had no need for sympathy. Action! First my financial affairs must be straightened out. Then I must find the toerag Rifuti, who, in a moment of revenge, had invented a disease and done his best to bring me low. Mighty indeed is the Rat's revenge!

I leapt to my feet, rocking on my heels, nostrils flaring, resisting the urge to squeal swinishly: the porcuswine drench was still in my system.

"To the bank!" I shouted. "All will be saved."

They shouted mightily and their cheers only died away when the intercom speaker on the bulkhead rustled to life.

"Now hear this. I have an interstellar message for Sire James diGriz. This is the communication's officer. A message . . ."

"To the bank—by way of the communications office!"

The officer was waiting when I threw open the door, holding a yellow slip of paper in the air. I grabbed and read . . .

ARRIVING TOMORROW AM YOUR TIME SPACER
KRANKENHAUS—JAMES

Clear enough; help was on the way.

"I got some other news for you," the operator said. I raised querying eyebrows. "I'm the only crewman left on this rustbucket. I don't know what you said to them, but they have all deserted."

"And you?"

"Unless you got more messages to send, my bag is packed and I'm outta here as well."

"Good-bye. Don't slam the airlock behind you when you go."

I put the whole sordid mess behind me for the moment. In the fullness of time I would track the weaseling Rifuti who . . .

"Later, Jim, much later," I cozened myself. "Mazuma first." I headed for the waiting car.

While my gilded chariot whisked me to the bank I called Angelina with the news; her happy laughter at our son's imminent arrival was indeed cheering. I disconnected the call as my golden transport pulled over to the curb. Next to a large refuse bin.

"This is not the bank," I said.

"A million apologies, Sire James," the chauffeurbot said. "But your payment has just ran out."

"Then tap my account for more."

"Assuredly . . . *krrkkk* . . . There has been a banking error. We cannot access further payment." The robot's voice now had a distinct chill to it. "However, you may deposit cash."

An empty drawer popped out of the armrest.

"Well, it just so happens—ha-ha—that I left my wallet home . . ."

The drawer closed and the car door opened. The voice grated, coldly.

"Moolaplenty Motors is ready to serve you anytime . . . you have the cash."

The air conditioner sent out an icy blast that was as chill

as my soul. I exited, the door slammed shut, I walked slowly to the bank.

By the time I arrived at the First Bank of Moolaplenty I had a spring in my step and determination in the set of my jaw. You can't keep a good Rat down!

"Welcome, dear customer, welcome!" the doorbot crooned as he threw the entrance wide: my spirits rose.

"Welcome!" all the tellers sang.

"Welcome to our dearest client—

"You but speak and we obey.

"With your money on deposit

"You bring such happiness to our day!"

I shook my hands over my head at this friendly display. Rotten poetry—but I'm sure the sentiment was real.

It had better be. After the last galactic bank crash—which left many star systems in dire poverty—a wave of anger swept through the galaxy. *"Never again!"* they swore. *"This is the end of financial failure!"*

And it was.

Terrifying words such as "subprime loans," "debenture bonds," "collateralized debt obligations," "credit default swaps," "derivatives" were now gone from the language and could only be found in ancient dictionaries. Banks were firmly watched and regulated by steely-eyed accountants. Money was deposited and earned interest. Loans and mortgages were cheerfully made—the banks profiting with the 1 percent spread. And— this was so revolutionary that the International Union of Financial Executives could not believe it—these instructions meant that they could only loan money that they *had in the bank*!

Stout bankers wept—there were rumors of suicides. But

the law was the law. Peace and fiduciary responsibility was the rule now.

Laughing employees ushered me through the manager's door. This functionary stood inside bowing and dry-wiping his hands.

"Welcome a thousand times over, Sire diGriz. Please take this chair." He pushed it in and I sat. He picked up his round black ball, that was secured by a chain to his ankle, so it wouldn't trip him, and seated himself behind his massive desk.

I always enjoyed the sight of the ball and chain. A constant reminder of the fate awaiting the bankers if their accounts were even a groat overdrawn. The balls were made of improvium and light as a feather. But if any larceny was detected in the bank's accounts more molecules of improvium were pumped in and the balls grew heavy. Their weight varied according to the seriousness of the crime. In the bank's cafeteria one could see manager's smiling and sweating as they dragged their balls after them. In matters of grievous financial funny business they could weigh as much as a tonne; unless fed by sympathizers it was said that many a manager starved to death. A suitable fate for the overweight, some have been heard to say.

"And how may I help, Sire Jim?" I ignored the smarmy use of my first name.

"My account—I have a query."

"Of course. Let me bring it up on my screen." He touched a button, looked—gasped and slumped back in his chair. "Empty, overdrawn. Past your limit—still being overdrawn as I watch . . ."

"Yes, well, that's my query. What do we do?"

"First—ho-ho—we try to turn off the overdraft function."
He stabbed down on a key. Sat back and patted his damp forehead with his handkerchief.

"Assets?" he asked.

"My home!" I said hollowly, trying not to think of Angelina.
"Yes, indeed!"

He punched keys, smiled at the screen, sat back with a sigh.

"Nine bedrooms, two kitchens, four bars, two swimming pools with poolside bars . . . a prime property indeed. It will fetch a good price . . ."

"Sell? Never! A mortgage!"

The smile became a frown. "Unhappily our mortgage funds are limited today, the law you know. Wait, a new deposit just came in. So we can offer you a loan—let me see after I deduct your overdraft—we can happily give you, after this deduction—four thousand and twenty three credits."

"For my luxurious home!" there was despair in my voice.

"Wait, another overdraft just came in. The balance will be three hundred and forty-two credits."

"I'll take it . . ."

"Too late—another payment-due just arrived. I'm afraid that if you mortgage your home now you will still be in debit to the bank." He turned off the screen, sat back and forced a smile. "Is there anything else I can help you with today, Sire James?"

I grated my teeth and forced a grin. Not speaking the unspeakable things that I would like him to help me with.

"Been nice talking to you," I said, standing, turning, exiting his office. By coincidence none of the bank staff was looking my way as, whistling, I exited the bank. I looked down the street; it was a long walk to the spaceport. As I shuffled slowly into the gloom of the afternoon I looked up. Three pendant gold balls. Was it by sheer chance that the hock shop was so close to the bank? I turned and looked behind me and lo— there was another one, balls glinting in the afternoon sun. Funny, I had never noticed them before. Bells chimed in the distance as I pushed the door open and strode firmly inside among the pianos, gold jewelry, stuffed cats . . .

When I left I pulled my jacket sleeve down to cover the pale stripe on my wrist where my watch used to be. I jingled the credits in my pocket and breathed a brief prayer.

Be swift, good son, James. Your rusty rat of a father is greatly in need of succor.

I jingled the coins again, turned to the curb, hailed a passing cab.

CHAPTER 5

"WHAT A PLEASURE IT WILL be to see our son again," I said cheerfully.

Angelina did not move; her face set in ice. My words fell leadenly to the floor. I could but persevere. "His spacer will arrive on time! See the announcement board. See the nice bar? Join me in a drink while we wait?"

"Are you sure that we can afford it?"

Yes, well, that was a consideration. The answer was a firm yes. It would be medicinal. I slipped away and stumbled over to the alcoholic retreat, rapped a coin to get the barbot's attention, drank deep of the libation he poured.

To say that my wife was not charmed by my financial report is like saying that an earthquake is a slight tremble in the ground. Oh, good son James, bearer of glad news—and hopefully mounds of mazuma!—please arrive soon. I emptied my glass and saw over its lowered rim that the first passengers were emerging from customs, their roboluggage trundling behind them.

And leading them—countenance beaming—was our son! Mother and son embraced while I looked on with paternal pleasure. I got a hug too; then James stepped back and brought forward a man who had been waiting patiently behind him.

"This is Kirpal Singh—I told you about him in my interstellargram."

We shook hands. He had dark skin, white teeth and his head wrapped in green cloth. A bandage? All would be revealed.

"Kirpal came with me because, you will be happy to hear, he is a spaceship broker."

"Welcome . . . doubly welcome!" I enthused.

"And does Mr. Singh have a firm credit line to cover any financial transactions?" Say what you will, my Angelina is not an easy sell.

"I am but a humble broker, dear Mrs. diGriz. Your son is the money bags in any transaction."

James held up the dark briefcase that was chained to his wrist. "Crammed with credits and ready to go!"

"Then all be well!" She exclaimed in an abrupt change of mood. "We look to you Kirpal for salvation."

"I am deadly in financial dealings, Angelina! We Sikhs are a warrior race."

"That explains the turban. I assume that you have your dagger and iron bangle?"

"I do, wise lady." He lifted his cuff a bit; metal gleamed. Then tapped his ankle. "You are indeed a student of ancient religions and customs."

My Angelina never ceases to amaze me.

"We'll have celebratory bottle of champers while you bring me up to speed," James said leading the way to the bar. He whistled and their wheeled cases trundled after us.

We clinked glasses and drank. Angelina, ever the pragmatist, outlined our problem while I downed a second glass of morale-raiser. When she was through she sipped daintily from her glass while we all applauded.

"What a worthy cause for a most charitable lady!" Kirpal cried aloud. "Count upon my expert help to save these rural refugees!"

"Which leaves us with only one problem—" she said, glancing at me. I nodded for her to continue, pouring another glass; she was doing fine. "Do we have the financial well-to-do to carry this off?"

"Alas, no," James said, then held her hand as her brow darkened. "But I am calling in a number of long-term investments that I made for you some years ago. However, even by warpdrive interstellargram this will take a day or two. In the meantime a million credits have been deposited in your account for day-to-day expenses."

"All's well that ends well," I said, and put my glass down. Enough sauce, Jim, this is a time for level heads. "To the spaceport and a showdown with Captain Rifuti."

We grabbed a cab—I wasn't using Moolaplenty Motors again if I could help it. We made a brief hotel stop on the way—where a checkinbot was waiting for us at the entrance to the Spaceman's Paradise. James signed in and passed over their luggage. We drove on and when we reached the *Rose of Rifuti*'s spacelock we were pleased to discover that a small welcoming committee was there to greet us.

"She was pinein' for you, Miz Angelina," Elmo said in his best cap-twisting toe-dragging servile mode. His voice was all but drowned out by Pinky's joyous squealing. She changed to a happy snurgle when Angelina knelt and gave her a good under-quill scratch. Elmo beamed as he led the way to the messhall.

Which was no longer the messhall. That scruffy nameplate had been replaced by a hand-sewn tapestry that read PARLOR & DINING ROOM in pink letters, surrounded by a floral wreath.

"I made a few improvements while we were waiting for you," Angelina said. "This—and the rest of the living quarters—were an ecodisaster." I was barely aware that Kirpal was slipping back down the corridor.

The messhall was no more. Stout farm-hardened arms, soap and water had scrubbed and cleaned so that the floors—and walls—were cleansed and shining. Colorful tablecloths abounded, pillows were on the chairs, while large holopix of prize porcuswine adorned the walls. We were quickly seated with pride at the top table and the air filled with merry cries as we knocked back the jugs of hard cider.

Then, suddenly, a hush fell over the room and joy was replaced by angry mutters. Captain Rifuti was dragged into the room, head lolling and semiconscious, firm in the muscular grip of two stout porcuswineherds. Engineer Stramm followed them, livid with anger. He had a small, fist-sized machine in one hand, a large wrench in the other.

"I caught this criminal messing with my engines. Got him with my spanner and called for help. He was stealing this atomic copraxilater. Cost a fortune—and the ship won't move without it. Thought you might want to have a word with him."

"Oh, I do indeed!" I said, dry-washing my hands with a sadistic rustle. "I'll take over now, thank you. If you kind people will leave us to it, you will have my full report soonest."

They exited. Each sneering or muttering a curse as they passed the wretched captain, now immobile in James's firm grip.

As the last farmer left Kirpal entered and locked the door behind him.

"I have inspected this spacegoing slum from stem to stern," he said warmly, nostrils flaring in anger. "A dump. The owner will have to sell it at a laughable rock-bottom price!"

"Sit, Rifuti!" I ordered as the door clicked shut. "Meet the honorable spaceship broker Kirpal Singh who will now arrange the sale and purchase of this miserable tub at the best price—for us—that is possible."

"Broke my arm . . ." he complained, holding up his wounded arm and waggling his cast at us. "Hit me on the head too. Got a lawyer, gonna sue!"

"Let's get one thing straight," I said, leaning over, my voice dripping venom, my breath washing him with hard-cider vapor. He cringed. As well he might. "Mention your arm again and you will be in jail for attempted swinicide, condemned, jailed, labeled a pauper by court order and have everything you own—particularly this ship—taken from you. Do I make myself clear?"

I did. Kirpal had no trouble proceeding with the negotiations at a distant table. The diGriz family clicked glasses, sipped a bit more of the cider, while James brought Angelina up to date on family matters. We were just refilling our glasses when Kirpal joined us, happily brandishing a sheaf of papers.

"Preliminary agreement for you to look at James."

They muttered, scratched out, rewrote, chuckled.

"You'll have to find a welcoming planet for our porcu-swine friends," Angelina said.

"The search progresses." Which was true. I had a search program running on my computer. Searching for a compatible planet that would take this mob. "As soon as I can, I'll see what the program has turned up."

"Good. The next question is what do we do with the house while we are away? Put it in stasis store or rent it out?"

I fought down the reflex gurgle and gape, choked out an answer.

"But . . . we're not going away . . . are we?" A desperate, doomed attempt at an escape.

"Of course we are. We can't let those sweet creatures travel alone—tended only by simple farmers—to face the troubles and tribulations of a new world. We'll go along to make sure they are settled in. Make it a holiday—it has been quite a time since we've had one."

Holiday! Squealing, rattling, rutting, groaning, grunting porcuswine forever . . . I had fought so long to leave the farm and the chuntering swine behind me. I was not going back.

"Never!" I cried aloud. "I escaped that life once—I can't go back!"

"Understandable," she said coolly, taking a small sip of her drink. "I do share your feelings. Perhaps it is too much of a good thing—like sweet little Pinky."

I shuddered—did I hear a rustle of quills?!

"But we must see that these people and their charges are settled in. Then, and you have my promise, we will say bye-bye and go on a relaxing holiday." She leaned over and kissed my cheek.

Disarmed, outfought on all fronts, helpless. I raised the white flag.

"Put the house in stasis. It will be so nice to come home to . . ."

"I agree. Now, how should we pack?"

"Congratulations," James said. Placing a thick folder of papers on the table before me. "You are now the proud owner of the spacer *Rose of Rifuti.*"

"Change the name." I heard myself say as from a great distance.

"To the *Porcuswine Express*!" Angelina said, and there were cheers of happy agreement. Behind them I saw Rifuti stumbling away; he turned and shook his fist in our direction, then left.

What would the future hold? I had no idea.

But I had some very strong and vile intuitions. Could there be a way to escape this desperate and tragic situation?

CHAPTER 6

I WRIGGLED ON THE HOOK.

"It will not be easy to get this ship ready. It will be impossible here on Moolaplenty to find a qualified captain . . ."

Kirpal smiled widely and white-toothedly at me. "You will be overjoyed, erstwhile employer Jim, to hear that I am a qualified and expert spacer pilot. I look forward to taking the helm of this soon-to-be-greatly-improved vessel."

"But the comm officer quit. Impossible to replace . . ."

"Already done! In my CV you will find my licenses, experiences and so forth as a qualified communications officer."

By now I was grasping for straws.

"You'll need a crew—"

"Only by law, as the previous captain showed with his alcoholic layabouts. The ship is fully automated. To satisfy the bureaucrats we can enlist some of your farmers. Sign them on as crew for the records."

Charming. A spacegoing sty manned by moronic yokels.

"Qualified off-planet spacer inspectors have already been engaged and are on the way here," Kirpal added before I could think of any more excuses. "Needed repairs will be made soonest."

"Kirpal and I will handle everything," James said. "Just do your packing and relax. And be prepared for the trip of a lifetime."

That's just what I was afraid of. My head vibrated as my sinaphone began ringing. In a moment of madness I had discarded my pocket phone and had this new gadget implanted in my sinus. Powered by body heat it would operate for decades. But I had to have the ringing tone turned down. Still in shock I muttered *on* and Angelina's voice rattled inside my head. *"I told everyone the good news and they are all celebrating."* Her voice was almost drowned out by the happy cries, clinking glasses, swinish squealing. *"They want to thank you . . ."*

"I am overwhelmed but too shy to face them. And I must rush—my computer has reported finding a possible planet for our pilgrims. I have to follow up the lead . . ."

Beating back all protests, I muttered *off,* indulged in a few moments of whining self-pity.

"Enough, Jim," I muttered after sadistically enjoying my own misery. I shook myself by my metaphorical neck. "Find the planet, transport these rube relatives and their porcine charges there, bid them all bye-bye and get on with your life. Think how pleasurable this pleasure planet will look upon your return."

I skulked through the corridors to avoid all contact and endless excuses. Exited and smiled at the guard sergeant's snappy salute earned by much financial largesse.

Once home I resolutely passed by the bar, entered my study and told the computer to turn on. Then tempered my prohibitionary resolution by getting a cold beer; that would have to do until I found a suitable planet.

I sat, sipped, stared at the screen—and muttered a sibilant curse as the apparently endless names of possible planets scrolled down the screen.

I wrote a quick filtering program to shorten the list. Climate, native population, form of government, average IQ of policemen, death penalty, proportion of incarcerated prisoners to general population, form of government, capitalization of the banking system—must always think of business opportunities—the usual things.

Hours later I straightened up and sighed. The beer had gone flat, thousands of planets had been turned to electrons—only three survived. I yawned and stretched and went for a fresh beer. There was a note on the bar.

"Didn't want to disturb. See you in a.m. Good luck."

I blinked at the clock: well past midnight. I hadn't even heard Angelina come in. I added a single whiskey to the beer, an ancient drink called a boilermaker for reasons lost in the immensity of time. I yawned again.

My synapses sizzling with the stimulation, I went back to work. Two more planets fell. I hit a key and the lone survivor expanded to fill the screen.

MECHANISTRIA

As soon as I did this sweet music filled the air. When I had accessed the planetary website an expensive, powerful message had punched right through my spam filters. An incredibly beautiful and underdressed girl smiled out of the screen and pointed a sweet finger in my direction.

"I want you . . ." she breathed salaciously. "If you are a farmer, or employed in the agricultural or food supply trade, then Mechanistria could be your new home. Let me explain . . ."

Music enthused, the girl faded to be replaced by smiling workers laboring at mighty machines as she explained in a lilting voice-over.

"Our happy workers are joyful in their labors for they know that work will make them free. We build and export vehicles and machines of all kinds to many planets in the nearby star systems."

Fading shots of planes, cars, engines, pimple removers, elevators, goatmobiles, machines beyond number marched across the screen. This changed in an instant as the music clashed, the machines vanished to be replaced by workers sitting down for a meal, smiling as they forked up their chow—and then stopping in mid-bite. They then stared and overacted horror at the food on their plates as drums rolled—then stopped. They froze and a male voice, oozing with distaste spoke.

"Yet we are being cheated, starved, taken advantage of. The planets who supply our food have joined together in a cabal of evil! They have raised their prices in unison and lowered the quality of their produce. To put it bluntly—we are being shafted! Our founding fathers were so busy building an enterprising planet that they neglected to provide self-sufficient planetary produce. But no more!"

An exuberant voice-over of scenes of laughing, jolly farmers, happy farm beasts, smoked hams, ripening crops and laden tables. "Our new policy is to encourage agriculturists of all kinds to come here to aid us in making ours a new and fruitful world! All expenses will be paid, as well as large bonuses, farm buildings, resettlement allowances, free medicare, free life insurances, cradle to grave . . ."

There was more like this, but I had seen enough. This was it!

In my enthusiasm I swallowed the rest of my drink too hastily and coughed until tears filled my eyes. Swept them away with the back of my hand and went to pour some Old Cough Killer.

I was saved! I sipped my poisonous potion and radiated sheer happiness. I could hear little trotters thundering down the gangways into the shining future. Hypocritical good-byes, a few tears shed, hosing out the decks—then up, up and away . . .

My pleasant dreams faded as I realized that my arm was being gently patted. I opened a gummy eye to see a smiling Angelina standing over me.

"Time to wake up. I've put the coffee on."

Sunlight streamed in through the windows. My neck hurt where I crunched it when I had slipped down in the chair.

"Good news . . ." I croaked, then coughed hoarsely.

"Save it until you are more lifelike," she cozened.

Good advice. I staggered into the shower room, hurled my clothes in the direction of the laundrybot—which snatched them out of the air—and dived into the shower, which inundated me as sweet music filled the air.

Washed, scrubbed, depilated, refreshed—I sat at the table and sipped at my coffee.

"Good news?" Angelina asked, raising one quizzical eyebrow.

"The best. I have found the planet of choice, a world that will welcome us with open arms, settle our friends, aid them and provide them with all the necessities for a happy future."

"Named . . . ?"

"Mechanistria. Just enter that into the computer, then sit back and be enthralled."

While she did that I whistled at the stove, gave it my order and tucked into an ample breakfast the instant it slid steaming onto the table before me.

"Just for a change you didn't lie or exaggerate," Angelina said entering the room with an armful of brochures from the printout. I was in too good a mood to defend this mild attack on my veracity and only smiled as I munched a mouthful. She sighed.

"I will be sorry to see them go, but it will be for their own benefit in the long run."

Sorry! I choked, gurgled, drank some coffee, smiled, spoke.

"See—it all came right in the end!"

CHAPTER **7**

I MUST SAY THAT OUR good captain Kirpal organized our departure with military precision. For two days he did not appear to sleep as he goaded the laboring technicians into frenzied activity. Loads of equipment arrived and were seized by eager hands. Without being asked he had torn out a number of cabins and had rebuilt them as a luxury suite for Angelina and me—complete with adjacent barroom. Welding sparks flew high, drills roared, hammers clanged, porcuswine squealed in angry answer. We went home to pack and I resorted to drink. I was not charmed by the thought of our coming flight. Moolaplenty had never looked better. I raised my glass at the thought of its myriad soon-to-vanish delights.

For all too quickly I would soon be many moons away from its warm embrace. I drank deeply to fond memories. Relaxed, muttered, dozed and sipped some more as darkness descended.

An indefinite period of time later, I awoke to find Angelina grasping my nose. I opened my mouth to register my protest and she popped a sizable pill into it. Followed by a healthy glug of water. I gasped, recoiled, vibrated like a strummed string on a bass viol as smoke trickled from my ears. I shuddered and writhed as the Sobering Effect pill had its sobering effect.

"Did you have to do that?" I croaked.

"Yes. I have been informed that the departure celebration on the ship is winding down and takeoff is scheduled to take place as soon as we arrive. We leave."

We left. The front door crunched tight behind us as a stasis field sealed it into place. Our chauffeur saluted as he held the limo door open for us. Efficiency ruled as well at the spaceport. We admired the polished and rust-free *Porcuswine Express* as it shone in the sunlight. As we approached it the elevator came down and James stepped off waving cheerfully.

"Have a great trip to your porcuswine paradise. I'll expect glowing reports."

His mother embraced him; his father exchanged hearty handshakes. Then we waved cheerful good-byes as he vanished into the sunset. I turned back, concealing a quavering sigh, to our interstellar sty. We stepped aboard the access gantry and the elevator bore us swiftly towards what, I am sure, would be an interesting future. The airlock door hummed behind us and closed.

"Positions for takeoff, please. Three minutes to go."

Our acceleration couches were waiting. Strapping in took but a moment. Angelina seized my hand and squeezed it happily. I smiled hypocritically and the spacer trembled as the engines rumbled to life.

Mechanistria here we come . . .

As soon as the acceleration ceased I unbuckled and headed—purely by reflex—towards the newly installed bar.

"Hitting the sauce early are we . . . ?" the chill voice of my beloved sounded in my ear. I turned towards her, discarded my glass and nodded grimly.

"You're right, of course. I have been feeling sorry for myself and I apologize. To work! You'll let me know when it's time for the cocktail hour."

"I will. And now I'm going to find Pinky! I'm sure that takeoff terrified her."

"I'm off to the bridge."

We parted. I climbed the stairs. Pining for that lost drink. Admit it, Jim. You're glugging the booze down because, truthfully, you're as useful as a fifth wheel on this trip. With a fine captain, a stout engineer—and a fully automated spacer— you're out of a job.

I went onto the bridge and Kirpal waved a cheerful greeting.

"The money for the overhaul was well spent. We are aligning now for our course and all systems are go—"

His enthusiastic report was interrupted by a crackling eructation from the wall speaker.

"Stramm here. We're having a little problem . . ."

"Boss diGriz is on the way!" I said into the mike, as I waved Kirpal back into his seat.

"You're needed here. I'll find out what's happening and report back."

"You're the boss, Boss." He sat back down.

I whistled as I headed for the engine room, drink and depression forgotten as I got my teeth into the bit.

I found Stramm staring gloomily at a large illuminated gauge set among the other readouts. He tapped it and sighed heavily.

"What?" I asked.

"Trouble." In a voice heavy with gloom.

"Tell."

He did. In far too great technical detail. Like all engineers with a captive audience.

"As you know this ship is a bit of an antique. It has no levitation field for takeoff and landing."

"But we took off!"

"With great effort. When is the last time you used an acceleration couch?"

"In the military . . ."

"Right. All modern civilian ships use acceleration neutralizers."

"But we did take off . . ."

"We did. But we are going to have a bit of trouble landing."

"Explain!"

He tapped the gauge again.

"Reads full. It's not. I began to think about how I found that swine Rifuti down here. I began to wonder if he had been up to any more sabotage as well. Then I checked this reaction mass tank for the atomic thrust jets. We had to use some of the mass for takeoff, but this gauge read full. That couldn't be right. So I used the override and reset—like this."

The needle quivered and jumped to one extreme and back to the other. Then slowly moved a short distance up the dial and stopped.

"Meaning?"

"Rifuti dumped most of the tank. We had enough mass left for takeoff and a bit left over. But there is not enough for deceleration when we have to land."

"Trapped in space! Doomed to roam the stars forever . . . !"

"Not quite. But we'll have to scout about and find a solar orbiting satellite station where we can take on more reaction mass."

"What is that?"

"Water."

Put the old thinking cap on Jim.

"Don't we have more water aboard?"

"We do. But not a lot. We can keep drinking—or use it to land."

"Not much of a choice,"

I chewed my lip—always a helpful cudgel for thought. But all I did was hurt my lip. Think, Jim!

"Is water the only reaction mass that we can use?"

"No, but it's the easiest to handle in bulk. Throw any mass away fast enough and you get a reactive force."

Newton's first law: you learned it in school. But what else besides water could we use . . . ?

With the question came the answer!

"Tell me, Stramm, what is it they always got an awful lot of down on the farm?"

He frowned. "I don't know—I'm a city lad. But . . . !" His

eyes bulged—and then he smiled broadly. "You can throw anything away!"

"Right! So this will be the first spacer to land using . . ."

"Pig Poo Power!"

I was quite pleased with myself for this keen bit of lateral thinking. Stramm was rubbing his lantern jaw, deep in thought.

"Logistics," he muttered, "logistics . . ."

"Not a problem. Call a specialist."

I grabbed the ship's phone, switched to all compartments, spoke in my most authoritarian voice.

"Now hear this. Will Elmo report to the engine room at once. Elmo needed below."

I was examining the seals on the tank's inspection hatch when he arrived, brimming with curiosity. This instantly became bucolic bliss when the nature of my request became clear.

"Why that is shore a great idea, Cousin Jim. I admit that this was getting to be a problem what with . . ."

"Work first, explain later. You will need buckets and wheelbarrows, shovels and pitchforks . . ."

"We got all them things." He rushed off, his voice dying in the distance. "When the boys hear about this they will be happier than swine with their trotters in a trough!"

It was quite easy to visualize what came next with the boys, and I wanted none of it.

"I leave you in control of the situation, stout engineer Stramm. Until things have been . . . finalized . . . I should avoid the corridors between here and the sty deck. Should there be any more problems please contact me on the bridge."

I fled. Buckets and barrows and hearty earthy oaths were already sounding in the distance. I joined Kirpal and accepted his kind offer of a cup of tea. His placid smile turned to a scowl when I told him about Rifuti's latest perfidy.

"I shall radio details to the planetary police. They may grab him before he goes off-planet."

"A possible chance," I muttered. Sure that he would long be gone.

A bell on Kirpal's computer pinged and he put his cup down. He muttered to himself, punched in some more figures and nodded happily when a throaty buzzer sounded.

"Good. Course alignment entered and correct." He pressed a large red button. "Done. We're beginning our first Bloat."

I scratched my finger in my ear, not having heard right.

"Earwax maybe. I, ha-ha, did not hear right. For a moment there I thought you said bloat!"

"I did. This spacer isn't exactly new . . ."

As he said this his face had the same gloomy expression as that of engineer Stramm when he talked about the ship. His voice echoed from the depths of depression.

"You've seen what antiques we have for landing jets. Well, the ship's main drive is not much better."

"No Faster Than Light Drive?"

"Hardly. We have what is an ancient, long-superseded, outdated and archaic form of transportation called the Bloater Drive."

My finger quivered toward my ear—but I resisted. "Would you mind, sort of, you know, explaining that in a bit more detail?"

"Of course." He took a pair of wire-rimmed glasses from

a drawer in the console and put them on, then steepled his fingers before him. Why did I think that he had been a professor in one of his many incarnations? "How acquainted are you with nuclear physics?"

"Use words of one syllable—or less!—and I'll be able to follow you."

He nodded gloomily and sighed. I could hear his thoughts: another microcephalic.

"Have you heard of molecular binding energies?"

"Positively! I have used a molebinding device most successfully in the past." In the profitable pursuit of crime, I neglected to add.

"Then you are aware of molecular theory. In this reaction molecular binding energy is weakened so that another molecule can actually penetrate the molecules in an existing structure. The Bloater Drive works like this as well, only on a far greater scale—to the square of two million in fact—with results equal to the forces released. It permits the ship's molecules to expand exponentially until they are literally approaching light years apart."

I wish I had some of what he was smoking!

"You can't be serious?"

"Regretfully, I am. The Bloat operates along the central axis AB. With no observable motion of point A and continual acceleration of point B . . ."

My head was beginning to hurt. "Simplification I beg!"

The captain took the steel glasses off. "The ship gets bigger and longer in one direction."

"Understood!"

"So, when one end of the ship is at its destination it begins to shrink again—from that direction. Like stretching a rubber band between your hands. You pull wide with your right hand. Then bring your left hand over after it. The stretched band contracts back to normal size. But it is now in a new place. The same way that the expanded ship contracts. This is done until the ship is small again, only now it is at the new location in space."

The professor put his glasses back on, scowling at the stupidity of the untutored.

"That's why it is named the Bloater Drive. It also uses a great deal of power and is very inaccurate. After it arrives at the target, star observations are made, a new course is calculated and the next Bloat is made. Usually a number of these are needed."

"Well, thanks . . ." But I was too late. He was in full Bloater Drive now!

"Gravitons are responsible. The graviton is an elementary particle that mediates the force of gravity and molecular adhesion in the framework of the quantum field theory. The graviton is massless, because the gravitational force must have unlimited range, and must have spin of two because gravity is a second-rank tensor field."

I was feeling third rank myself by this time and badly in need of rescue.

"And how is all this powered?" I asked desperately, maybe forcing a change in subject.

"I explained that in detail that I thought was quite clear. Gravitons are orientated in the tensor field as you can see here."

He pointed to a glowing screen, looked away, then pulled his attention back to it sharply. His jaw fell and he reached out and almost tapped it. Grimly he whipped off his steel glasses and thumbed a switch, spoke sharply and abruptly.

"Engineer Stramm to bridge—code red."

CHAPTER 8

THIS WAS THE FIRST TIME I had seen our highly efficient captain loose his cool. He punched the buttons angrily, ran a quick program in the computer—growling under his breath—then wiped it from the screen with a muttered curse. He became even more active when Stramm hurried in. They bashed at the control console, ran equations. Even tapped dials.

"Something wrong guys?" I asked.

I must say that Captain Singh exercised great self-control and did not strike me down on the spot.

"Gravitons . . ." Stramm muttered darkly and they sighed in mutual disgust.

"Might I ask you to expand on that just a bit?"

"That treacherous swine Rifuti . . ." The captain growled. Then grabbed his self-control and was in command again.

"More sabotage. He was the wily one, making acts of double sabotage in the hope that when we were dealing with one we wouldn't notice his second dark deed." He tapped a meter. "He bled off over eighty percent of our gravitons."

"Weren't they seen?"

"Hardly. Since they are invisible, infinitesimal and exist only in quantum terms. The ground might be heavier for a few microseconds before they vanished into the planet's core."

"So . . . what do we do?"

"Hope there is a graviton refueling depot waiting at the other end—when we finish our Bloat."

"They are not very common." Stramm said, adding to the general gloom. "The collection stations are located on massive high-G planets where there are plenty of gravitons lying around." He raised his finger and smiled. "But we do have a graviton concentrator on the engine room!"

"I've seen it," the captain said, gloomily shaking his head. "It's an antique like everything else on this ship. Working flat out, on a one-G planet, it would take about two years to collect enough for our needs. Three months on a three-G planet would be fine. Except we would all be dead."

I dropped the obvious question into the growing silence.

"Then . . . what shall we do?"

Captain Singh took himself in hand—sat up straight and shook himself like a dog.

"We'll get out of this." He looked at his watch. "Our first Bloat will end in about five hours when we are scheduled to make a navigation check. We'll have to forget about getting to Mechanistria until we have had the opportunity to refuel."

"Where we will end up after the first Bloat?"

"Hopefully we will be close to a solar system that contains a single inhabited planet named Floradora."

"Sounds nice!" I said chipperly.

"The cheerful names usually stand for very repellent planets," Stramm said, bringing the gloom level back up again. The captain read from the screen.

"Inhabited planet. Early technical world type Alpha-X. No orbiting satellites or space stations at time of survey."

"When did this survey take place?" Stramm asked.

"Four hundred and two years ago come next Groundhog Day."

"Gosh, a lot could happen in that time!" I said brightly. This sally was greeted with cold silence. The captain hammered at a program he was running. When he finished he actually sat back and smiled.

"I estimate that when this first Bloat ends we will have enough gravitons for two more Bloats of the same distance." The smile vanished. "I hope we will be able to load gravitons at one of the two destinations." His voice grew cold. "If not, be prepared for quite a long visit."

I could think of no snappy answer to that. But I did have an important question.

"Instead of carrying on this course, why don't we simply return to Moolaplenty?"

He shook his head. "It's not that simple. When the Bloater Drive is in operation it leaves a virtual tunnel through interstellar space. These tunnels gradually die away, but sometimes take years to disperse. But they are easily detected and avoided."

"Then there is no way of going back?"

"Not the way we came. And we don't have enough gravitons for a more circuitous course."

I went back to our cabin under a cloud of gloom. I was mixing a lethal weapons-grade cocktail when I heard soft footsteps and the clatter of little trotters. I doubled the quantity of drink and filled a bowl with curry puffs. I cooled the drink mixture and poured it into two glasses over ice.

Pinky sniffed the air and burbled happily. I threw her a puff.

Angelina raised an eyebrow at the sight of the drinks.

"Are we celebrating?"

"Yes and no," I said handing her a glass. "Yes we are celebrating a successful takeoff and first Bloat—"

"How many of these have you had?"

"Like you, this is my first. Here's to a successful journey." I raised my glass and drank deep.

"But . . . ?"

"There are difficult times ahead. Sit, drink, nibble a puff. And I'll explain."

She listened in attentive silence to my tale of woe. In the end she nodded and held out her glass for a refill. She sipped and, in a steely voice, said, "I should have killed Rifuti when I had a chance. At least I sent a message to the Moolaplenty police about his first sabotage. Someday I will kill him. But that's for the future—after we have refilled the graviton tank."

"Have another curry puff," I said extending the bowl. Still glaring she took one, crunching down hard on it as though it were Rifuti's neck. An inquiring snuffle drew her attention and she fed one to Pinky.

"What's this Floradora planet like?"

"Don't know. All contact was apparently lost during the breakdown and the records were wiped."

"We'll just have to play it by ear."

She smiled. "I hate to say it, Jim, but I suddenly realized that I have had it with our pleasure planet sojourn. It will be a relief to see a new world. To deal with whatever problems come up."

The nature of the problems we might face was obvious when a small and wicked-looking knife appeared in her hand. She tested the blade delicately with a fingertip, frowned slightly and went into the kitchen. She returned with an atomic sharpener, which put a molecule-wide edge on the blade. Then smiled cheerily as, with a quick swipe, the blade cut a good chunk out of the metal table. "I think Floradora will be fun!"

We clinked glasses happily—smiling at each other at the same time.

THE DAYS PASSED SWIFTLY AS the end of the first Bloat approached. But the air seemed to smell sweeter—despite a certain lingering memory of the farmyard, although the constant topping up of the reaction mass tank did tend to improve this. The thought of more interesting and attractive times to come made the food taste better, the drink stronger, the future more appealing.

We were just finishing our evening meal when Captain Singh's voice crackled from the speakers.

"Boss Jim to the bridge. Unbloating has begun."

Angelina smiled and we even held hands as we climbed the stairs. We didn't know what to expect from this new world, but we did know that life was sure to be more interesting in the very near future.

"That's the primary," Kirpal said, pointing to a star in the center of the screen. "I'm holding position here while I get off a signal to Interstellar Emergency."

Angelina declined a visit to the communications room and went to see after Pinky. I followed Kirpal and watched while he switched on comm power.

"It will take a short time to align . . ."

I don't know if it aligned or not, but there was a brief thudding sound. Followed by a great gout of flame that blew the front panel off. Smoke billowed out as alarm bells sounded throughout the ship.

I dived for the rear wall and tore a fire extinguisher from its mounting, pulled the pin and sprayed the opening with suppressant powder. The fire roared, fizzled and died just as Stramm burst in waving an even larger extinguisher. He doused the last bursts of flame and smoke, then took a flashlight from his utility belt and peered inside the blackened opening. Then, muttering guttural curses, he reached in carefully and removed a blackened, twisted box.

"Very ingenious."

"More of Rifuti's work?" I asked.

"Obviously. A Bloat detector connected to some explosives. It wasn't activated until the Bloat was switched on. The transmitter would work fine until then. But now, after our Bloat, it exploded nicely."

"No communication . . ." Kirpal said hollowly. "Let's hope there is a transmitter on Floradora."

Drenched in gloom we went slowly back to the bridge. Angelina was waiting there with Pinky.

"Trouble?" she asked seeing our dark expressions.

"Lots of it," I said, bringing her up to speed about the latest sabotage. Pinky sensed our mood, shivered and retreated to the corner. Kirpal went to work

"I have directed a low-power Bloat field towards the planet. We'll be in orbit around it in a few minutes."

The primary grew larger even as we watched, then moved slowly off center.

"The planet has been detected and we should reach it as soon as the Bloat ends."

There was slight tingling in the air and a slight pop as the Bloater Drive shut off. A distant spot grew to a disk then loomed large and filled the screen. Blue skies and white bands of clouds.

"Looks quite nice," Angelina said.

"We're getting strong television signals on a number of stations," Kirpal said. "Let's see what they have to say."

He thumbed a button and loud martial music boomed from the speakers. It died away to the background as a harsh male voice rasped out.

"Welcome to the *Happy Kiddies Hour.* Today little friends we are going to have a jolly time talking about your gas mask and how it protects you from all nasty poison gasses . . ."

I gaped. "They must be joking . . . Try another channel." The sound gurgled then steadied.

"Welcome to the preparedness evening broadcast. To-night's topic is titled 'How to Build Your Own Bomb Shelter.' "

"At least he's talking Esperanto," I said.

Angelina frowned. "Not that I care much for the choice of topic. Do you think there is a war on?"

"We'll take a look," Kirpal said. He made adjustments to the controls. "I've put us into a geostationary orbit over the source of the broadcast. Viewing is fine . . . the electron tele-scope has high resolution . . ."

A walled city swam into focus. It appeared to be sur-rounded by fields of some kind. A cloud of dust was clearly visible from one of the fields. The telescope zoomed in on a farm tractor pulling a plow.

A moment later the scene changed. The tractor stopped and the gray-clad driver jumped down. He took one quick look at the sky before he began running. He ran to the city and through a large gate, which began to close behind him. At the same time the radio burst into life on the emergency fre-quency.

"Alien spacer identify yourself. Ten seconds. Identify yourself. Five seconds . . ."

"What happens when they hit zero?" I asked.

The answer was quick enough in coming. A rocket zoomed up from the city—and burst well below us. Kirpal hit the controls and we moved quickly out of range.

"Welcome to lovely Floradora," Angelina said. And laughed wryly. "I think I'm going to enjoy it here!"

My dear wife was a woman of a different disposition. Where others might flee or seek safety she went boldly forth. I laughed too, catching her mood. Captain and engineer looked at us as if we were mad.

"Let us leave these paranoid peasants behind us and take a look at the rest of the countryside," I suggested. "Get below the horizon and make a wide circle out of their sight."

"Why not," Kirpal muttered for lack of better inspiration.

It was a pleasant enough planet once the city was left be-hind. The plowed fields ended abruptly and were replaced by sylvan forest. There were streams and ponds, even a few small lakes.

"Looks like good fishing," Stramm said, revealing that he had a pastoral side to his nature.

"More plowed fields ahead," Kirpal said zooming the image in on the countryside below. Unpaved, rustic roads meandered away from the fields—all heading in the same direction. We followed them, passing over green fields filled with grazing cattle, until low structures appeared ahead.

"Do those buildings have thatched roofs?" Angelina asked.

"Indeed they do," Kirpal said, zooming in on them. "Wattle and daub walls too if I am not mistaken."

Flowers abounded, while fruit trees lined the roads. I pointed to a large grassy open space next to a small grove, just beyond the buildings. "Why don't we put the ship down there—and see if the natives are friendly."

"Done," the captain said, "but my hand will still be on the throttle if we have to leave abruptly."

Barnyard power flamed out and we settled gently to the ground. Waited. Nothing stirred. Doors remained closed.

"Anyone home?" Stramm asked. "Maybe they're suspicious of our intentions."

"You would be too—considering who their neighbors are." Angelina said. "I think I'll take a stroll and see what happens."

"Not alone," I said. Patting the small of my back to make sure my weapon was secure.

The lower hatch opened as we approached it and the gangway rattled out and down. There was the clatter of tiny hooves as Pinky joined us. She sniffed the balmy air and squealed happily. Holding hands we followed her down to the grassy ground—where she burst into frantic squealing as she galloped away.

I had my hand on my gun when Angelina put her hand on my arm.

"Relax," she cozened. "It appears to be a nut tree of some kind."

"The edible kind," I said to the sound of happy munching.

"There is someone watching us from the building behind you," Angelina said quietly. "I saw the window curtain move."

"The other buildings too. One of the closed doors is open a bit now."

"Let's reassure them," she said, as she bent and gathered a small bouquet of white flowers from a nearby patch. Then she turned towards the house of the twitching curtain—and held them out, smiling as she did.

It worked like a charm. The curtain dropped back and a moment later the door opened. Hesitantly, a rustically dressed woman emerged. Angelina walked slowly across the green towards her—and handed her the flowers.

Other doors were now opening and men and women cautiously appeared. One gray-haired, gray-bearded man left the group and walked over to us. When he came close he raised his hand, palm outwards, in what could only have been a gesture of peace; I responded in kind.

"Welcome peaceful strangers—and fine animal—welcome to Floradora," he said formally. "I am Bilboa of Burgansee."

"My thanks and I return greetings, oh fine gentleman of Floradora." This kind of thing was catching. "I am Jim of diGriz."

From behind me I heard the all too familiar nasal tones of Elmo.

"Hi there, Cousin Jim. That fresh air shore do smell great. The swine think so too—can we let them out to root around?"

Why not. "But just the sows and piglets first." I didn't want the thundering boars to spoil the party.

There were oohs and ahhs from the growing crowd of Floradorans as the porcuswine swept out. In a moment their joyful squealing died away to be replaced by happy rooting and munching. One of the women swooned with delight.

As I turned back to Bilboa I saw that Angelina was in close conversation with an attentive circle of women. So far so good.

"Nice planet you have here, brother Bilboa."

"It is indeed a world of wonder, brother Jim. Legend has it that we came here from a planet of darkness where we suffered and were despised for our pure beliefs. But we, the Children of Nature and Love, did flee the darkness and impurities and did come to this planet of shining peace for lo—millennia. Until . . ." He groaned aloud and shook his fists at the sky.

"Then they came and brought great evil with them . . ." He shivered and lowered his fists. "I beg your indulgence and pardon, brother Jim of diGriz. I sully this happy day of new friends, both two-legged and four-legged, and beg you to excuse me."

"No problem, brother Bilboa, let's enjoy . . ."

The radio buzzed in my head.

"Jim—what's happening out there? I see quite a crowd."

"It's going great, Captain. I'll call you back soonest."

Bilboa was interested. "You speak to your friends in the ship of space?"

"I do indeed."

"Perhaps they will join us—as you see we prepare for a feast of greetings."

While we had been shooting the breeze men had been carrying out tables and chairs. Moments later burdened women had spread them with cloths, plates of food, bowls of flowers. And interesting jugs of liquid refreshment. I was beginning to like these simple folk. I quietly said *radio on.*

"It's party time and the fun is about to begin—and you're all invited."

"Enjoy. I and Stramm are staying here. I'll let the passengers out—and lock the airlock after them."

"Understandable after the way our luck has been running. We'll bring you back a picnic basket."

There was laughter—and even cheers—when the company emerged. Oohs of admiration greeted the appearance of the boars, each carefully tethered by a hind leg. They trotted across the field, rumbling with pleasure, and joined the rest of the herd in a good root under the trees. There were excited shouts of greetings on all sides: I seized the moment to investigate the chilled jugs of liquid.

I sipped from an earthenware mug. Fresh fruit flavors—and a hint of something else. Alcohol? I chugalugged some more. Yes indeed, my old friend Ethyl, if I was not mistaken. And I rarely was.

"I see that you are enjoying our tinkleberry wine," Bilboa said, pouring himself a good mug full.

"Health and happiness," I said. We thunked jugs together.

"Nature and love."

We smiled happily and he poured refills.

The party was now in full swing. I nibbled on some delicious baked cheese biscuits. Then Angelina joined us and, in the spirit of the day, put her radio on the table and switched on some pastoral music.

"A wondrous device," Bilboa said.

"Don't you use radios?"

"Happily, no. The simple, natural life is sacred to us. We left all the machines behind when we sealed and abandoned the vessels that brought us here. Along with other evils like money, property tax, income tax, guns and goatmobiles—or so legend has it. Though I know not the meaning of these words."

"You're better off without them. So . . . no machines, music players, radios, interstellar communications machines?"

Casually mentioned . . .

"None of those." My spirits fell. Still, the city had machines—if TV and ground-to-air missiles counted.

I waited until we had knocked back a few more mugs of Old Relaxing Juice before I worked the conversation around to more serious matters.

"Dear friend Bilboa, I so welcome your many kindnesses. But, at the risk of offending you who offers such hospitality and largesse, I must return to a topic of great importance to me. Those who live in the walled city . . ."

He sighed tremulously and his smile vanished as I made my pitch.

"Though we approached them in peace they used a weapon in an attempt to destroy us. For our own protection I must know who they are and why they fired on us. We have an expression: know your enemy. I must know more about these people for our own protection."

The day appeared to darken and the warmth was gone from the air.

"You are correct and I was wrong to keep this knowledge from you. It has been written that one black day our peaceful and loving existence—alone on this friendly planet—was broken by the thunder of their great ships landing. Like us they came here seeking escape and the solitude to pursue their own philosophy and ends."

His eyes sparkled and he shook his fist at the defenseless sky. "While we are one with nature, they attack it with foul machines and great stinks. They attempted to force us to join them in their evil beliefs. We could only flee in horror. In the end they tired of attempting to convert us to their Church of the Vengeful God and retired behind their city walls."

"Then you no longer have any contact with them?"

Bilboa sighed again, most unhappily, and shook his gray head.

"Would that were so. Perhaps we are weak, but we welcome their medicines that cure us of illness."

"But these Vengefulers don't sound like the type to indulge in generosity . . ."

"They are not! We pay a high price! Not in this money thing you talk of, but in toil and labor in exchange for these vital needs."

Getting close now! "And that is . . . ?"

"Flowers."

That was a stopper. Interstellar flower power? Religious nutcases with a weakness for blooming buds? I managed to gasp out a query.

"But . . . I mean what . . . why flowers?"

"When their machines break down they must be repaired, replaced. Or so it has been explained to me although I know not the details."

This was it. Interstellar contact for replacement and re-pairs.

"Do you know what they do with these flowers?" I asked humbly.

"By some devious means they turn the blooms into per-fume. It has been said that the flowers of Floradora make a perfume of such beauty that it is prized throughout the galaxy."

"You wouldn't know how this perfume of delight reaches said galaxy?"

"They summon spacers who bring things they require in exchange."

Bull's-eye! Contact could be made!

CHAPTER 9

I STROLLED OVER WITH THE jug and refilled Angelina's mug with the potent Floradora fruit punch. She smiled her thanks. I bent close.

"Good news from the local capo. They trade flowers with the city people in exchange for medicine."

She raised a quizzical eyebrow. "How very nice for them. And you have a reason for telling me this?"

"Indeed. The war-happy city citizens turn the flowers into perfume—which is picked up by off-planet traders . . ."

"Contact!" she said, clapping her hands with pleasure. She glanced over my shoulder at the lowering sun. "Time to go back to the ship and report the good news."

"I'll bid our good-byes and start the pigs and people moving."

"And I'll fix a picnic basket for Kirpal and Stramm. I hope they don't mind vegetarian food."

"Is it? I never noticed."

"It was so good it didn't matter. You'll have plenty steaks on the ship."

I saw Bilboa carrying out a fresh jug and joined him for a stirrup cup. We thudded mugs.

"Fine as this day was—new friends and fine food—all good things must end," I said. His face dropped.

"We have much to talk of, new friend Jim."

"We do indeed, fine friend Bilboa, but it will have to wait until another day."

"Can we say tomorrow? You must see our dairy!"

"First thing in the morning. Your milk and butter—and cheese—are more than excellent."

"Warm thanks! Until the morning then."

The party was slowly breaking up. Tables were being cleared, good-byes rang out and reboarding began. Stomachs full, the swine trotted happily back to their pens. So did the farmers—though not to their stys. A number of hearty handclasps later we waved our good-byes and rejoined the others. I rolled in the ramp and sealed the port. By reflex— since I didn't think the Floradorans meant us any harm. In the dining room I found the ship's crew tucking into the lavish spread.

"Farm fresh and delicious!" Kirpal sounded like a TV commercial. Stramm wasted no time on talk only nodded and crunched. I joined them in some fruit punch until they were sated.

"The good news is that the city dwellers, who are followers of a cult religion called the Church of the Vengeful God, have interstellar communication."

I nodded agreement with their happy cries.

"That's the good news. The bad news is that they may take some persuading, for they are a surly and bigoted lot—as their surface-to-air missile proved."

Kirpal rubbed his jaw and frowned. "Church of the Vengeful God? Never heard of them."

"No reason you should have. There were a great number of nutcase religions during the breakdown years." I pointed to the communicator unit on the wall. "Does that connect to the ship's central computer?"

"Of course—by law. A mini mainframe with almost unlimited memory banks."

I put the communicator on the table and the captain ran a Gurgle search. "There it is." I leaned close and read—

CHURCH OF THE VENGEFUL GOD

During the Breakdown Years on Earth (or Dirt), thought to be the original planet that was home to mankind, there were a number of remarkable, and distasteful, religions that sprang up. All of them died out—though it is possible that some of them spread to other of the colonized planets.

The Vengefulers, as this odd religion was called, had a rather obnoxious philosophy. They believed that God was really the Devil—having displaced the true God and chained him in Hell. Only by practicing a rigid discipline could they satisfy the Devil-God and convince him to finally release God from Hell so they could join him in heaven. To this end they mortified the flesh, since they believed it to be intrinsically evil, and forewent all pleasures and luxuries. They also believed that the rest of mankind was jealous of them and waged eternal war against them. To say that they were extremely paranoid understates the case.

It is reported that this cult died out when they fled to other planets to escape what they saw was an eternal holy war.

Many centuries have passed since the last report that they had been seen.

However, there is still an intergalactic warning out not to approach them or attempt any contact.

"Nice people," Kirpal said, curling his lip with distaste.

"I can handle them," I said briskly.

With more surety than I really felt. Yet I must do it—or resign myself to a vegetarian life with plenty of flowers. But I needed more information about the city. And I knew where to find it.

"Captain Singh. A question, please. When we were above the city, and they attacked us with their missile, we had a fine picture on the screen of everything that happened. Was that image recorded?"

"Of course. Automatically."

"Wonderful! Can you print out some good pictures of the city?"

"Of course."

"Then, after you eat, will you make some blow-up prints? Know your enemy and all that."

"Good as done."

It had been a long and busy day and it appeared that everyone had retired early. But I had too much to think about. I dug into the bar supplies, which I had carefully restocked for any emergency before we left. I found a bottle of Old Cerebellum

Tickler and poured a tall one with plenty of ice. With Mozart playing softly in the background I pulled over the transcribing screen and a stylo.

After many minutes and a number of glugs it remained infuriatingly blank.

"Come on, Jim, put the thinking cap on. You are the only one—you ingenious old Rat—who can find a way out of this mess. Outwit the Devil-Gooders, contact the galaxy, convince the porcuswiners that they would all be very happy remaining here. That done you can forget all about Mechanistria and go home for some peace and quiet."

It sounded wonderful.

Now how would I go about doing just that?

Why, by remembering the old diGrizian axiom: turn everything on its head. All too often strong beliefs revealed a flaw. A perceived strength would often contain an inherent weakness.

So what were these pseudoreligious nutcases really good at? Ask a question, get an answer.

Paranoia.

They thought everyone hated them.

Therefore I must make that come true! And extract great pleasure in doing so.

I finished my drink, patted my lips dry, turned off the lights and, fatigued yet happy, went to bed.

It is understandable but inconvenient that there are no portholes in deep spacers. Yawning myself awake I switched an outside image to the screen. Another bright and sunny day in what I hoped would soon be a porcine paradise. How I would treasure the sight of the last retreating hams on the hoof. I could not help but whistle cheerfully.

"Someone is all bright-eyed and bushy-tailed this morning," Angelina said, covering a yawn.

"I'm a genius—and I am the first one to admit it!"

"Not before I've had my coffee. Desist."

I was spreading a last piece of toast with marmalade when Angelina emerged. Coiffed and glowing with health—in a fetching outfit I had never seen before. Not that I would have remembered if I had.

"I've been invited by the Floradoran's Women's League to a sewing bee."

"Sounds delightful." Sounded like death warmed over. "Do you know what this bucolic ritual is?"

"No, but I'm sure they will tell me."

As she said this I felt a surge of inspiration. Lights flashed and bells rang.

"I imagine it has to do with sewing clothes, since without machines I don't think there are any factories here. And, if that is what it is, why, you and the ladies will be of immense help in our leaving this planet."

She clapped her hands and laughed aloud.

"Has my genius elaborated an ingenuous plan to leave this planet?"

"Your genius has done just that!" I said as I buffed my fingernails on my shirt front, then blew upon them. "Complete with a new and powerful bureaucratic establishment with galaxy-wide authority."

"And the name of this newly created omnipotent organization?"

I drew myself up, took a brace and proudly said—

"The Intergalactic Department of Religious Control."

"You're serious?"

"Never more so. In my position of authority as First Galactic Inspector I will investigate a reported violation of the Galactic Religious Code."

"And what may I ask is that?"

"I don't know yet, but it's going to be a humdinger. But—first things first. We must have a design for my uniform for you to take to your ladies' sewing circle."

She frowned at the tiny watch set under her pinky fingernail. "Will you be long?"

"Hard to tell. Why don't you join your sisterhood and find out more about their sewing skills. I'll join you as soon as I have completed the design."

I was humming with creative ardor as I signed onto the terminal and brought up a surfeit of splendor. My, how mankind does love its military glory!

Uniforms of every color and gaudy display raced across the screen. When I had picked out the most splendid and eye-dazzling, I saved them in a file of martial magnificence. A quick search through the computer index found a design program that let me combine elements of the most stunning. When it was complete I hit print and a large and glaringly colorful picture emerged. I held it up at arm's length and marveled.

"Truly impressive, Jim. The Vengefulers can but shiver before its majesty!"

First off it was black, a deep jet as dark as interstellar space. Set against this were many glistening and glowing features. Large epaulettes on the shoulders, heavy with gilt bullion. Rows of gold buttons, looped braid, glistening cuffs, exotic awards and medals heavy on the chest. To design these medals I rooted through the history of religion and made copies of all the symbols of many creeds. There were crossed swords next to a crescent moon. Then five joined stars next to a five-pointed star, a burning sun inside a black coffin—next to a plain cross. Oh, the wonders that man doth create!

The only quiet note in this glorious uniform was a white clerical collar. I held the printout at arm's length and nodded with appreciation.

"And you are just the man to wear it, Jim." I was never one for false modesty.

Now, construction. The sewing circle would do their part. What about the medals? After a little thought I called Stramm.

"What's up, Boss?" his screened image said.

"Do you have a laser lathe in your engine room?"

"Of course. Need it to machine spare parts."

"Then fire it up. I'll be right down with a little job for you."

When I handed him the printout I swear his eyes bulged. Whether with horror or appreciation it was hard to tell.

"What in . . . ?"

"Don't ask! All will be revealed eventually. What I need are 3-D replicas of all the fruit salad on the chest. Can do?"

"Of course. I'll scan them, then laser-form them in brass. There will be no problem filling in the details in colored ceramic."

"Then go to it—while I see about the uniform."

The lower ramp was down and the porcuswine were already grunting and rooting in the woods under the watchful eyes of the swineherds. I waved back to their shouted greetings and hurried on, not wanting any swineyard chat. Well away from them I used my phone to ring through to Angelina; who sent one of her coworkers to find me. A shy young girl soon joined me, blushing when she curtsied, then hurried away towards one of the bigger buildings. Following her lead I entered a good-sized room where a score of ladies were industrially plying their needles. Angelina, who thought little of home economics, was serving cups of tea.

"Is this the masterpiece?" she asked. Then stepped back stricken with awe—or horror—when I proudly displayed it.

"Well," she said, "it certainly is something different . . ."

"It is indeed. But remember it is not designed to astonish this gathering, but to make an impression on a far sterner audience."

"It surely will!"

"Can they do it?"

"I don't think it will be any problem. They've created some wonderful designs. Not only clothes but drapes, bedding—just about everything."

"Then I'll leave you to it."

I exited—with the sewing circle gasping with awe over my design.

Or were they vibrating with shock?

CHAPTER 10

IT HAD JUST GONE NOON when I reentered the ship. I had intended to hold my meeting on the bridge, but the sight of the sun just above the yardarm was too tempting. But just one drink, Jim, I promised myself. I flipped on the ship's speakers as I entered the bar.

"Now hear this. All crew members—namely captain and chief engineer—to important conference. In the bar. And will the captain kindly bring those printouts of the city."

I had just filled three glasses with ice when my loyal crew came in.

"Gentlemen, what are you drinking?"

The captain shook his head. "Sorry. Never drink on duty."

"I do," Stramm said. Thus upholding the noble artificers' tradition. "Whatever you're having."

"Pink gin. A traditional midday tipple."

I poured the captain a fruit juice. We clinked glasses and sat.

"I can now reveal my plan for our leaving this divided planet. We all know about the loathsome pseudoreligion of the Vengefulers. I intend to now use their rampant paranoia to assist us. Since they live in fear we will use that fear against them. Or rather the Intergalactic Department of Religious Control will. Since this organization is charged with monitoring all religions it must be all powerful."

"What will you tell them?" Kirpal asked.

"I don't know yet. I'll play that by ear. I'll find out where their worries and uncertainties lie—then take advantage of them." I saw that Kirpal was frowning and I nodded.

"I agree. It is a dirty business taking advantage of a person's greatest fears and reinforcing them. But we need help— and I'll see what I can do to aid the Nature and Love people at the same time. Nor will it, I hope, cause any lasting harm, since we know their paranoia is already well-institutionalized."

"I still don't like it."

"Nor do I. And I won't say it is for a greater good, which it is not. That excuse won't wash. I'm digging in dirt and I'll be soiled by it. We'll all benefit but that doesn't excuse what I'm doing. And I'm sorry."

And I was. But there was no going back. Despite my promised one-and-no-more I poured myself a stiff guilt-expiator. Plus one for Stramm. Though free of guilt he was happy to join me.

"Now we must devise a plan for opening contact with the sinful city dwellers. Any thoughts?"

My only answer was a numb silence. It was obvious that

fine captain and stout engineer were empty of any ideas reeking of cunning chicanery. I sighed silently; we needed crooked thoughts now from a crooked brain.

"We must make a memorable impression with our first contact. Catch them off balance and keep then tottering."

The juices of inspiration were beginning to flow; I sipped my drink to keep them lubricated. I pulled over an aerial picture of the city.

"We will strike at the first light of day, while they are all asleep. We will bring up our forces during the night and they will be concealed, here, under cover at the forest's edge. At dawn we will move into action."

"What forces?" Stramm asked, puzzled.

"I don't know yet. But I do know that we must make a strong and instant impression. I imagine that you can whip together a portable amplifier with loud and impressive speakers?"

"No problem."

"Then I must make a truly imposing appearance. Strike them with shock and awe. Too bad I can't ride up in a tank—or at least an armored car . . ."

"I have a motorcycle in the hold," Stramm said, getting into the spirit of our endeavor. "But it's bright yellow—"

"Spray it black to match my uniform!"

"Good as done."

"Then I blast up to the gate, screech to a halt and issue my orders . . ."

"With a remote mike patched through to my amplifier."

He was really getting into the spirit of the occasion—as was the captain as well.

"What you need are troops to back you up. What about all of the farmers behind you just at the edge of the clearing?"

"With the dungarees they all wear dyed black," Stramm added.

"And wooden rifles also black," I broke in.

"It's a good plan," the captain said, draining his glass.

"But next—what will you do after you get to the gate?" Stramm asked, suddenly worried.

"Fear not! With this buildup they should be rattled enough to follow my orders—at least in the beginning. I'll just have to stay on top of the situation."

I hoped. It was a pretty mad plan—but I had to make it work. I reached for the gin bottle. Then stopped and put the empty glass down. Time, Jim, for a clear head and some detailed cogitation.

Stramm hurried back to his shop to start work. The captain went to the bridge—while I found a memory tablet to make notes. A good deal of time passed while I planned my attack. My concentration was broken only when Angelina appeared at the bar door. Of stern expression.

"I thought I'd find you here. Isn't it early to—" Her eyes widened when she looked at the table before me. "Jim DiGriz . . . is that a cup of coffee in front of you . . ."

"No—" Her expression grew grim. Until I added "it's a cup of tea."

She blew me a kiss. "Congratulations on a booze-free day."

I nodded acceptance and kept silent. Not wanting to change her happy mood.

"How long will you be?" she asked.

I held up my notes. "Just about done."

"Good. I want to clean up and change and then we'll declare the cocktail hour open."

"I'll be here."

When she returned I was flipping through the pages of the barputer.

"I have been searching through the history of drink—and reams of recipes for cocktails. Amazing! Would you like to try a Horse's Neck, or a Manhattan? A Sheep Dip Special? Consider a Rusty Nail, The Widow's Kiss or a Hound Dog's Hair?"

"Surprise me."

"Done!" I entered data and hit the MIX button.

The machine gave a mechanical rattle and a deep chunter. Ice crackled and a chilled pitcher and frosted glasses appeared on the delivery tray. I poured and passed her a glass.

"A Very Dry Martini with a Twist."

"Sounds terrible—tastes wonderful!" She sipped—then sipped again, then put her glass on the table.

"Your uniform is going well—although we had to make some minor changes—and one major one."

"Which is . . . ?"

"We have a problem with gold braid and the gold buttons. There is simply nothing that even resembles gold to hand. We tried various kinds of yellow fabric with mixed results. The braid looks cheap and nasty. And the buttons are all carved wood or bone. They can be died yellow but with very poor results . . ."

"In adversity lies the answer. Let us forget the military glitter and stay with all black. Gloom and doom! Very impressive. But do they have enough black dye?"

"They do indeed—a deep, dark and impressive one. Made from a species of lake shellfish."

"Let's do it." I glanced up at the bar clock. "There are still a few hours of daylight left. I want to have a conference with Bilboa. Unless we want to move this ship we are going to need some help getting to the city."

"See you at dinner. I want to take Pinky for a long walk. All that rooting and eating under the nut trees has made her more than rotund."

"A porcuswine's job."

"The others maybe, but I want her to keep her figure."

We parted at the foot of the gangway and I was not surprised to find Bilboa waiting patiently at a nearby table. He was tucking into a mug of drink and I was more than happy to join him in a jar.

"I have been talking with your kinsman named Elmo and he has revealed many important things to me."

I could only smile and nod since I could think of nothing Elmo might possibly say that would be even remotely interesting.

"It seems they raise a number of crops to supply feed for their porcuswine. He had a wondrous book with pictures that moved as if blown by the wind. Many of the plants shown are grown here, but others were unknown, like the yellow corn. They have golden seeds that he said are quite nutritious and with great kindness gave me some."

I did not share his agricultural enthusiasm.

"That's nice." I groped for a way to change the topic but he was well into full flow. "In turn for some of these we will give him seeds of the manna plant. Which supplies the ground flour that makes the fried cakes which, as I remember, you greatly enjoyed."

"Enjoyed is not the word—paradisiacal might be closer! And from a plant too—I thought they were meat patties—"

I stopped as he reeled back, eyes wide; his tanned skin paled. He gasped aloud.

"Are you all right?" I asked. Wondering where the nearest medikit was. He gurgled something incomprehensible, started to stand—then slumped back. And spoke in a halting, pained breath.

"Don't speak again—ever—what you just said. We eat the fruits of the earth. We could not, impossible to . . ."

He grew silent, his pallid skin turning bright red.

I realized that these people were vegetarians—with a vengeance.

"Corn—cornmeal . . ." I said. Changing the subject quickly. "Makes lovely porridge and corn bread. Even better boiled on the cob and served with butter."

He shuddered once and relaxed. Pulling a large bandanna out of his sleeve and mopping his brow.

"But enough talk of food, ha-ha," I ha-ha'd. "I want to ask you how you bring your flowers to the city?"

"Yes, of course. We take them by oxcart. They are strong and willing creatures."

"Does it take very long?"

"There is an easy road through Burnham Wood. A half-day's travel at the most. But, I beg you, do not go there! Nothing but evil comes from the city." He drank deep, our early perilous conversation seemingly forgotten.

"I must see them—and deal with them. For our mutual

benefit I assure you. Nothing but good will come of my visit there."

"In that case we will assist you, Jim of DiGriz, for you are a man of great wisdom."

"I sincerely hope that I am, Bilboa of Burgansee. We will talk again in the morning."

I returned to the ship in a somber mood—to see my darling wife in the nut grove, waving a greeting. I waved back and when I drew close I saw that she glowed with good spirits. Holding the leash that was tethered to a panting and very glassy-eyed Pinky. Even her bristles were drooping.

"We had a lovely stroll by the flower fields. Then a nice run back. She'll sleep well tonight. And so will you."

"Me? Why?"

"Because the ladies told me that your uniform is finished and ready for a fitting."

"Now?"

"Indeed!"

Pinky squealed a feeble protest when she was awakened and forced to walk between us. The ladies of the sewing circle must have been watching out for us because they emerged from the building en masse. When we drew close they parted ranks and proudly held aloft their sable garment.

"Tre tre bonega!" I gasped for it was indeed a beautiful creation.

"It's not quite dry yet," Angelina said.

"It may dye my skin but not my soul!"

There was a small dressing room just inside the front door. I stripped down, then happily slipped into the uniform's clammy embrace. My dark image in the mirror was truly stupendous. I threw the door wide and emerged to resounding applause. I bowed in response.

"A work of art that exceeds my wildest expectation. Thank you, kind ladies of Floradora, thank you."

I carried it back to the ship in triumph. To the welcome news that Stramm had finished all of the metal religious badges. We called a council of war on the bridge where my new uniform was greatly admired. With the badges attached it was even more impressive.

"I went through all your shoes," Angelina said. "You have a pair of black climbing boots that will really fill the bill. But you need a uniform hat of some kind."

"As good as done. I'll do just what I did with the uniform— amalgamate all the most repulsive headgear into one repellant black and frightening cap. Will your ladies be able to make it up?"

"They have some wondrous holiday headgear, so I know they can."

"Things are shaping up to perfection," I said. "I can see it all happening now. Our convey of oxcarts leaves here at dusk and we reach our destination before morning. The troops line up on the forest's edge. The amplifier is set up and I am ready on the motorcycle. On the signal there is an ear destroying blast of trumpets and I gun the motorcycle forward. And . . ."

My voice ran down and they all leaned forward expectantly, waiting . . .

"And . . . something is missing."

"What . . . ?" Angelina breathed softly, speaking for them all.

"And we must have something truly impressive happen. Something as dramatic as a pillar of fire . . ."

"No problem," Stramm said. "I doubt if you have ever heard of thermite?"

"Indeed I have. I have used it in . . . errr . . . construction." Destruction would be more correct.

"It's new to me," the captain said.

"It's a mixture of finely ground iron oxide and aluminum," Stramm said. "Used mostly for welding."

"Or making a great fireball!" I added. "But it's dangerous to handle."

"Not with the correct igniter. And a launcher of some kind. I'll see what I can come up with."

"Please do that!" I chortled. "Gentlemen—and lady—we have a plan!"

"Do we?" Angelina said, with an edge to her voice. "And just what part am I to play in this plan?"

"Light of my life—you have made it possible with this fine uniform."

"I see. The little lady stays in the sewing room while the brave men go off to war . . ."

"Not at all! It's just a one-man job . . ."

"One man, one woman. I'll run up a black uniform for myself and go along as your assistant—and bodyguard."

There was an air of finality in her voice that brooked no argument. I opened my mouth to protest, but words would not come. I looked to Stramm and the captain for aid, but they were looking away.

"Yes, indeed. That certainly is a good idea."

CHAPTER 11

IT TOOK THE BETTER PART of three days to make our preparations. And all of that time I was living in a fool's paradise. The future looked so bright! We would storm the city with flame and threat and—seemingly—armed strength. Subdue the Vengefulers, make interstellar contact, then leave this planet forever. Elmo and Bilboa were now good buddies and both seemed to like the idea of the porcuswiners staying here on this friendly world. The future was bright and beautiful.

Until it all came crashing down. Elmo tracked me down to the engine room where I was helping Stramm to construct a thermite bomb thrower.

"Cousin Jim . . ."

I looked up to see him in best cringing mode. Slumped over, wringing his hat, shivering.

"Yes?"

"Could I kind of talk to you, mebbe outside . . ."

"Tell me here, good cousin many-times removed. I have no secrets from engineer Stramm."

"It's, maybe, I . . ."

"Speak—for we are all literally in the same boat together."

"Well . . . I kind of gave our friend Bilboa a present, you know, friendly like. Strange feller, took it the wrong way. Got angry. Told me to tell you that we all gotta get off this planet at once. Or even sooner, that's what he said."

There was a clang as Stramm dropped his wrench. We were both now staring straight at the quavering Elmo who shied away.

"And what, may I ask, was this present you gave him?"

The frigid silence lengthened before Elmo coughed and spoke so quietly I could barely hear him.

"I thought shore he would like it . . . them feeding us so well and all. I didn't know he would take offense . . ."

"Elmo! What was it?"

"A nice big slab of smoked porcuswine ribs . . ."

My wrench also clanged to the deck.

"You microcephalic moron! They're all vegetarians! Why didn't you offer him your grandmother's smoked leg as well . . ."

He fled, Stramm's thrown hammer just missing him.

All our careful plans were as naught in the face of this disaster. Or were they?

"What do we do?" Stramm asked.

"We'll not change our plans. We tell Bilboa that if he doesn't help us get to the city he'll be stuck with our carnivorous presence for a very long time. We must get there to summon off-planet help. He'll do it—if only to get rid of us. We have to go ahead with our plans . . . nothing has changed."

"Right. Let's start by taking this catapult out and testing it."

We needed some muscle to move the bulky contraption out of the ship. So I summoned up some swineherd help. They all looked most impressive in their black-dyed dungarees. Quite a crowd had gathered by the time we were ready to go. Angelina and the captain were there, but this was no time to tell them about Elmo's major crime. He was prominent by his absence—with good reason.

Stramm had designed his machine around a heavy steel spring. A geared-down, battery-powered motor bent the spring until a hook locked it into place.

"I'm glad I got the flint from the locals," Stramm said. "Before that moron dropped us all into it."

"Flint?"

"Best way to ignite thermite—nice hot spark. I took a chance there was flint on this planet. And there is. Plus I got some flint igniters that they use to start their stove fires." He picked up a heavy bag. "Sand bag, same weight as the thermite bombs. Now, let's see what kind of range we get."

He shooed the gawking spectators away from the line of fire, then pulled the release knob. The catapult twanged and the sandbag flew a good hundred meters before it thudded to the ground with a puff of dust. Stramm smiled with satisfaction

"I measured the distance on the photo of the city, then paced it out. The bag hit just about as far as the city is from the edge of the woods."

"Wonderful. Could we test one of your thermite bombs as well? To make sure we are all right on the night?"

"Of course. That's why I made some extras."

The spring was bent and locked into place. Stramm removed one of the igniters from a box and plunged the ignition spike through the bag and into the thermite powder. Then he carefully sealed it into position with twisted lengths of wire. He did this slowly and patiently while the onlookers stirred and muttered to one another. He would not be hurried. The final touch was hooking the looped end of the igniter cord over a knob on the catapult.

"Done," he said, straightening up. "When it's released, the spark will ignite the thermite and—bang—it should burst into flame." He turned to Angelina who stood close by and pointed to the release knob.

"Would you like to do the honors?"

"Delighted."

"Ready, Jim?"

"Go!"

A quick tug released the spring—and the instant the firebomb was airborne there was a brilliant flash and a sudden trail of smoke. There was a concerted gasp from the onlookers as it hit the ground with a great gout of flame.

"I imagine that will get their attention," I said. "Congratulations, stout Stramm."

"Just good engineering, Boss."

"Then we are ready to go?"

"Whenever you say the word."

"Tonight?"

"We're on!"

But only after I girded my loins and had a heart-to-heart with Bilboa.

However, when Angelina and I strolled over to the settlement we found that all the houses had drawn curtains and locked doors. Even when I knocked loudly there was no response. Angelina watched my frustration grow and put a gentle restraining hand on my arm.

"I'm going to talk to some of my sewing friends about this. Never underestimate the gentler way."

With some reluctance I nodded agreement. "You're right of course. Do it—I'll wait here."

Nor did it take long. She soon reappeared, smiling happily.

"Good as done. They see the wisdom of a high-level conference and a number of them are talking to Bilboa right now."

What unseen pressures lurked behind that simple statement! Why did I feel sorry for him?

Only a short time passed before a gray-haired woman appeared and waved us over. "He's in there," she said, pointing to the open door of a nearby building.

"I'll leave you to it," Angelina said. "I've been invited to tea."

"Enjoy. And thanks for the gentle touch."

But there was nothing gentle about Bilboa, or the score of gray-beards who were sitting beside him and scowling furiously.

"Well, gentlemen," I said coldly, just as grim as they were. "We are facing a problem that must be solved."

WHEN I RETURNED TO THE ship, Angelina, ever understanding, handed me a large glass of cool amber liquid when I had dropped into a welcoming chair.

"It wasn't easy convincing them, but I had to win eventually. I finally persuaded them that the only way they would be rid of us, and our repulsive eating habits, was by taking us to the city. We leave tonight, as soon as it is dark. When we get there the oxcarts will wait deep in the woods to bring us back. If they do that, I promised we would be gone within twenty-four hours."

"I think I shall miss Floradora and my new friends. They are really very nice people."

"Agreed. But I'm afraid they don't think very much of us. Now—I feel it is time to get a bit of rest. It is going to be very, very busy come dawn tomorrow."

THE PROMISED OXCARTS WERE WAITING—a long line of them for our troops. The soldier-farmers chattered among themselves, excited by this break in their daily routine. I don't think they truly understood what we were up to. Nor did they have to. We had rehearsed their assigned roles and they had mastered all the complexities of hiding behind the trees. Step forward into the clearing when ordered to. Shout loudly and shake the wooden guns. To then step back behind the trees. It took a number of rehearsals before they got this hideously complicated procedure right. They carried baskets of food and jugs of hard cider and treated the whole affair as a holiday. A fool's paradise.

Enough! I wasn't going to spend the trek worrying. I knew what must be done and I would do it. I grabbed the jug from a passing yokel and took a long drag. Angelina appeared at this moment—fetchingly dressed in black.

"Your hat," she said, passing over a cloth-wrapped bundle. "They had to smuggle it out, but they were as good as their word."

I peeled away the cloth and gasped. "Formidable!" And indeed it was. The blackest of blacks. A deep, dark visor and above, circling the crown, a tasteful line of skulls and cross-bones. I pulled it on and Angelina clapped.

"Most impressive!"

"Thank you." I pointed to the oxcarts. "On to victory!"

Or axle-squeaking boredom. I did manage to nap a bit as we lurched on through the night. There were almost three hours to dawn when we reached our destination, what Bilboa assured us was the correct location. There was enough light from the two moons to pick out the path among the trees to reach the edge of the clearing. And there, looming up above us, was the dark and menacing bulk of the city.

Standing below the high walls, looking at its sinister outline, I was suddenly depressed. Were all my plans just smoke and mirrors? How could my bluffing approach fool anyone?

Angelina put her arm around me and gave me a warm hug.

"You can do it. You are probably the only one in the known universe who can."

She knew me so well! I returned the hug warmly and thankfully. Cheered and grateful.

"We'll knock 'em dead!"

"That's the Rat I know and love!"

"Now we can move all our gear into place. I checked out on the motorcycle and I hope you will sit behind me when we storm the bastion."

"Of course—it will be a fun ride!"

Fun? Not quite the word I would normally use. But, perhaps she was right.

We could do it.

CHAPTER 12

THE TROOPS DOZED UNDER THE trees through the warm evening hours. I was resolutely awake, planning the encounter to come. At first glimmer of light on the western horizon I walked back under the trees and woke my sleeping soldiers, then pushed them stumbling to their positions. Angelina joined me and shushed the waking farmers when they started talking loudly.

Stramm had all the equipment in position and gave me a thumbs-up, clearly visible in the light of dawn.

"Just tell me when," he whispered, holding on to the launching handle.

"Very soon now."

I climbed aboard the motorcycle and Angelina slipped up behind me. The gate in the wall was clearly visible, with the dark forms of soldiers on the wall above.

"Now!"

I hit the ignition button just as the loudspeakers placed among the trees blasted out the ear-shattering bugle call, drowning out the roar of the exhaust. The burning glare of the thermite bomb sizzled by over my head to crash into the wall with an explosion of flame.

Angelina held tight to me as the bike gunned forward, the front wheel rising high.

I had the throttle wide open as we roared towards the gate. Only hitting the brakes at the last possible moment so we screeched to a stop.

A second thermite bomb sizzled past—just over my head—and exploded against the gate. In seconds the wooden gate had caught fire and was now burning nicely.

"Very dramatic!" Angelina said, slipping off the bike. I touched the mike switch on my cap and the amplified roar of my voice replaced the blaring bugles.

"NOW HEAR THIS!"

What they heard was the shout of our troops as they stepped out from the cover of the trees, shaking their weapons over their head. As they drew back my amplified voice replaced their throaty roar.

"Obey me and you will not be harmed. My troops and weapons are here. My spacer is in orbit, armed with atomic weapons, and awaits my instructions. Open your gate for me—NOW!"

I paused for dramatic effect, then spoke with the voice of destiny.

"I am General diGriz, First Galactic Inspector of the Intergalactic Department of Religious Control."

Carried away by enthusiasm Stramm launched another

sizzling firebomb against the already burning gate. I walked towards it, felt its heat on my face. Stood, hands on my hips, staring up at it.

"OPEN!" my amplified voice boomed—followed by an ear-blasting blare of trumpets.

More figures were moving about on the wall above now. But nothing was happening. I had to keep them off balance. I switched off the mike before I spoke to Angelina.

"Put a shot through the gate—up high."

Before I finished talking a shot blasted a gaping hole in the wooden gate—and the gun was already back in its holster. I switched the mike back on.

"Followers of the Church of the Vengeful God, I command you: open—or die in sin!"

A little stir of their paranoia was called for here.

Was it moving?

Yes—the gate was opening!

We stamped our way in past the wall of flame.

Black-garbed soldiers stumbled away across the courtyard before us. I reached out and seized the nearest one of them by the collar and shook him a bit.

"Take me to your master," I ordered, my words echoing from the speakers behind me. I thumbed off the mike as we followed after him into the grim building beyond.

Daylight was streaming through the high windows now, lighting up the building's interior. Dark and shabby. The only touch of color coming from some badly framed painting of figures burning in leaping fires. Repulsive.

We followed our stumbling guide up a flight of stone stairs and through a gilt-framed doorway. The large room beyond was lit by stained-glass windows depicting more scenes of diabolic torture. I did not have a chance to look at them because my attention was drawn at once to the black-clad man seated on a heavy chair before me. I had been right: black was the new black.

I had been even luckier with the skull-and-crossbones cap design, for he was wearing a large silver skull on a chain about his neck.

"I have never heard of you or your organization," he said. Words dripping with venom.

"That is because you are on this backward and forgotten planet. Your name?"

He was silent for long moments, glaring at me, his hands gripping tight on the arms of the chair. Then, reluctantly.

"I am Father Coagula, prime rector of the Church of the . . ."

"Then you are the one I am here to see. We have had grave complaints about your church."

He wasn't getting up and I wasn't going to stand before him like a penitent. There were chairs against the wall: I caught Angelina's eye and pointed towards them. She nodded grimly back and brought one over.

"Females are not permitted in this chamber," he hissed.

"They are now. Where I go Sister Angelina goes."

I sat and matched him stare for icy stare. He blinked first.

"What do you want here?"

"I told you—we have had complaints." I took out a black-covered notebook, thumbed through it, then read . . .

"You have attempted to subvert another religion, namely that of the Children of Nature and Love, with whom you share this planet."

"They are idolaters and worship a false god. We simply showed them the Way—"

"You oppressed them, drove them from their homes and now cheat them of their rightful gain."

"What are you saying?"

Was there a touch of defensiveness in his voice? Naturally he would cheat the Children out of the true worth of the flowers they traded for.

"We have had complaints from those to whom you sell the perfume."

"They lie!"

"They speak only the truth. Our agents have talked to them. Other skilled agents have penetrated your ranks and found the secrets of your stills that are used to make the perfume you trade."

Coagula leaned back as though struck a physical blow. "You can't—"

"We can . . . and we will. Distillation is a well-known process on all civilized worlds. We will disclose every secret of the perfume process to the Children of Nature and Love. Then give them the materials to construct the stills. These are the people you have so viciously cheated. Unless you agree to our terms."

"What . . . are they?"

I tapped my notebook. "They are written here. Bring in your scribes to write them down as I read them out to you."

He was slumping now, defeated in every way. After a moment he seized the bell hanging from the arm of his chair and rang it.

"You are being wise. I will order my troops to stand down."

Then I added, in the same bored voice. "We will use your communication facilities to contact our ship."

He looked up and shook his head.

"But . . . we have none."

"Do not test my temper," I roared at him. "We know that you contact the traders when you have perfume to sell."

"But . . . we do not. They come whenever they want to. They have refused to give us communication apparatus. They did not want us contacting others of their trade."

Zero. Nothing. The best-laid plans . . . I drew myself up and salvaged what I could from the ruins.

"It matters not." Angrily. "Where is your scribe?"

"He comes." He shouted instructions at the priest who had answered his bell.

Depressed, I pondered the future.

We must leave Floradora.

But . . . where would we go?

I HAD TO PLAY OUT this farce to the very end. Dictating the terms of agreement that, in the future, payments for the flowers would be doubled. The Vengefulers also agreed that no future attempts would be made to convert anyone to their sadistic religion. They could keep it to themselves. I made a silent oath—if and when we returned to civilization again—to report their presence to the Galactic Authorities. Let them ponder over responsibilities here. Of course they respected the rights of all religions to believe what they would. But how did they feel about children on this world growing up to a life of paranoia and superstition? I had heard rumors that there was a Psych Corps that aided and abetted the spread of reason: I can only hope the rumors were right. Copies of the agreement were made. Read, signed, witnessed, signed again. Father Coagula turned away and averted his eyes when we left.

Still depressed by the failure to open communication, I felt slightly better that we had at least brought some aid to our vegetarian friends.

Bilboa was waiting by the oxcarts. I gave him what I hoped was a cheerful thumbs-up. He looked surprised.

"Your hand gesture means that the food is very good—is that what you mean?"

"Sorry, to us it means things are going well."

"In what manner?"

"The Vengefulers have signed an agreement for a happier future. First off they will stop any future attempts to convert anyone to their dismal religion."

"I thank you, friend Jim."

"You are welcome, friend Bilboa. They also agree to double their future payments for your flowers."

"Oh joy and happiness! We can buy more medicines from them. There are some illnesses we cannot cure—now lives will be saved . . ."

Then he stopped—stepped back—and an expression of deep sorrow spread across his face.

"I beg your forgiveness, dear friend. I have wronged you, disparaged your people—and you are the one to turn the other cheek, as taught in holy scripture. I took such offense at your horrifying eating habits that I wronged you, the wise and generous man that you are."

He reached out impulsively and took my hands in his. I felt more than a little embarrassed for there were tears in his eyes.

"Glad to help . . ." I muttered. "No big deal. Only fair thing to do."

"Still, I cannot forget that I wronged you and your people. I humbly apologize. They and their fine beasts can stay here on Floradora—for are we not our brothers' keepers? We already share our world with the loathsome city dwellers. Certainly there is room for everyone—far from us of course. And you and your shipmates must stay as well."

This was indeed a morale builder. My spirits rose with the good news. Free at last of Elmo and his crew! Our future still wasn't clear, but at least there would be no porcuswine and their keepers in it. I joined the others boarding the carts.

When I broke the news to Angelina and Stramm they were as excited as I was. As soon as we got within broadcast range of the ship I would tell the captain.

Elmo could wait—particularly since he was sound asleep, as were the others.

With very little effort I put my head down and did the same.

BACK AT THE SHIP IT was a grim and silent group that gathered on the bridge.

"I think we better discuss our future before we tell Elmo that they will be able to stay on Floradora."

"Whatever we decide it will be a pleasure to have them off the ship," the captain said.

"I go along with that!" Stramm added. "We can use water as reaction mass again." He smiled at this blissful thought. Then frowned and dug a crumpled bit of paper from his pocket and read from it.

"I have been running the graviton collector ever since planetfall. As of today it has added two thousand and twenty-two units to the tank."

"Which means . . . ?" the captain asked.

"Forty-three more minutes of Bloat time." He sighed. "You must remember that it is an old machine." Only silence followed.

"At least the reaction mass tank is full—drinking water tanks as well. We can get into orbit as soon as you say."

Angelina had the only encouraging news.

"While the elders were arguing about their future dealings with us carnivores, the women brought aboard loads of fresh cheese and produce."

"Hurray for them!" I said brightly, trying to improve the mood of the day. "We've agreed among us that we will leave here after we unload the pigs and people." Then I frowned. "I was forgetting that we had to move them and their repulsive gustatory habits away from the flower folk. We'll put a call throughout the ship. Arrange for the conference to be held in the dining room."

It took some time to stir Elmo and company awake and goad them to the meeting. Sensibly, the captain and engineer were prominent by their absence. Angelina sat chatting among the women—while I faced the bleary-eyed men.

"Gentlemen," I said, starting off with a lie. "You will be pleased to hear that our little adventure was a complete success. The Vengefulers will venge no more and not bother the other kind folk on this planet—and that means you as well. Angelina and I, and the rest of the crew, must leave this fair world. But you—you lucky lot!—have been invited to make this your home. You can look ahead to a prosperous future— though I must admit you will have limited means of disposing of your excellent pork products—"

"That's a real kind of a problem, Cousin Jim," Elmo said, breaking in with newfound determination. "Without no income, why how we gonna live?"

"You can trade with the city," I said, with a touch of desperation in my voice. Elmo gloomily shook his head.

"From what the locals tell us we best stay away from them."

"And we got us other problems," a burly swineherd called out. "The only television we got is from them city people and it's no good at all."

"All shooting and killing and praying and such and no soap operas," a woman in the front row said, and the sisterhood nodded fiercely.

"But . . ." I said, and it was a pretty feeble *but*. Any arguments I produced could not sway them from the lost pleasures of TV. I looked at their determined features and had to admit defeat.

"Yes," I said, fighting to hold back a heartfelt sigh. "You had better start bringing the animals aboard as soon as possible."

I went to break the news to the crew. Who took it in stoic silence, bad news being the order of the day.

"I never liked this planet from the moment we arrived and were shot at," Captain Singh said. "Let us get off-planet as soon as we can then plan our next Bloat jump." He swung about in his chair to face the control board. "Let me know as soon as everyone and everything is aboard. Tell them we'll pull a maximum of one-G during takeoff. Make sure all the livestock is secured. One of the sows broke a leg when we landed and I have had nothing but hassle from our passengers ever since."

I went to say my good-byes to Bilboa and friends, which

was a time-consuming process. Even then I found that the boarding was slow and tearful, with many good-byes. I went to the bridge where I joined the equally depressed captain, who was gloomily watching the slow preparations for departure.

"I checked and everyone's aboard," Angelina said happily as she joined us. "I'll miss the nice people here." The silence that followed was thunderous.

"Best go to our cabin now," I said.

We went. Angelina gave me a quick hug before lying down on her acceleration couch. "You did everything possible, Jim. We were all so sure that those Vengefulers had interstellar communication. And the vegetarians should really thank you for the way you improved their dealings with those dreadful city people."

This cheered me slightly, but I still had great fears for the future. "We should change the name of this ship." I said as I buckled in. "Did you ever hear the old myth about the *Flying Dutchman*?"

"What's a Dutchman."

"I have no idea. But it was an ocean vessel of some kind that was supposed to be sailing under a curse. That meant that it could never reach port and was doomed to sail on forever."

"How awful. But I'm sure that won't happen to us."

The buzzer rasped loudly and the recorded voice announced *"Ten-second warning."*

Takeoff went well. At least something did for a change.

Angelina unbuckled and stood up. "I'm going to see how the porcuswine fared after this takeoff."

"Right. I'll be on the bridge."

Captain and engineer were laboring at the computer; cabalistic equations ran down the screen. After much muttering they seemed to reach an agreement. The captain pushed his chair back and pointed to the screen.

"I've gone through the galactic ephemeris and this seems to be the optimum balance of all the factors."

I nodded—although the spatial coordinates were just a meaningless series of numbers.

"I've balanced out favorable locations that could be reached in one Bloat, against stellar density. This is our best choice."

"Do it!" I said. "Let's see if our luck is better this time."

"Beginning Bloat," he said, hitting the RUN-PROGRAM button.

Floradora began to shrink slowly behind us, growing tinier and tinier until it blinked out of sight.

"The bar is open!" I said with false enthusiasm. Then I remembered that the captain never drank on duty—and Stramm was already on the way to the engine room.

Hopefully Angelina would share a cocktail with me. If not, I was sure Pinky and I could split a bowl of curry puffs . . .

THE DAYS CRAWLED BY. I saw little of Angelina, who was exacting a great deal of pleasure from her unexpected female companionship. I began to realize that women were far better than men at enjoying the company of one another. The thought of socializing with Elmo and friends—what could their conversation possibly consist of?—was a frightening one! I did extract some enjoyment—and a good workout—from helping Stramm strip down and reassemble one of the major thrust bearings on the landing jets. I still welcomed warmly the captain's announcement over the ship's speakers.

"Getting radio signals now . . . I'll see if I can amplify them."

I must say that the elapsed time between emergencies was getting shorter and shorter. I relaxed after we had finished work and had just made my first drink, was stirring the ice to chill it, when the wall speaker rustled and the captain spoke:

"Boss Jim to bridge."

I sipped, then frowned. Had there been a touch of anxiety to his voice? Yes, there had. I put the drink down and headed for the stairs. He was frowning at the viewscreen when I came onto the bridge.

"Something is wrong?" I asked.

"There certainly is. Come look at this."

This was a bright star slightly off-center on the screen. He pointed to a much-dimmer star in the center of the screen.

"This is the star system that is our target destination. The brighter star should not be there."

"Which means . . . ?"

"I'll tell you in a moment, as soon as the spectral analysis is complete—there it is."

The computer pinged, the printer hummed, then ejected a printed sheet. He took it and scanned it quickly: the frown became a scowl.

"Helium, carbon, nitrogen and oxygen—in that order of quantity . . ."

"Which means?"

"Ejecta."

"Explain if you please—physics was never my best subject."

He touched a changing number low on the screen. "It is getting brighter and hotter the closer we get." He was not happy with this. "What we are looking at is a star gone nova. If we stay on this course we'll be a smoking cinder before long."

"Cut the power! Go back!"

"Impossible—as I have explained. We cannot retrace a Bloat course. What I can do is gradually reduce the power and shorten our Bloat time. But we can't activate a new course until the Bloat is over."

"We'll be toast . . ."

"I hope not."

I was still not sure what was happening. And what was the nova star doing there?

"Wasn't this nova in the stellar ephemeris when you plotted our course?"

"Obviously not." He groped in the drawer for his glasses; it was obviously lecture time again. He put them on and we were back in the classroom. "Although stellar surveys are being made constantly, it is a big galaxy out there and this nova was obviously not at this location when the last survey was made."

"But a star doesn't go nova just like that."

"Normally, I agree. But there are exceptions. Some novae are recurrent, albeit on a time scale ranging from a thousand to a hundred thousand years. The recurrence interval for a nova is less dependent on the white dwarf's accretion rate than its mass . . ."

The lecture ran its course but I tuned out. The only thing that mattered was how hot it would be when we popped back into normal space. I cracked my knuckles and brooded until the lecture mode ground to a halt. Only when the captain took off his glasses did I venture to ask a question.

"Do you know how hot it will be when this Bloat ends?"

"No. I can measure it, but of course we won't be able to feel it until the Bloat terminates."

"Why?"

"Because of the attenuation of our molecules during Bloat, all the wavelengths apparently change. Only when we have resumed our normal dimensions will the temperature change be felt."

"Which will be when?"

He looked at the control panel. "I'm shortening the Bloat time steadily. As of now we have five hours to termination. But there will be updates."

I looked at my watch—then set the alarm. "I'll be here again in a few hours."

I made my way slowly back to the bar and my tepid drink. Angelina came in just when I was making up a shaker of refills.

"Someone is looking very glum," she said.

"With good reason I'm afraid."

I poured out drinks for us both. Then spoke to the point since I knew that she could handle any occasion—and loathed secrecy.

"We will be having a spot of trouble in a few more hours."

I couldn't repeat all the physics data that the captain had made so murkily clear, nor did I try.

"The details are both complicated and inescapable. One thing that I can say is that at the conclusion of our Bloat we may be in trouble. That is, we may be fried. All we can do is wait and see."

"Then there is nothing more to talk about. Let's finish this drink and go see the captain. We must try and cheer him up."

My level-headed darling was even cheering me up!

Nor was the captain just sitting on his hands. Engineer Stramm had joined him and they were working deep within the control board. Panels had been opened and cables ran to a newly constructed apparatus that had been bolted to the top.

"Ready for test—" Stramm said.

"Now!"

The captain threw a switch. Nothing happened.

That we could see. Obviously the engineer could see more. He smiled and tossed his screwdriver high, caught it as it fell.

"Total elapsed time—a shade under two seconds."

"Can we reduce that any more?" the captain asked.

"Not possible. The Bloat termination signal is only three milliseconds long. This has to be transmitted, modified, electronically amplified, relayed—and the new course activated. We've already made the activation time as short as we can."

"All right—we can live with that. But we better test it a few more times."

"Could the humble peasantry be informed just as to what is going on?" I asked.

"Simplicity itself," the captain said. "The electronic circuitry we have installed here will be automatically activated the microsecond the Bloat ends. A new course has been calculated—pointing ninety degrees away from the original course. We will be in normal space-time for less than two seconds—then we will again be safe from outside radiation."

"And just what will happen during those two seconds?" Angela asked.

"Radiation from the nova will hit our hull. It will be quite high and quite sudden. I will not hazard a guess as to just what the results will be."

"Do we tell the passengers what is going to happen?" I asked.

"As captain of this craft that is now in powered flight, I am in command. I have decided there would be no point in informing anyone else about what is happening. Though she is old this spacer is soundly built and has plenty of shielding. I think she will survive . . . or . . ."

The silence lengthened—until Angelina spoke.

"Or we will never know what hit us."

He nodded. "That is correct."

After that, it was just a matter of marking time. I went to refresh our drinks—and supply Stramm with one since he was now officially off duty. When I got back to the bridge with the tray I found that Pinky had joined the party. Since she had learned how to climb stairs she had the run of the ship. She was mumbling with pleasure as Angelina used a steel brush to comb out her quills.

"How much more time left to end of Bloat?" I asked, putting the drinks tray on the plotting table.

"About twenty-six minutes," the captain said. "I'll switch on the countdown at zero minus one minute."

The silence grew as we sipped our drinks. There was nothing more that could be said. Perhaps it was a time for introspection not conversation. In fact I was startled when the recorded voice said . . .

"Sixty seconds and counting . . ."

Angelina reached out and took my hand. I squeezed back.

"Thirty-one."

The seconds remorselessly ticked by.

IT ALL HAPPENED IN AN INSTANT

A shudder hit the fabric of the ship and the steel wall vibrated, while the floor twisted horribly under our feet.

Three different alarms screeched and roared out sound. The lights went out and at the same moment all the control boards went dark. I fell against the wall and felt it warm, then hot against my skin.

Then the alarms died away, one by one, as the red emergency lighting flickered and came on.

I stumbled over to Angelina and held her tightly—and she smiled.

"Let's try not do that again," she said.

The captain was feverishly working at the control board, restoring power to the instruments one by one.

"No hull damage. No air leakage," he said. "But all of the pickups, monitors and aerials on the outer skin are gone."

"Not all of them," Stramm said, pointing to two glowing readouts. "These were on the far side of the hull, away from the nova flare."

"They will have to do as long as we are in Bloat space."

"Do you have replacements."

"Of course," Stramm said. "Required by law. That and a spacesuit for external repairs."

"Can someone go out and do that now?" I asked.

The captain shook his head. "Not while we are still in Bloat space. People have gone outside during Bloat . . ."

Stramm spoke into the silence. "None of them ever came back."

It was Angelina who suggested the obvious.

"Shouldn't you make an announcement to the passengers? Give them a little reassurance after the shaking up they just had."

"Of course," the captain said. "Please excuse my delay." He switched on all the speakers throughout the ship. Tapped the microphone and got a happy amplified thud in return.

"This is your captain speaking. While making course adjustments to our main drive we encountered a spatial anomaly, which are quite common in this area of space. The jarring you felt was transitory and brief, though it did actuate some alarms. Rest assured that everything is under control again and there was no damage. Sire diGriz has asked me to extend his apologies for the incident and wishes every table to have two bottles of wine with dinner tonight.

"Have a good day."

He turned the speakers off and winked at me. "Hope you don't mind my spending some of your money to take their minds off this little matter."

"You speak with my voice. But, one question. Do you know where this Bloat is taking us?"

"No. But we'll find out in ten hours at Bloat's end. Since we are moving away from the nova, on a course only ninety degrees from the original one, I allowed enough time for us to be clear of the radiation."

Stramm started for the door. "I'm going to crack out the space gear. As soon as the Bloat is over I have to inspect the hull for damage."

"A question before you go—" I said. "How many hours spacewalking time do you have?"

"Well . . . offhand I'm not sure . . ."

"I am. Since I have a senior license and over three thousand logged spacewalk hours," I said. I didn't bother to add that this all happened during a little prospecting I once did. On a carbon satellite with diamond infarcts that I, just by chance, happened to be on when the owners were absent.

"I think it would be wise for me to go out and inspect the damage after you tell me what to look for. Then I'll make any needed repairs. Now, let's go see your space gear."

"Time to take tea with the passengers," Angelina said. "Build a little morale among the ladies. The men will be busy enough by now calming down the porcuswine."

We all left the captain to brood over his control panel. The hull had cooled down by this time and everything seemed back to normal.

The secure section of the storeroom was locked and sealed. Stramm had to call the captain to get the correct code to open it. The spacesuit, in its own sealed container, was hanging from a hook on the back wall.

"Wonderful," Stramm said, brushing dust off the inspection label that was just visible through the thick, transparent wrapping. "Last inspected a little over ninety years ago."

"They last forever—very durable," I said. With more enthusiasm than I felt.

We struggled it out of its wrapper to reveal the cheerful label.

ACME SUPER SPACE GEAR
ONE SIZE FITS ALL

"That's impossible," Stramm said.

I was tempted to agree but stayed silent to keep the morale up. Not his—mine. I've seen these bargain spacesuits before.

However, this one seemed to be pretty functional. The fits-all was accomplished by a built-in series of pneumatic chambers and pads—and a control panel on one sleeve to activate them. I entered my height, weight, body-fat content, arm length, shoe size and everything else barring marital status. Then switched it on.

"Here's hoping," I said, not too enthusiastically.

It crackled, writhed, swelled and contracted—groaning all the while as if going through birth pangs. All this activity finally stopped: a green light came on and a tinny bugle sounded a brief battle charge.

"Try it on," Stramm said. He had been watching all the activity with widened eyes.

Then all movement stopped. A red light flashed and a rasping voice said: "Low battery, low battery, recharge . . . krrrk . . ."

Everything stopped, then the light blinked out.

Stramm unsealed the battery compartment and pulled the battery out.

"Not too bad—considering how long it has been since the last charge."

"How long will the recharge take?"

"At least five hours—if it takes a charge at all considering its age. But I have replacements in stock."

A rumbling borborygmus sounded from my stomach. With all that had happened it had been a long time between meals.

"Time to take my wife to lunch. I'll see you later."

CHAPTER 15

PINKY JOINED US FOR LUNCH and, since she was inescapably a swine, made a pig out of herself. We left her sleeping deeply under the table, her bristles rustling softly with her breathing. We had just finished when we were called to attend the captain.

Stramm was already there when we reached the bridge.

"Fifteen minutes to Bloat termination," the captain said. "Because of spatial attenuation we only have a very vague idea of space ahead."

"But no novas this time?" Angelina said.

"Indeed not. From what is visible it seems normal enough. But remember, this is an emergency hookup to the one remaining pickup that survived the heat. It's designed for landing approach use and has little magnification."

"Better than nothing," I said. "We'll at least have some idea of where we are."

We were all grouped in front of the screen when the Bloat ended. With a soft ping the screen cleared and the stars swam into focus. Rather, one star did. All of the others were dim and distant, barely visible on the screen."

"Not too promising a start," I muttered. And tried to smile when the others glared at me.

"That's the best we can do now," the captain said, looking at me. "It will be necessary to restore the hull instrumentation components before we can know any more."

"Good as done," I said. Hopefully. Because I had the strong feeling that it was not going to be that easy.

It wasn't. Getting into the spacesuit proved to be the easiest part of the job. Getting out of the ship was much harder.

"The stern exit lock won't open," Stramm said. "I should have known."

"Why?"

"The nova. Those three seconds of radiation melted all the external fittings. Essentially . . . the outer door is welded shut."

I was feeling welded shut too, since the spacesuit coolant could only be turned on when it was sealed and in space. I laboriously climbed out of it while the engineer tested all the controls in every hull sector.

"Got it!" he announced happily. "There is a single emergency inspection port that was on the shadow side of the hull when the nova blast hit us."

"Let's take a look."

We ran into trouble at once.

When we tried the opening cycle on the inner door the motor and the gear train squealed and protested for a moment— until the safety override popped open. Stramm looked closely at it and growled angrily. "Hasn't been used in years. Practically welded itself shut with disuse."

Brute force was the only answer. Only after an hour of hammering, prying, oiling, cursing did we get it open. Squeaking loudly it finally swung wide and a puff of stale air blew out.

"Maybe the outer lock will be easier," Stramm said hopefully, wiping his streaming face with an oily cloth.

It was not. Particularly since I had to do it alone. Because of all the interlocks that prevented both airlock doors from being open at the same time. Which would of course let all the ship's air into space.

I put on the spacesuit and, with the engineer's help, squeezed into the airlock. It was essentially a tube about two meters long. I went in headfirst, lying on my back as he passed me the tools I would need, pushing them in past me to the far end.

"Better seal your suit before you start banging anything."

Happily, I thought, as the cooled air was pumped past my face. Once the helmet was closed—and the inner door as well—we had to communicate by radio. Static crackled in my ear.

"Facing the hatch, the hinges will be on your left . . ."

"I know," I growled, sweaty and not a little claustrophobic. "I'm trying the opening handle now."

Of course nothing happened. I cursed and banged, first by hand and then with a pry bar and extension. In the end we had to open the inner hatch and laboriously push a hydraulic jack in over my tender body.

With the hatch sealed again I positioned the jaws of the jack under the outer door handle and started pumping. I worked the pump and sweated and was rewarded with a squeal of metal.

I pumped again—and saw that the steel handle was beginning to bend. I stopped and caught my breath.

"How's it going?" The voice rasped in my ear. I could only growl in response as I did one slow pump after another.

The handle was bending—then with a sharp squeal it moved a fraction. The end of the jack jumped free and I bruised my knuckles nicely as my hand slammed against the metal.

"It's moving," I said as I repositioned the jack.

Two more slow pumps did it. The air puffed out through the dark crack and I was looking out into interstellar space. I pushed hard and it swung wide.

The stars were brilliant pinpoints, sharp and bright. But not as bright as the disk of the sun that we were approaching. Our destination, growing darker when I turned towards it and the helmet faceplate polarized in the glare.

I made sure that the magnetic anchor of my safety line was secure, then pushed my way out of the lock and into interstellar space.

The hull's surface—like that of all spacers—was roughened by the abrasion of dust particles. Moving slowly I passed the outer lens of one of the instruments and worked my way around the hull.

Then the surface changed abruptly. It was now glossy and free of any protrusions. All the attachment cleats were gone and only the magnetic clamps kept me from drifting away into space.

"On," I said to actuate the radio. "The hull has been melted smooth by the blast from the nova. Mirror smooth. All instrumentation and hull fittings are gone. I'm coming back. This is going to be a bigger job than we thought."

Once back inside with my helmet off I downed a liter of water with almost a single glug.

"There is only one thing we can do," Stramm said as he pulled out the suit's absorption pack and put in a dry one.

"Drill?"

"Right. Locate the site of the melted instrumentation. Seal the compartment. Drill out through the hull and put in new cabling. Reseal and install the equipment from the outside."

"A big job."

"I'll find out from the captain the minimum instrumentation that he needs."

I finished the water and sighed. "Let's get going."

AFTER THREE DAYS OF SINGULARLY long and hard work, the electronic and ocular pickups were in place. Along with a broadband aerial that would have to handle all communication. I had slept very well indeed and ached in a number of spots that had never ached before. When everything had been installed and inspected, I crawled out of the spacesuit for the last time. Angelina helped me open the last clamps and a frosted glass was waiting when I emerged.

"The captain asked me to relay his thanks," she said. "And invites you to the bridge to take a look at our target destination."

"Let's go!" I said. I didn't want to ruin this happy moment by saying that I hoped all the labor had been worth it. We climbed the stairs to the bridge and were joined by Pinky who squealed greetings. Which probably meant feed me in porcuswinese.

We looked on as the captain ran a stellar scan, modified it, then put the software to work identifying the location.

"Not good," he said. "It appears that we have hit an unrecorded sector of the local galaxy. It is so empty of stars that apparently it was skipped by all the earlier stellar scans."

"So what we see is what we get," I said. "We either take a look at this one star—or make another Bloat."

"Correct," the captain said. "Since we are in close proximity I suggest we expend a few more gravitons and get close enough to make a spectral analysis. That will tell us if it is worth the expenditure to examine any planets that we find more closely."

"Do it," Angelina said. And we all agreed.

It was a short Bloat and a successful scan.

"Four planets. One with an orbit that is just one astronomical unit from the primary."

"Habitable location?" I asked.

"Very. And I am detecting what could be very weak radio signals."

"Worth a look," Stramm said; no objections were raised. "May I make a suggestion?" he added.

"Of course," the captain said.

"We are short of gravitons, but not of reaction mass. Which grows by the day. At an acceleration of one G it won't take us long to get within radio contact."

The captain looked at me. "Let's do it." I said. "The ship will be all the better for large evacuation of reaction mass."

CHAPTER 16

"Boss Jim and crew to the bridge."

The captain was actually smiling as well, as he pointed to the figures displayed beside the planet's disk, enlarging and glowing in the center of the screen

"Most satisfactory," he said. "Habitable, oxygen atmosphere. And it gets better. Figures flowed down the screen, mostly colored amber or gray. Then one set of numbers turned green and a distant buzzer sounded.

"Amplify," the captain said.

"Habitable planet. Gravity one point zero three . . ." There were more specifications to which he nodded happily. "Now look—and listen to this."

He touched the controls and a new window opened on the screen, with a grainy, out-of-focus TV image of a weather map with a rasping voice-over.

"Light rain moving in from the east into the area. It will clear by morning and be another sunny day for all you folk enjoying the Founder's Day holiday . . ."

We broke into hearty cheers and pummeled one another on the back.

"Good news I gather?" Angelina said as she entered the bridge.

"Party!" I said. "Time to celebrate.

"Shouldn't that wait until we see just what is down there?" Angelina suggested, ever the practical one.

"I have a suggestion," the captain said. "We are close enough now so that it will take nominal gravitons for an approach Bloat. It will save us many days of deceleration . . ."

"Do it!" I said to happy nodded agreement. "If they have TV they almost certainly will have interstellar communication . . ."

"Can we be sure . . ." Angelina said.

"No, but I feel it's worth the chance."

No one disagreed. It had been a long trip.

It was a quick Bloat. The few stars drifted across the screen and the blue dot of a planet centered on the screen, then grew quickly into a cloud-bright world. The captain worked at the controls.

"Getting more TV and better radio signals now . . . I'll see if I can amplify them."

Static crackled, then dim voices could be heard—just as clear images appeared on the TV screens—most of them were talking heads.

". . . tell me Pyotr—why does a turkey cross the road?"

"Don't know, Vassily. Why does a turkey . . ."

The heads swam into focus. Two men in funny hats, wearing clown makeup. The channel changed to a nature program with screen-filling volcanoes belching flames.

"Elmo and his TV-watching friends will be right at home," I said. "See if you can find some music."

The captain obliged and eventually found a not-too-new jazz concert that would surely please the viewers belowdecks.

"Considering the contents of their TV, I have to agree with Jim. They must be in touch with off-planet broadcasts," Angelina wisely said.

I looked around at the others. "I'm for making contact with these people. Agreed?"

There was a concerted nodding of heads. I went and sat down at the ship-to-planet communication console. "Are we close enough for our signal to reach the surface receivers?" I asked.

"Well within range," the captain said. "Power on."

"Just a moment," Stramm said. "There is one thing that we have to consider first." There was a sudden silence as all eyes were on him.

"What?" I asked.

"We can land all right, but how do we get out of the ship? One at a time through the emergency lock?"

"Yes, that is a good question," I said, speaking for us all. "How do we get out?"

"Quite simple, really. But we can't do it while we are in space, which is why I didn't mention it before this. We will have to unseal the lower port, so we can lower the ramp. This can only be done when there is normal pressure outside the hull.

Then we open the inner door. Use the override so both doors can be opened at the same time. Then we cut our way out. Burn away the outer seal, which was welded shut by the nova blast."

"It will require extensive repairs if you do that," the captain said, worried about the integrity of his ship's hull. Stramm nodded.

"It will. But it must be done. And I'll fit a new seal as soon as possible. We'll do it—unless anyone can think of a better plan?"

Only silence followed, since this was obviously the only way to go.

"Let me see what kind of reception we will have," I said. "Then we'll worry about the next step."

I turned to the transmitter that was already set to the ship-to-ground frequency that all planets used. I thumbed on the microphone.

"Spaceship *Porcuswine Express* now in orbit. Can you read me? Over."

I repeated this message twice before I had any response. I just hoped it would be a little more friendly than the ground-to-air missile of our last encounter. The speaker crackled, a distorted image flowed across the screen—then steadied as the control circuitry sorted it out. A white-uniformed man with pleasant dark-skinned features swam into focus.

"Southampton Spaceport here. I read you loud and clear. Over."

"Hello Southampton. Seeking permission to make landing."

"Hold your altitude and orbit, spacer. Am contacting health officials."

"Roger that. Some information, please. You're not in our

planetary ephemeris. Could I ask—who are you?" My contact laughed out loud.

"You need to update your files, orbiting spacer. You'll find the corrected listing under United States of England. President Churchill. This is an elective democracy on the British Continent—the only habitable landmass on the planet." He looked off-camera and nodded his head. "Yes, sir." He turned back. "I'm putting you through to Admiral Soumerez, Port Commander."

The screen flickered and rolled, then swam into focus. A sturdy gray-haired man in uniform, sitting behind a desk taking some papers from another uniform. They had interesting pigmentation—pink skin on the admiral, sallow yellow on his aide. Who exited as the admiral looked up.

"You wish to land here?"

"We certainly do."

"Do you have medical clearance records from your last port of call?"

I looked over at the captain who nodded.

"I have them to hand."

"Good." A number appeared on the screen beside him. "That is the radio frequency of the spaceport. It will also guide you to the quarantine landing area. A medical inspection team will be waiting."

"They are going to have to wait a bit. We were hit by a solar flare that sealed our outer locks shut. We will have to cut our way through it after we land."

The admiral picked up a sheaf of papers, obviously losing interest in our problems.

"That's fine. Open contact again when you have unsealed."
The screen went blank.

"I have the frequency and landing coordinates," the captain said. "I'll do a visual and radar scan of the site. Then we can land."

"Can we put a hold on that?" I asked.

"Of course. But why?"

"The skin colors of these people—" Angelina said.

"The lady gets a prize!" I kissed her and she smiled. The crew were simply puzzled.

"It is a bit of a mystery," I said. "And I don't like mysteries." I had their attention now. I was about to get my own back at the captain and give *him* a lecture for a change.

"It is a matter of genetic history that mankind was originally composed of different races. I forget what they were called. But I do remember that there were various physical differences as well. One of which was skin color. Once mankind became integrated most of these differences slowly vanished. But traces still remain. I'll wager that Captain Singh comes from an isolated community."

"I do indeed! A happy refuge surrounded by mostly hostile territory. We Sikhs are proud of our heritage."

"As well you should be. You must have a strong and beneficial culture to exist this long. But neither Angelina nor I remember visiting a world where different skin types exist. They should have been bred out centuries ago."

The captain was puzzled by all this. "So—how does it affect our course of action? Should we not land here?"

Now I was troubled. "We don't want to take another Bloat

without at least determining if they have off-planet communication facilities."

"We could ask them," Stramm said.

"We could, but how could we be sure they were telling
the truth?" I was a creature of dark suspicions, which had
saved my skin more than once.

"Let's land," Angelina said. "After taking all possible pre-
cautions. There must be a simple answer to our questions."

We were in agreement on that.

"We'll head for the spaceport," the captain said. "Get into
orbit above it and examine it as well as we can before we land."
He entered the coordinates and our final approach began.

"Looks like any other spaceport," Angelina said as the
clouds drifted away and the image filled the screen. A large
cleared area was completely surrounded by verdant forest. A
single long, straight road cut through the greenery and stretched
off to the horizon.

"A good-sized one," the captain said. "There are six spacers grouped on one side, by those buildings . . ."

"Come in orbiting spacecraft. This is landing control,"
the speaker rasped.

"Hello control. Do you have landing instructions?"

*"Positive. Do not land near other craft until you have
cleared your medicals. The contamination zone is away from
other craft. The pad is marked with our national flag."*

"Roger and out." The captain zoomed in and a large red flag
painted on the landing area swam into view. It was decorated
with a golden hammer and a curved instrument of some kind.

"Twenty minutes to landing," he said into the ship's intercom; we hurried to our acceleration couches.

It was an easy landing—the safety of the animals was still a consideration. Before the passengers started milling again, the captain told them about the planet—and the fact that there would be a slight delay, because of access difficulties, before the port was opened. Stramm went to get the oxyacetylene torch; I had the inner lock opened and the interlock switched off by the time he arrived. My ears popped slightly.

"I've opened the exterior air pressure vents," he said. "Very slight difference from our ship pressure."

It was a hot and nasty job of work. He sparked the igniter, put on his welding mask and went to work. It was easy enough at first, though the smoke from the burning gasket was annoying. I had to fetch a ladder when the cutting area became too hard to reach. When his arms grew tired I spelled him and the unsealed area grew. Until the circle was complete and we reached the opening cut.

"Done," I said and turned the valve; with a pop the flame died. "Now let us see if the motor still operates."

Stramm flipped open the safety cover on the control box and pressed the actuator. The sound of the electric motor was music to our ears; at least something was working. The gears ground and the door opened wide. Then the ramp slid out and fresh, warm air poured in. I sniffed happily.

"I forget what the outdoors smelled like." Stramm nodded agreement.

"Ship's air gets a little ripe after a long trip. Particularly on this ship." The sound of distant squealing behind us was a poignant reminder.

The end of the ramp thudded down on the tarmac and we saw the waiting health reception party. Two uniformed men.

On horseback.

"Do you have the health documents?" One of them called out. His skin was deeply dark; his companion pallidly sallow. Stramm handed me the folder and I held it up.

"Please place them on the landing pad," he said, swinging down to the ground. "Then you must return to your ship. I'm afraid no one can exit until the health documents are processed." The sound of distant squeals and grunts registered a protest.

"No problem," I said, and did as requested. He took the folder, remounted and they both galloped away. I sat down on the ramp, still sniffing the air. I called the captain to put him in the know, while Stramm joined me.

"I wonder why the horses?" he said.

"Fuel shortage maybe. And you saw their different skin color."

"Hard to miss. Is it important?"

"It might be. Or maybe I'm too suspicious for my own good." My radio buzzed, then turned on when I said *radio*.

"Jim here, Captain," I said. His hologram image floated in space before me.

"They just radioed through a medical clearance. The customs team is on the way."

"They don't seem to be in any hurry . . ." I muttered.

"Meanwhile we have permission to leave the ship—as long as we stay within two hundred meters of it. That's as far as the trees."

"What about the animals?"

"They can exit too—before they break out."

Even as he spoke we heard a happy squealing and the thunder of hooves. We jumped to one side as the boars crashed by, closely followed by sows and piglets. As they entered the nearest stand of forest their human minders hurried after them.

"Shore nice to smell all this fresh air!" Elmo cried out as he followed after. A master of spelling out the obvious.

The women were next—in a very holiday mood. They carried folding chairs and baskets; let the jollity begin.

"I still don't like it," I muttered, scowling after their retreating backs.

"I agree completely," Angelina said, following the others down the ramp. "Nothing—other than the fresh air—smells right."

I pointed to the satchel she was carrying and raised my eyebrows.

"Ship's registration and assorted paperwork the authorities asked for. What I didn't like is that they asked for the commander of this vessel to bring it. I took it from the captain before he could leave. I said that you were the owner and would take care of it. I also told him that he must stay on the bridge until you told him otherwise."

"You have read my mind!"

"I didn't have to. I'm as suspicious as you are." She handed me the satchel.

"Did they say what I was to do with this?"

"The authorities are on their way to pick it up."

"On horseback again, I suppose?"

"Come over here away from the others," she said quietly. We sat on the grass in the sun and she pointed to the spaceships grouped together at the other end of the port.

"Have you had a chance to look closely at those other spacers?"

"Negative. I have been too busy burning open the lock."

"Well I have. There are no people there—or vehicles. No one going in or out of the buildings. And the lower locks on the ships appear to be open. But there is no movement in or out. We're too far away to tell, but they have a very deserted, abandoned look about them. And . . . where are the workers in those buildings?"

"I like nothing about this planet at all, nothing!"

I was puzzled and frustrated—and positive that things here were very, very wrong.

"Something is finally happening," Angelina said, pointing across the field to the road that led into the forest.

Indeed there was. First one, then two vehicles came onto the field. They were covered over and the only people visible were the two drivers, sitting on raised platforms at the front of both wagons.

Each holding the reins of the six horses that were harnessed to them and pulling the contraptions in our direction.

"Not good!" Angelina said.

"Agreed!" I agreed, already in motion before she spoke. Running towards the forest, shouting back to Angelina over my shoulder.

"Get the women back inside. I'll do the same with the men."

The wagons were closing at a good gallop. As they rushed closer I recognized the drivers.

They were the same two men who had taken away the medical papers.

They were reining in the horses now, so close that the screaming women were hurrying to get out of the way, rushing up the ramp. I called again to the men, who were gaping at me as though I was demented. I was.

"Follow the women, you morons!" I passed the ship's papers to Elmo as he ran by. "Back to the ship. What we have to do—" I shouted, but never finished the sentence.

Armed, uniformed men were pouring out of the back of each wagon. Armed with what looked like, could only be, bows and arrows. Just as this fact registered I realized something far stranger still.

Their skins weren't black or pink or brown . . .

Their hands—their faces—were all bright green.

CHAPTER 17

IT WOULD HAVE BEEN A bizarre comedy had it not been so serious.

The women, shrieking in terror, were running up the ramp—
leaving behind a scattering of chairs and overturned picnic
baskets. The men, some of whom were trying to round up the
porcuswine, were starting to hurry back. When they heard the
terror of the screaming women even the laggards began to run
as well. I turned back to our green attackers—and discovered
that Angelina was ahead of me. Her gun was small but powerful; her quick shot blasted out and exploded by the first wagon
with a great gout of flame.

The attackers instantly panicked. One managed to fire an
arrow—straight up into the air. The others were either fum-
bling with their bows or throwing them away. To hurry them
along I fired a shot into the ground just before the horses.
They whinnied with fear and bolted.

"Well done," I said.

"I didn't want to hurt the horses," Angelina said. "As for the green-skinned soldiers . . ."

"In full flight." And they were. Only the two drivers remained. Trying to rally their troops—with little success. One of them actually kicked a soldier, who scuttled away on all fours. They were the last to leave the field of action—now strewn with discarded quivers, bows and arrows.

The frustrated driver with the quick boot turned and shook an angry fist back at us, cursed and shouted.

"Green is great—pink is putrid!"

Angelina's next shot—between his legs!—spattered him with clods of earth. He turned and fled after the others.

The last of our passengers were now running up the ramp. But the porcuswine were still rooting under the trees, unbothered by our little dustup.

"What happens next?" Angelina asked.

"Good question."

"While you're deciding, might I draw your attention to a large number of wagons that are now arriving on the field."

And they were too, one after another—soon almost too many to count.

"Do we try and herd the porkers back aboard?"

"Not enough time before the troops arrive. If they remember to use their bows there is no way to stop them."

The thought of the possibility of porcine butchery made my mind up. The pieces of a possible plan clicked into place. I turned on my phone.

"Tell Stramm to crank in the ramp and close the outer port."

"What will you do?"

"Angelina and I will join the beasts in the woods. We're free and mean to stay that way. These green guys seem to be pretty dim for the most part . . ."

"Did you say 'green'?"

"Take a close look—over and out."

Angelina nodded. "A fine idea. Fresh air and a nice stroll in the forest with our four-legged friends. I agree. But let's bring some of these baskets with us—unless you intend to root for food like our swinish companions."

"Most practical," I said and picked one up. "We need to know more about these pea-green thugs before we can figure out what to do next."

"Reluctant thugs," she said pointing across the field.

Far across the field more and more bowmen had emerged from the forest—but they weren't going very far or fast. They huddled together, clutching their bows, and only advanced slowly when a few of their officers kicked and pushed them forward.

Then we reached the shelter of the trees, among the friendly snuffles of the rooting animals: there was a shrill squeak as Pinky emerged from the herd, her snout covered with loam, and enjoyed a quick scratch from Angelina.

"While the Greenies are being kicked into action," I said, "I think it might be wisest to put a little space between them and us."

With a little gentle prodding the herd moved deeper into the woods, away from any pursuit. I kept in radio touch with the captain, who reported very little action among the attacking troops. They milled about, but appeared to be reluctant to approach the ship. Some of them had been goaded into apparently starting after us, but little by little they filtered back into the woods.

They were soon left behind and out of sight as we moved steadily away. After an hour of slow progress we were far enough from the field to take a break. We stopped on the shore of a small lake where the porcuswine drank their fill.

"I have been thinking," I said digging out a crock of cider to slake my own thirst.

"Well, I should hope so—and kindly pass that over. After all it was your decision to land on this planet."

I could only pass the jug to her in silence. Feeling that this was not the time to apportion blame. If ever.

"I think everyone on this planet has green skin," I said. A foolproof subject-changer.

"But the other people we talked to on the screen. Black, pink, brown—"

"Makeup to hide their green skin."

"Why?"

A good question. I could only shrug my shoulders and respond feebly. "Solve that and we are a lot closer to finding out what is happening here."

"I know what they did. They tried to con us into landing by having the same skin color as we have."

"But why so many different colors?' I asked.

"It is obvious: they didn't know our skin color—so they gave us a selection to chose from."

I shrugged. It was as good an explanation as any until we could find out more.

We ate in silence, wrapped in our own thoughts. Pinky

snuffled over for a handout. The other beasts were resting and dozing. That was a good idea. It had been a long and busy day that had ended with a lengthy walk. I spread one of the table-cloths on a mossy bank, then pulled two others over for a blanket. As warm dusk descended so did we, emulating our four-legged friends.

IT WAS DARK WHEN I awoke, the darkness tempered by a large pinkish moon just visible through the trees. One of the boars was rumbling angrily deep in his throat as he sniffed the evening air. It had been many years since I had heard that sound, but its meaning was clear. There was something out there he didn't like. I slipped out of our rustic bed, without waking Angelina, and walked over to the boar. It was Gnasher, top pig in the pack. I gave him a quick scratch under his quills but he had other things in mind. He gave a quick shake and rose, still sniffing and grumbling.

"Let's go see what it is," I whispered and he gave an answering grunt.

On silent hooves he moved his tonne of porker silently through the trees. I followed him, doing my best to be quiet as well. He stopped at the edge of a clearing, sniffing the air and staring intently at the cover on the far side of the opening among the trees. Was that a dark form moving against the darkness under the trees there? We were both silent and motionless.

Watching as a man stepped into the clearing. The silhouette of a bow rose up over his shoulder.

With a thunderous crash Gnasher burst through the undergrowth and was on the stranger before he could move. Banging into him and tossing him aside as he did. The soldier screamed shrilly and I was grabbing him. Holding him to the ground with one foot while I tore the bow from his shoulder.

"Good swine . . . good Gnasher!" I said. Turning to face the foam-flecked tusks of the irritated animal.

"Sweet little swine!" I cried desperately as I dug the bow into the spines along his shoulders, prodding and scratching.

For long moments he grumbled in anger while I sweated and scratched. Then the grumble died away and became a burble of pleasure. The man writhed under my foot and I crunched down harder. Then I grabbed his collar and hauled him to his feet.

"You are coming with me, Greenie. One move to escape and you are pig meal . . ."

Gnasher rumbled agreement and my prisoner shivered like a leaf in the wind.

Our crashing about in the forest had roused the herd. They milled about in the growing light of dawn, the boars grumbling angrily, the sows protecting their piglets. I made all the soothing sounds to cool them down. Gnasher had had enough excitement for the night. He flopped down and soon muttered himself to sleep. The rest of the herd followed his example and calmed down as well.

"And dare I ask: what was all that about?" Angelina asked, stepping out of the cover of the forest and slipping her gun back out of sight.

"This," I said, holding my prisoner by the neck and shaking him a bit. In the growing light we could see that he was shivering with fear.

"He's just a boy," Angelina said. "You've terrorized the poor creature."

"With good reason—those arrows in his quiver go with this bow. I really don't enjoy being shot at in the dark."

"You're twice his size," Angelina said. "He doesn't look like much of a threat now."

He was clearly visible in the breaking dawn. Staring around wildly, still terrified, his pale green skin dotted with sweat. His uniform was crude, made of a coarse fabric of some kind that had been stained brown.

"I have some questions for him to answer," I said, stepping forward. He whimpered with fear and shied away.

"Stop being a bully, Jim diGriz. Now let me try talking to him." She faced him, smiling and talking softly. I grumbled a porcuswinish grumble, sat down and reached for the jug of cider.

"Relax, young green friend—I just want to talk with you," she said. My private feelings were that a touch of the boot in the right place would extract answers a lot faster. "Why don't you tell me your name . . ."

With great reluctance he finally muttered an answer.

"Grinchh . . ."

"Is that a name—or stomach trouble?" I muttered. And was rightly ignored.

"Are you a soldier, Grinchh?"

"No—no soldier." He drew himself erect with a touch of pride. "Tracker. Best tracker in Mittelflop!"

Wonderful claim to fame, I thought, but wisely kept this to myself.

"But why were you following us?"

"Bad Ones come! Tried to hide in hay, me and Pssher, but they push in sharp hay fork. Pull out—take away. Momma . . . !"

"Now don't you worry. There are no bad ones here . . ."

It was more than I could take. Muttering under my breath I went over to the picnic basket, shooed Pinky away and dug into it in search of some breakfast. Behind me the interrogation continued—obviously not needing my help.

It was some time before Angelina left the prisoner sitting dejectedly under a tree and joined me.

"If he makes a run for it the pigs will eat him alive."

"Don't be cruel, Jim, that's not like you. He's a simple country bumpkin—and a long way from home. He's far more frightened of what he calls the Bad Ones than he is of us."

"That's good to know—maybe we can raise a peasant rebellion."

"I doubt that—he's far too afraid of them."

"And just who are the Bad Ones he talks about?"

"It's hard to tell exactly. Other than that they are all-powerful, all-ruling. But one thing is obvious. He is simple and stupid, illiterate too I am sure. Not so the ones we talked to with the painted faces. I don't know how or why, but relative intelligence seems to be a powerful factor in the equation."

I sat up, intrigued by the idea. "Makes a lot of sense. That's why the two men who asked us for the paperwork later drove the wagons! They have a limited supply of intelligence—the Bad Ones! A planet full of peasant morons led by an elite few with a monopoly on the brains. But why?"

"Answer that—" she said with grim certainty "—and you answer the big question about this puzzling planet. So, master planner, what do we do next?"

What indeed?

I had no answers to that riddle.

It was full daylight now. All the food baskets were empty and we—or I—had drained the last of the jugs. I saw a future of pond water and starvation. The porcuswine might be able to live on their bosky resources, but we humans couldn't.

"We will have to go back. Contact the ship . . ."

"I wouldn't do that if I were you," the man said stepping out of the shelter of the forest. "Not yet at least."

IT WAS REFLEX, PURE AND simple. As the first words were spoken Angelina's gun—and mine too of course—appeared. Pointing dead center at the intruder.

"I mean you no harm," he said, smiling and holding up the bow he was carrying. "I use this for hunting only. I'll place it on the ground to prove that I wish only peace."

Angelina smiled at the thought of his causing us any harm and her gun vanished as fast as it had appeared. As did mine.

"You surprised us," she said.

"I'm sorry. But it was necessary for me to contact you."

He wore a kilt of tanned green leather, shoes made of the same material. The bow was carefully constructed, as were the arrows protruding from the quiver.

Most important was the color of his skin. It was tanned a light and healthy brown.

"My name is Bram. Might I sit? It has been a long and tiring night following that one who was tracking you."

He dropped to the ground and leaned back against the thick bole of a tree. "Again welcome strangers, to our unhappy world."

"And a hearty welcome to you, good Bram," I said, sitting down as well. "Since you are here by your own choice I hope you won't mind a few questions?"

"I am delighted to help in any way I can."

"What are you doing here?" Angelina asked, getting in the first question.

"A runner came to our camp and told us the wonderful news of the arrival of an off-planet spaceship. It has been over five years since the last one. We have been waiting—and hoping to make contact this time. The Rememberer tells us that we have always failed in the past. But could we do it now? I must say there was great jubilation when word was passed that a number of domestic animals and two people had left the ship and escaped capture. You were followed by a small party of our people as soon as you entered the forest. You were not approached until we had captured most of the trackers the Greens had sent to follow you. The one remaining tracker was kept under surveillance until you took possession of him. Then I was chosen to have the honor of greeting you."

He sprang to his feet and bowed.

"Welcome, good travelers. May the future be a wonderful one."

"It would be more wonderful," Angelina said, pointing to our captive, "if you would tell us why he is green and you are not."

"Would that I could—but I am not conversant with the details of the history of this unhappy planet. But I will be more than happy to take you to the one who can tell you. The Rememberer, who at this moment is being joyfully rushed to meet with you. It has been agreed that we will join him at our campsite. It will be my pleasure to guide you—and your domestic creatures—there."

He was intelligent—unlike our prisoner—and happy to talk with us. But it appeared that there was little he could add to what he had already told us. Angelina walked with him as the trek began, attempting to find out more of what he knew about this world.

"It seems pretty clear the way he tells it," Angelina said to me later, when we had stopped at a running stream that bubbled down a green valley. "And he gave me this bag."

She opened the soft leather pouch she was carrying and took out what looked like a handful of dark chips of wood. "It's the meat of some nameless beast. Smoked and dried. Delicious."

"It is," I said crunching vigorously away.

"He apologized for it. Said we will have much better fare when we reach their encampment. This is a far more friendly reception than we got from the Greenies."

I could but agree. "Did he tell you much about this world?"

"Little more than what we already know. The planet apparently has two separate races or groups, divided by skin color. The Greenies who guided us to this world dominate everywhere—and greatly outnumber those of a different skin color."

"Are there many other skin colors?"

"No, just the two. And that was makeup the Bad Ones used on their skin when they met us. They really do hate the pale faces of other races. At least the intelligent ones do. Most of the Greenies are simpletons like the soldiers who so feebly attacked us. The green minority bosses work hard to kick them into line. Our friend Bram was a little vague about this—kept telling me to save our questions for the Rememberer."

"Not that we have much choice."

Half an hour later the track we were following ran through a stand of what looked very much like chestnut trees. At least the porcuswine thought so and chomped happily at the windfalls.

"There is no way we can get them moving now," I said gloomily, disinterring my youthful memories of swinish husbandry.

"There is no need to," Bram said. "My people are waiting just beyond these trees."

And they were. The track we had been following opened out into a green field where some cows were grazing. Beyond them was a small group of bowmen—with pink skin. There was a ragged cheer when they saw us and they hurried across the field to join us. They stopped and their leader, with gray hair and serious mien, stepped forward and spoke.

"I am Otmar, first among others in this part of the forest. I have been appointed to take you to the Rememberer." As he spoke his hand rested on the hilt of what looked very much like a sheathed knife on his belt. I tensed, ready for anything that looked like an attack. He slowly pulled out a gleaming iron blade, placed it on his open hands, and held it out towards me.

"I, Otmar, give you my blade and declare our friendship," he said with utmost gravity. I took it and nodded—then passed it back the same way. And spoke carefully just the way he had.

"I, Jim, give you back your blade and declare our friendship."

There was a quick murmur of approval from the men behind him.

"We will now go to the Rememberer."

"It's not quite that easy," my wife said, stepping forward. "And my name is Angelina." Spoken easily, but with chill overtones. Otmar was no dummy and picked up on it at once.

"My pardon, friend Angelina. What is it that disturbs you?"

"Our herd. I don't think it will be easy to move them."

"That will not be necessary—that is why these men are here. They are the shepherds who tend our cattle. They will care for your animals, guard and protect them."

"Then we are ready to go," Angelina said.

Otmar was a quick learner and nodded agreement. We hadn't seen any women yet and knew nothing of their status in this society. But now he knew their status in ours.

The porcuswine merely chomped on, uninterested in our departure. Except for Pinky, who grunted an interrogative grunt—but then tucked right back into the feast.

While we had been talking more people began to arrive, smiling and curious about the off-world strangers. Some of them were women, in leather skirts—with woven baskets on their backs.

"Well, guess who does the heavy work," Angelina said.

This was the kind if statement for which there is no answer.

"There is food," Otmar said. "We will eat before we leave."

I launched a preemptive strike and spoke quickly before Angelina could.

"A great idea—isn't it, my love?"

A chilling glance was my only answer. It could have been worse.

The fresh air and exercise had given us ravenous appetites. There were more of the dried meat chips—undoubtedly beef. Fresh cheese, crusty loaves of bread, washed down with skimmed milk from pottery crocks. I don't know how the Greenies fared, but there was nothing wrong with the Pinkies' food. I was quickly sated—and thankfully at peace.

"It is time to leave," Otmar said, looking up at the sun. "We want to reach the camp before dark. The Rememberer is no longer young, but his students have brought him there to meet you."

"Students?" Angelina asked as we started down the trail. "What does he teach them?"

"To remember." Of course. "There is also an art called reading, which I am sure you have heard of. He teaches that . . ." He stopped abruptly and turned to Angelina.

"Of course, you have heard of reading—you must excuse my rudeness. And . . . perhaps it is that you can read as well, lady of great wisdom?"

"Of course," she said. And smiled. "Where we come from everyone can."

Otmar lowered his eyes. "You must excuse my lack of

knowledge," he said. "You will understand that life here is not easy, with the Grønner always in pursuit of us."

"Don't worry. We're going to see to it that there will be some major changes on your planet."

He gasped at her firm resolve.

"It will be different, Otmar," I said. "I promise you that it will."

He looked from Angelina's face to mine and could not talk. I could understand why. If we spoke the truth then this world, as he knew it, would indeed be turned upside down.

In silence we started back along the forest track towards their campsite and what we all hoped would be a glowing future.

It was dusk when we arrived. A little tired but not terribly so. Give Moolaplenty that, we were in good shape. A pleasure planet where the pleasures included skiing in the winter—and surfboarding in the summer—saw to that.

The trees were taller here, providing concealment from observation. Beneath them were hide tents that blended into the forest. Otmar led us to the largest one but paused at the entrance.

"I will wait outside for you. May you gain wisdom and share it in return."

There was little that I could say. Angelina had no such reservations. She reached out and took Otmar by the hands.

"Thank you," she said. Then turned and went into the darkened building.

In the flickering light of the fire, in an open hearth, we saw the elderly man who was waiting for us. He was seated on a dais of some kind. Behind him was a small group of young men. As we approached one with a black-beard and wearing a cowled robe, he stepped forward and raised his hand.

"You will stop there," he said in a cold and demanding voice. "I am Student Prime. You are now in the presence of the Rememberer. You will . . ."

"And so we are—and we intend to talk to him," Angelina said coldly. Tired and out of patience. "Step aside."

The color rose in his face. But before he could protest I raised a fist—that Angelina could not see, as I waved him aside. He was smart enough to close his mouth and move out of the way. The Rememberer started to rise but sat back heavily. Angelina smiled at him.

"This is my husband, Jim diGriz. My name is Angelina. We have been told that you are the only one who can tell us exactly what is happening on this planet."

"I can indeed, kind lady. Welcome to the troubled world of Salvation and her unhappy inhabitants. Let this sad story begin."

CHAPTER 19

He raised his shaking hand and his students moved into well-rehearsed action. One of the smaller children carried over a low table and placed it before the old man. Student Prime made a great show of putting a very large, leather-bound book onto it, then stepped to one side.

"In the beginning was the Book," Rememberer said. "This is a true copy made by the ancient scribes. So it begins." He pointed at the thick tome and Prime leaned out and opened it.

"This is the log book of the deep spacer named *The Spirit of Free Enterprise*. It came from the planet of Das Kapital and was manned by our ancestors, who were called the Tory Party. They were fleeing oppression on their home world. The voyage was long and arduous and beset by difficulties most terrible. A disaster called a Radiationleak struck them down. We do not know what this word means. But we do know that many were ill and many died. Then they reached this world, which they named Salvation, where they fled the ship that had cursed them. Though many had died, and many newborn children died as well, our fathers' fathers' fathers lived and we bless their memory."

He nodded and the page was turned. Then he looked up at the visitors. "There is now another word I must use that no one knows the meaning of. Generations of learned men have discussed it but the import has never been made clear. It was a curse, we know that. A curse that made the world as you see it today."

"And that word is . . . ?" Angelina asked.

He took a deep quavering breath and said—

"Geneticradiationdamage."

"That word—really those words—are known," I said. "Please tell us the rest of your history and the meaning will be clear."

Rememberer fell back in his chair. "Then . . . you do know?"

"We do—and all will be explained."

There was a great stir and shouting among the students. One of them collapsed and was dragged aside. The old man was brought a bowl of water and he drank deep. Student Prime finally restored order, cuffing the smaller students about the ears and pushing them into line.

"Please continue," Angelina said and the old man nodded.

"The curse was upon our people. Mothers who suffered from this curse had babies who were not like us. Their skin was green and they were not as we were. Although the mothers loved all their children alike, this love was not returned by the green ones. They cried and screamed and were only quiet when they were among others of the same skin color. A green generation grew to adulthood and rejected their parents who loved them.

"Many were born and joined with others of their kind when they grew up, until there were more with green skin than that of pink. The greens began to live apart from us. But there soon were far more of them and they were most cruel. They watched us closely and when a baby was born they came and looked at it. If it had green skin they tore child from mother with great violence. As the years passed fewer green ones were born to our people until there were no more among us. That is the world as you see it now. There are far more of the Grønner—as our fathers called them—than there are of us."

He drank more water and fell back into his chair.

"But why are there more greens than pink people now?" I asked, puzzled.

"Because," Angelina said. "They are obviously more prolific then our friends here. Whatever mutation caused this massive genetic change must have been accompanied by increased fertility."

"What you say is true," Rememberer said. "Their women have babies when they are very young, even as children—and many more of them. They also die when they are still young."

"Is it possible that the fertility was accompanied by lowered intelligence?" I said. Angelina nodded.

"Of course," Angelina said. "Rapid maturity and early fertility left no time for developing intelligence. You end up with a prolific race of green morons—lead by the very small minority of their kind with something close to normal intelligence."

In the following silence I saw that the old man and his students were listening to what we said, but understanding little. I smiled as I turned to them.

"I will now, hopefully, explain what has happened on this world. If you have any questions as I go along just speak up."

"And please . . ." Angelina said, "could you find two chairs—and some water to drink. It has been a very long day." The students hurried to help. The chairs were folding stools, but we weren't complaining.

What had happened to these unhappy people was now painfully clear to us. Explaining it to them was going to be the difficult part. Rememberer had a lifetime behind him of learning one text. He was probably not equipped to assimilate new stores of knowledge. Most of the students could probably only memorize by rote and would not be able to handle these new concepts. Only Prime seemed to understood what we were saying, and his questions were all highly relevant.

"Then this radiation you speak of is a strong force that damaged the parts of our bodies called genes. These are small, but powerful, and shape our bodies before we are born?"

I nodded. "Bang on."

"They make us be male or female—tall or short."

"Right."

"And also make our skin color—like making some of us green?"

"You've got it! Whatever happened in the ship released a blast of radiation . . ."

"And caused the genetic radiation damage. That is the meaning of the word!"

"You have it—all is explained."

"To you only, Student Prime," Angelina said. Pointing to the mass of sleeping young acolytes—as well as their elder in the chair. But Prime was too excited by this new knowledge to care about them.

"Now we know what happened, know why we are this way—and why the Grønner are as they are. But what do we do with this newfound knowledge? How does it help us defeat them, to live in a world at peace?"

I sighed. "I'm afraid there is nothing your people can do but survive—as you have done in the past. Genetic damage cannot be reversed."

"On the contrary," Angelina said. "You now have hope. The powers that practice peace rule all the known worlds out there in space. When we contact them they will know what must be done to end this terrible battle."

I found it took a distinct effort to smile and reassure this young man, who expected so much of us. Because it was not going to be that easy. He could not know what trouble we were in ourselves.

"We'll continue this in the morning," Angelina wisely said. "I don't know about you two, but I am more than ready for some sleep."

Bram had managed to stay awake, though he was looking very much the worse for wear. "A place has been prepared for you to sleep. It is this way."

A corner of one of the tents was walled off with hanging skins, giving us a measure of privacy. A flickering lantern supplied enough light to move around. Fresh green boughs formed a bed of sorts. They were spread with coarsely woven blankets. Angelina rubbed them between her fingers.

"This is the first cloth I've seen here—leather seems to be the fashion of the day."

"The Greenies have cloth uniforms—maybe our lads stole this from them."

"That is a mystery that can wait until morning." She smoothed out the blanket and tested the temper of the bed.

"Fine." She slipped under the covers. "I don't know about you, but I need a swim—or at least a wash in the morning." She sniffed the air. "And you do too. Good night . . ."

LIKE THE OTHERS, WE WERE up at dawn. A bowl of fresh fruit was most welcome. Angelina went with some of the women to a bathing spot; for the moment I just scratched. When I stepped out of the building I was greeted by a very bleary-eyed Student Prime. He looked as if he hadn't slept at all.

"I have some questions, friend Jim . . ."

I waved him to silence while I finished chomping on a piece of fruit, juice dripping from fingers and chin.

"Wash first, talk later. How do I clean this off?"

"There . . . behind those buildings."

It wasn't much of a washroom, but it would do. A lean-to of leafy branches with a large wooden basin of water. There were scoops—made of dried gourds—to dip into it. Refreshed and slightly cleaner I found a bench outside where I could dry off in the sun. Prime sat by me.

"I need to ask you some questions," I said.

"I sincerely hope I will be able to answer them."

"I notice that your people wear leather clothes—by choice?"

"Forced choice. Deer are plentiful, both for food and skins. We have some cloth—all stolen. The Grønner have vast fields of cotton. Something we cannot do since they would easily be discovered by their scouts who are constantly looking for us. We have small vegetable patches that we can sometimes harvest before they are found. We are always on the move, always staying ahead of them. It is easy to find and extract the dye from a certain forest plant. We use it to color our leather, so it blends with the forest. We have no industry, no permanent homes. We only own what we can carry."

"I saw some cows in the clearing."

"Yes, we have a few that we move with us. It is a life of constant traveling, constant fear."

We were both depressed now, but I still had to learn more.

"When the tracker, Bram, first contacted us, he was very excited to be able to speak with us. He said something about not being able to contact the other ships that had landed at the spaceport. Including one that arrived five years ago. Why?"

"Because we must find a way to contact the other worlds in the universe out there. To seek help, make our predicament known. To end living like outcasts on our own planet! But before you arrived, all the other people who landed in the machines from space were seized and taken away."

"Why . . . and where?"

"I know not. But there have been sightings of prisoners from time to time. Always far from here. Most recently there was a possible off-worlder seen at a cotton mill, but it was dusk and the tracker was not sure of the man's skin color."

"What about the buildings at the spaceport. There must be people there?"

"We cannot get close. Trackers have tried, but there are many wire fences, all of them heavily guarded."

The scarcity of knowledge was annoying—and frustrating. The Greenies had obviously lured us here—as well as the other spacers at the field.

But why?

"What will you do now?" Prime asked.

"Good question." And it was. The answer was obvious. "I must contact our ship. Do you know what is happening there?"

"We have watchers in the forest. They report no change. The Grønner tried to break in once with no success. The metal of your flying machine resisted their wooden battering timbers. Then something happened—there was a sudden great cloud of smoke and the soldiers all ran away. They coughed and fell down and did not attack again."

At last some good news. The captain and Stramm must have cooked up some noxious gas. Score one for the good guys. I turned my radio on—but all I got was static. With no satellites to relay my signal I would have to get nearer for line-of-sight contact.

"If we can get closer to the spacer I can talk to them. Find out what is happening."

He looked horrified. "You will be seen—captured!"

"Not that close—nearby among the trees will do." How did I explain what a radio was to these peasant people without machines?

"I have a magic way of talking through the air that I can then use to contact them."

"A radio of some kind?"

So much for the illiterate peasant; I had forgotten he was in the educated very minor minority.

"Yes, a radio. It is called a headphone."

"But . . . I do not see it on your head?"

"That's because it is inside my head, in the bone."

"What wondrous things there are—that we know nothing of. We are like pink rats scuttling around in a green world, barely surviving."

His analogy cut to the bone. Brother Rats—that is what these people were. Here was an intelligent man, shut away from almost all knowledge. I vowed to myself that this errant planet must be brought back into the wide realm of mankind. Another important reason to get back in touch with the family of worlds. Do it, Jim!

"You are looking your most serious," Angelina said, sitting down beside me in the sun.

"We must end our woodland idyll. As much as the porcuswine enjoy the easy life, we can't. We have to find a way to get out of this mess. But first I have to talk with the ship."

"A great idea. I feel clean now, but still badly in need of a change of clothing."

"That too . . ." I said, turning to Prime. "When can we leave?"

"Now. Those who will take you are waiting over there."

I stood and stretched. "Are you joining in the party?" I asked Angelina.

"Only when you are sure we can get back into the ship. I want to check on Pinky and the pack. I'm sure the poor creature is feeling lonely."

Feeling fat is more like it, I thought—but had enough sense not to speak my thoughts aloud.

Bram was waiting with the small group of men at the forest's edge. Instead of bows they carried stout wooden cudgels.

Fine for close-up contact. Student Prime was waiting with them.

"I must leave you here, to return with the Rememberer. But I will be back to join you as soon as I can."

"Do that. We will need your help."

The scouts fanned out ahead and the trek began. It was a lot faster than the outward trip had been—because we weren't going at a pig's pace now. When we reached our objective two of the scouts were waiting among the trees at the spaceport's edge.

"There are many of their men all around your sky traveler," one of them said. "But they are afraid to go too close after what happened with the gas."

"Great—so let's open contact. Radio on. Hello the ship— the Boss is back . . ."

CHAPTER 20

"*WELL IT'S ABOUT TIME,*" THE captain said, his voice resonating like thunder in my skull.

"Volume down!" I said. "You will be cheered to hear that we are safe—as are the swine. How are you faring?"

"Fine so far. Those Greenies tried to break in a few times, but we drove them off. However, the passengers are growing restless. The frozen food is tasteless, the water is running low—and they have nothing at all to do with the animals not here . . ."

"Sounds great. We need to have a meet and make plans for the future. Is there any way I can get back aboard?"

"Talk to Stramm about that."

It took awhile to work out a strategy. It was obvious that the lower hatch could not be opened without risking an attack by the waiting troops. However, there was a chance we could use the emergency lock that we had first unsealed.

"I'll look into it and call you back," Stramm said.

We rested out of sight in the forest, with guards out on all sides. It was well after dark, and I must have dozed off, when Stramm's voice inside my skull brought me quickly back on line.

"Are you ready?"

"Speak—and I obey."

"The hatch will be open in ten minutes. I'll lower the rope when I get a signal from you. Grab the ring on the end . . ."

"And climb?"

"I have a motor here to reel you in. Don't fall off."

"What encouragement . . ."

As planned, Bram and some of the sturdier scouts were waiting under the trees at the forest's edge. By the light of the waning moon I could just pick out the dark opening of the emergency lock. It seemed very small and very high.

"I can see the airlock . . ."

"Rope dropping—now!"

We ran—as silently as we could. And ran right over the soldiers who sprawled on the tarmac. A few startled cries were cut off by the quick thudding of wooden clubs.

Then I slammed into the landing fin and groped for the metal ring swinging slowly above me. Just out of reach above my head.

There were shouts from around the field now as the Greenies stirred to life.

"Bram, give me a lift."

He threw his club aside, bent and seized me by the waist—and heaved. I grabbed at the ring—just managed to get my fingers onto it—then clutched at it with my other hand.

"Take your men back!" I shouted as the rope started up with a sudden motion—almost tearing lose my grip.

I clutched with grim desperation, as I swung about and looked down. My troops were pelting back to the safety of the forest—leaving a few sprawled green bodies in their wake. As far as I could tell they all had made it.

I turned my attention back to my swift ascent. Crashed against the hull, kicked myself clear. Then the motor stopped grinding and a mighty hand clutched my wrist. With my waning strength I hauled myself through the lock and collapsed onto the floor.

"Let us . . . not do that again . . ." I gasped.

"Captain's waiting for you." All heart our engineer.

I just lay there enjoying a good gasp as the outer door closed. By the time the inner door ground open I was on my feet and ready to go. Stramm went with me, morose and silent. The captain was no better, but at least he made an effort to welcome the wanderer's return. He poured a glass of strong cider from the jug on the plotting table. I drank deep, and sighed.

"Thanks. I needed that."

"We are in deep trouble—and getting in deeper," was his grim prediction.

"Welcome back boss, welcome!" I said. Feigning happiness. "Shall I tell you what I have discovered—and how we will get out of this mess?"

"Yes, do," he sighed, uncheered in the slightest.

But they did listen intently as I told them about our adventures during our escape. Our new friends in the forest—and what we had discovered.

"So what do we do next?" Stramm asked. I poured another

glass and groped for an answer. My mind was blank. When in doubt—and was I ever!—answer a question with another question.

"Have you been in contact with the Greenies?"

"Far too much . . ." the captain gloomed. "First they said it was all a mistake, some renegades, since caught. Told us to come out and talk like reasonable men. Then came the threats—and the attack. When the gas drove them off all pretense ended. They even wiped off their makeup—green as grass, like the rest of them. That's where it stands now."

"How long can this impasse hold?"

"No one in the ship likes it, but we can get by for a while. There is more than enough food, but water is a different matter. We're going to have to fill the tanks fairly soon. The passengers aren't in open rebellion yet—but it won't be long."

"Can you hold out for a few more days? Then we'll move the ship away from here. Land it and board the beasts, fill the water tanks—and blast off before the Greenies arrive. But before we leave this dismal planet I want to find out if they have interstellar communication or not. Agreed?"

"Agreed—but first, how are you going to get out of the ship now—with all these angry natives surrounding it?"

"Another drop of cider, please." I pushed my glass forward and smiled what was surely a fake smile. "Let me give that a moment's thought."

It was a brief moment, because seconds later there was a loud hammering on the door. The captain's gloomy face grew even gloomier.

"They didn't take long." He nodded to Stramm. "Better let them in."

Elmo was first through the unlocked door. Followed closely by Miz Julia who, for some unknown reason, was carrying a rolling pin.

"What's happening with the herd?" Elmo cried, shaking his fist. "Is they all right?'

"Tell us!" Miz Julia shouted, waving her strange weapon. "The sows—the piglets . . ."

"All fine and feeding in the forest. Angelina is looking after them with the greatest care."

"We gotta see them . . . and get outta this ship!" Elmo said, more concerned with self than swine.

"Let me reassure you that plans are already under way to do just that. As soon as I leave this ship—"

"And how you doing that?"

I was getting a little tired of Elmo. "You'll just have to leave that up to us," I growled, then turned to Miz Julia, stood and offered her my arm.

"May I escort you back to your quarters? It has been nice talking with you again."

She looked suspicious—with good reason—but accepted the offer. I chatted amiably as we exited the bridge.

"The sows are rooting in a walnut grove . . . and the piglets grow plump on the rich diet . . ."

"My—that is wonderful to hear!" Her weapon, forgotten, swung by her side.

"It surely is. Now, while we are having this nice little talk— could I ask you a favor?"

"Of course."

"I was just wondering—do you, or any of your ladies— have any skin cream?"

I responded quickly to her wide eyes and dropped jaw.

"Not for me! It's for Angelina. Living rough, the sun, she is so worried about her skin . . ."

"Why, the poor child. Of course . . . I know that Becky Sue has some."

"Could you bring it to my cabin, if you please. I'm packing up some clothes for her as well."

"I'll do just that!" She hurried away—as did I—snarling as I passed Elmo as he tried to open what was sure to be a mind-destroying conversation.

I thanked Miz Julia when she brought the cream, and asked her to thank the cosmetic-conscious Becky Sue as well. I put it in a light backpack with the clothes, and made by way back to the bridge.

"I'm leaving now," I told the surprised officers.

"How . . . and why?" the captain asked.

"Why? Because the not-too-bright Greenies are now passing the word of the evening's excitement, then slowly considering what to do, while at the same time they are being thoroughly confused. The sooner we act the better the element of surprise. As to how I will get out—I will exit in just the way I came in. And the quicker the better. I'll count on speed and my reliable and alert troops to stay one jump ahead of the Greenies. All right?"

They were reluctant but had no choice.

"Sounds like suicide. But when—and if—you manage to get clear, you will let us know what is happening?" the captain asked.

"As soon as I can."

Stramm led the way back to the airlock. "Grab onto the

ring," Stramm said, "because I'm turning the lights out before I open the outer lock. And I don't want to run the motor to lower you—they'll hear the sound. I threw a couple of bights of the rope around a stanchion, so I'll brake your descent."

The moon had set; the night was dark and silent. I hoped that it would remain that way. And hoped even more ardently that the engineer's good right arm . . . was a good right arm.

I settled the pack on my back, grabbed the ring and wriggled my way out of the lock.

"Ready," I whispered, easing my weight out onto the rope.

And fell! Stramm had either lost control or was overly enthusiastic about my rate of descent.

The ground rushed up towards me.

An instant before I hit I kicked hard against the hull. Thrust away with both feet and tumbled into a shoulder roll. The pack punched my back—and then I was down and gasping for air. The wind knocked out of me.

There were shouts and whistles on all sides, running green men looming up out of the darkness. I stumbled, dropped, staggered to my feet again—and they were onto me, clutching at my arms.

Then getting clubbed down.

It was a murderous melee in the darkness.

More shouting and more men appeared. The Greeny holding my arms grunted and fell limply away.

"To me," sounded in a loud whisper and this time I was seized in a more friendly grip and hurried from the field of combat. There were low whistles now—a prearranged signal I imagined.

"We'll wait here for the others," Bram whispered. "We leave no one behind."

Nor did we. When the count was complete we moved silently and quickly away.

"One unconscious," Bram said. "We're carrying him. Brkur has a broken arm—you can hear him cursing." And I could. Other men were laughing, that was understandable. But I felt sorry for Brkur as well.

When we were well clear of the field we made our first stop. There was some pained gasping as the broken arm was wrapped and immobilized, then we moved on again.

Dawn was just breaking when we came to the encampment. Angelina was waiting there.

"Are you all right?" she asked, clutching my arms.

"Fine—as well as all our loyal troops. The ship was attacked—pretty ineffectually—and those within are bored but sound. Plans have been made and I'll reveal all as soon as I have a drink of water."

I passed her my pack.

"And here are some clean clothes."

She gasped, laughed—and kissed me on the cheek.

"You never cease to amaze me! A Stainless Steel Rat . . . with a heart of purest gold."

CHAPTER 21

WE SAT ON A GRASSY bank and watched the sunrise. Another nice day in what should have been paradise, but was a green purgatory instead.

"I have worked out a rough plan of action," I said as I reached into the pack. "And this may be the key."

I took out the jar of face cream and held it proudly aloft.

"No more puzzles—or jokes—if you don't mind."

"I'm deadly serious. Before we leave this wretched planet we must find out if the gruesome Greenies have interstellar communication. After all, that's the reason we came here in the first place. And we certainly can't ask them for all the obvious reasons. But our new friends told me that pink prisoners have been seen from time to time. And there is the possibility that there is one in a cotton mill less than a day's walk from here . . ."

She clapped her hands and laughed: no dummy my Angelina.

"So you are going to dye your skin—and break in so you can break the prisoner out!"

"Right in all ways! The pinks use a green vegetable dye for their leather clothes. A quick mix and I'm ready to go."

"Clothes?"

"Our tracker prisoner, Grincch, is just about my size . . ."

"I'll have him stripped now so I can wash his clothes before you even think about putting them on."

"While I get the dye—and put the proposition to Bram."

Who understood at once—and ran with the plan.

"I will get the dye and tell the others. They will all want to come!"

"Not all of them. A small war party is all I need."

"But you must know more about the mill and the cotton fields. I am going to send one—no two is better—of our fastest trackers to meet our people nearest to the fields. We will need their guidance. You really want to just, well, walk in among them?"

"That's the plan."

"You are indeed a brave man . . ."

"Lots more would say I'm incredibly stupid."

"Not us! You must pick a time—perhaps at dusk?"

"Perfect."

"That means we should arrive there when there is still some daylight left." He looked up at the sun. "It is too late to leave today . . ."

"Not to mention getting a bit of sleep before we go—"

"That too, of course." He didn't sound convinced. Trackers were made of stern stuff.

The green dye was a whitish powder that turned a brilliant green when mixed with a little water. I stirred and blended, working it into the face cream until it took on a satisfactory hue. I rubbed some on the back of my left hand and held it up to admire.

"I get a cold chill just looking at it," Angelina said and held out the still-damp, burlap clothes.

"My size?" I asked.

"We'll soon see. They really are baggy and shapeless so I don't think it will be a problem. But his sandals are falling to pieces, a disaster—"

"Not a problem. I'll wear my own boots. Scuff them up and cover them with mud, until they look like everyone else's footwear."

Next morning we were all up before dawn. Angelina worked by the light of a guttering lamp to spread the dyed cream smoothly over my hands and face.

"I suppose you are not inviting me along on your little expedition," she said casually but most meaningfully. I sighed and shook my head.

"If there were something you could do to help I would ask in a flash. But it is a one-man job. That I will do all the better if I know that you are here and safe."

Her slow nod was answer enough. She was realist enough to know that—this time at least—her talents could not be of any use.

"Done," she said. Holding up the lantern to admire her cosmetic skills. "You look utterly loathsome."

"My thanks! I aim but to blend with our equally loath-some adversaries."

"Don't go near any of the children here—you'll only make them cry."

Bram was equally taken. He actually reached for his cudgel when he turned and saw me in the dim light of dawn.

"For an instant, I thought we were being attacked! Come, we must show the others."

My makeup and outfit were an instant and horrible success. Men gaped and twitched their weapons: women screamed and fled.

"Just the five of you are going?" Angelina asked.

"They'll get me there—and safely back. And there should be plenty of help waiting for us when we arrive."

A lot was left unsaid. I had to do this alone, we both knew that. We started our journey just as the sun was breaking through the trees.

The trackers were hard men and experienced. Twice whispered word came back of danger ahead, and we made a quick circle around the trouble. Two of my companions had dried meat in their shoulder bags; we ate as we walked, then drank from a stream that cut through the woods.

The sky darkened and by late afternoon there were ominous rumblings from the clouds. A thin mist began to fall: I could only hope that my war paint was waterproof.

It was not an easy trek, so I was more than happy to flop down when Bram signaled a halt. The rain had stopped—and my skin coloring was still intact.

"The cotton fields are just ahead," Bram said. "We'll meet the others, the ones who left before us, here in this grove."

We didn't have to wait very long before dark and silent forms began to filter through the trees. More and more of them—the local trackers had joined them, most of them carrying bows. A tall man, obviously their leader, stepped forward.

"You are Bram. I knew your father well when we were growing up."

"Then you must be Alun."

"I am." They clasped hands. "And your father is in good health?"

"He's dead. Killed by them."

"A curse on all Grønner."

Bram nodded; a fate all too familiar to even talk about.

"Have there been any more sightings of the person we seek?" Bram asked.

"Just one," Alun said, pointing at the low building just beyond the field. "A positive identification. They had ropes tied to him and he was not green."

"Can you get me close to him?" I asked. He nodded.

"Let me show you what this place is like." He bent over a dry patch of ground, used the tip of his bow to trace a square shape in the dirt.

"This is the cotton field—and we are here, on the forest side of it. On the other side," he traced another box, "is a building with machines of some kind. I am told they make the cotton into cloth in some way."

Beyond the mill he traced out more squares. "Here there are many buildings where the cotton workers live, more and more of them. We want to stay away from them. Many guards there, many more of their people." He tapped the largest square.

"The field workers will be leaving here very soon. When they do, we'll let you through the fence so you walk after them." He looked at my green face in disgust. "You will do fine, just fine."

"They are leaving the field now!" Bram called out. "You must go and follow them."

Two of the trackers bent over the wooden fence, holding open a gap they had forced between interlocked boughs. As I wriggled through Bram pointed to the grove of tall trees we had just left. "We'll be waiting here when you come back."

Then I was through, standing and walking behind the others. On my own.

Which was just the way I liked it.

Some of them carried wooden hoes, shambling, tired from a long day's work. As I walked closer no one even looked my way.

First step done, Jim. You are just one more green among Greenies. Now all you have to do is find your target.

My fellow travelers shuffled past the building, going around it to their quarters beyond. I slowed and lagged behind. I paused at a door and pulled on the handle. It was open.

I closed it and waited until the last worker had trudged out of sight. Pulled the door open just enough to slip through. Closed it behind me.

A large open space with many wooden supports to hold up the roof. There were rows of hulking machines—crude looms— just visible in the darkening gloom. People—women perhaps— were grouped together at the far end of the building, leaving through the doors there. A few smoking lanterns lit their way. I worked my way towards them, moving furtively from loom to loom.

There was a sudden scuffle and some angry cries. I

crouched low, looking through a gap between the machines. I heard loud male laughter and shouted commands. The women moved aside and three men came into view forcing themselves through the crowd.

The shrill voices were angry now as the men emerged. The one in the center appeared to have his arms tied behind his back, was bent over trying to avoid the grasping hands. When he finally straightened up I could see bloody scratches on his face.

Red tracks on his pallid pink skin!

Got you!

I skulked after them, among the dark looms, and moved closer.

"You morons are supposed to protect me," an angry voice said. I could see the prisoner rubbing his face along his shoulder, smearing away the blood.

"You just shut them face," one guard said—and followed with a hard blow to the man's ear. His companion laughed at the good fun.

Then they stopped under a lantern; I hunkered down behind a loom. They fumbled with the lashings on his wrists, taking an unconsciously long time to free him. Then he was pushed, stumbling, through the doorway into what must be a room beyond. The warders struggled a heavy beam into place, sealing the door shut.

"Don' go long time!" The remaining man called out as the other guard shuffled away.

"Come back when sr'gent say come back."

"No long, no long . . ." The man wailed.

Better and better. One against one now; good odds. I

slipped between the rows of machines. Then stood and walked silently towards him. He caught the motion, spun about, his jaw dropping.

"Who you? What here for . . ."

"See this finger," I said quietly, holding out my fist, thumb rigid.

He stared and gaped. Drooling a bit too.

I stabbed forward, my thumb catching him hard, just on the ganglion in his neck. He grunted and folded, thudding silently to the filthy floor. I stepped over his inert body and took the lantern off its hook. Looked around carefully.

Silence. The lamp guttered and smoked as I put it down. Then I worked the beam free from the retainers on the door and set it quietly aside. Picked up the lantern and opened the door.

"Go away," the voice said hoarsely from the darkness. "Don't beat me again. The loom was broken when I got there. It was that cow's fault—I told you what she did . . ."

"Quiet," I said and walked towards him. "I'm a friend."

He stared, eyes wide as I approached.

"I have no friends," he said through bruised lips. I could now see the scabs and unhealed bruises on his face, matted filthy hair. I felt a surge of hatred at the malicious, stupid creatures who had done this to him.

"Look at my skin," I said pulling up my jacket to bare the undyed skin at my waist. "You have a friend now."

He collapsed against the wall, sobbing and gasping—pulling back in fear when I reached down to help him to his feet.

"Questions—and explanations—later. Now just come with me. We're leaving this place."

There were voices in the distance. I blew out the lamp, threw it aside, pulled him to his feet, dragged him after me.

There was a fierce whooshing sound behind us and flames lit up the darkness. The fuel from the lamp had caught fire. I wasn't going to worry about it. The approaching voices turned to shouts and there was the sound of running feet.

We met at the doorway. Two of them. Wide-eyed, gaping green faces.

I struck out with my free hand, knocking the first one to the ground. The second guard raised a club. I jumped for his wrist, seized it and kept his arm coming up and over until the man screamed with pain: I silenced him with a quick blow.

Two down. No more in sight. Behind me the flames roared as the dry wood of the building caught fire.

"That should keep them busy," I said to my new companion. "Just keep going."

We ran between the looms, easily avoiding them in the flickering light as the flames flared in the dry wood. We were still unseen by the locals who had all of their attention focused now on carrying the unconscious men from the burning building.

I stopped for a breather at the same door I had used to enter the building. Though it felt like hours had passed since I had come through it, there was still light in the eastern sky. And the field was empty.

There was more shouting now—but all of it well behind us.

"You ready to go on?" I asked.

"Yes . . . of course. Lead the way."

We stumbled between the cotton plants, towards the forest beyond.

The figures by the gap in the fence were friends. Willing hands helped us through.

We were safe.

CHAPTER **22**

THE NEWLY RELEASED PRISONER FELL to the ground as soon as
I let go of his arm.

"We were watching," Bram said. "You weren't followed.
So I don't think you were seen leaving the building. But still,
we must get away from here before the search starts." He bent
over the man who was crumpled on the ground, still gasping
for breath.

"Soon . . . give me a minute . . ."

"He'll slow you down," Alun said. "We'll come with you
until you are well clear of this place. We will have to take
turns carrying him."

With an easy motion he lifted the man and slung him over
his broad shoulders.

"Follow me."

The trackers trailed quickly away into the forest.

By taking turns to carry the exhausted prisoner we made

good time as we returned the way we had come. Another one of the three moons had risen, which made it easier to find the trail. It was Alun who finally raised his hand and brought us to a halt in an open glade.

"You will be safe now. Their trackers aren't good enough to follow us this far. But my people will go back the way we came. In case a few of their trackers might still be after you. They won't get past us."

"I thank you for your aid," Bram said.

"We are as one. My son here, Tome, will go on with you. He will return and tell us what you have found out after you talk to this man."

"He is welcome to our food."

The escaped prisoner was sitting up, listening to us.

"Who are you people? What will happen to me?"

His confusion—and fear—were obvious to see. I sat down beside him.

"We are your friends," I said. "From off-planet. We have a spacer and you will be leaving here with us very soon."

"Gott im Himmel!" He cried out in some tortuous tongue. "To believe it . . . after all these years . . ."

He was sobbing with relief, clutching my arm. "You cannot understand . . ."

"I certainly can. These Greenies embody evil and stupidity in equal portions. But most important is the fact that you were their prisoner. There is every chance that you may be able to help us . . ."

"Whatever you ask!" He struggled to stand and I helped him to his feet. He braced himself erect and clapped his right fist across his chest; a salute of some kind. "Hans Steigger, Second Mate of the research ship *Rumfahrtroman.*"

"A pleasure to meet you. Jim diGriz. Civilian. Unemployed." I hit my fist against my chest too. "Can I ask you a few vital questions?"

"Anything!"

"When you were captured . . . were you taken into any of the buildings at the spaceport?"

"They lied to us! Said they would make us welcome . . . They told us their inspectors would come aboard only to look at the ship's quarantine and medical records. A common thing. But when we opened the spacelock we were overwhelmed! There was a rush of green thugs—they clubbed us down. Killed poor Klaus—dragged us into the buildings at the spaceport."

"You've been inside then?"

"Of course. We were all taken there. The one we had talked to on the radio was their leader. He actually had skin makeup on. Laughed at us when he wiped it off. Then he spoke to us one at a time. Wanted to know what position we held in the ship. He really only wanted the comm officers. The ones who knew about radio equipment. They were taken away and we never saw them again."

"What happened to you—and the other men?"

"Slave drivers—that's what we were. These green bastards are morons—cretins!—stupid beyond belief. They put them into work gangs with one of us in charge. We were guarded, watched all the time, by thugs with clubs. The workers—you can't believe how incredibly dim they are—like retarded chickens. No, chickens are smarter. You put a hoe in their hands and guide it for them. Hoe between the plants, you tell them, keep on doing it."

He spat with disgust. "A few minutes later they have forgotten what you told them to do. If you don't stop them they actually dig up the plants you are trying to grow . . ."

He fell back, breathing heavily, exhausted. I patted his hand.

"That's great, thanks. You better rest a bit before we go on."

Communication gear inside the spaceport buildings! This was the news we needed. The rescue effort to free Hans had been more than worth it.

"We must keep moving," Bram said. He turned to Hans who was sitting up. "Can you walk by yourself now?"

"Of course—but not too fast I'm afraid."

"This will help—" Bram said, passing Hans some of the dried meat. "When you finish that we will leave."

His only answer was muffled mastication.

The trek continued, but within a short time it became obvious that the stumbling Hans was in no shape to go on. I, not to mention the exhausted Hans, could not match the iron endurance of the trackers. He had to stop. I agreed—it was a most attractive option. Apparently not to my sturdy companions. As I was falling asleep I was aware of a murmured conversation, that ended when two of them slipped away into the darkness. So did I.

I awoke, reluctantly, soon after dawn when, what the military would call a relief column, appeared out of the morning haze. They had a warm greeting, particularly when they put down the bundle they had been carrying. When it was opened out it became a simple litter, soft leather skins stretched between two stout poles.

We made much better time now, and by late morning reached the encampment. Angelina took one look at the tattered and bruised Hans, injured flesh showing through the rents of what was once a uniform, and had him whisked away at once. I huddled with Bram and made plans.

"A flat field not too far from here," I said, "some place where we can safely land the ship."

"How big should it be?"

How big indeed? There could be no talk here of square meters or other accepted measurements. I looked around at the glade where the encampment had been set up, then pointed past the tents and the grazing horses.

"Do you see those trees over there? The ones with the yellow blossoms."

He shielded his eyes against the glare of the newly risen sun and nodded.

"That is not very far."

"It isn't. What we need is an open area at least twice this size."

He found a stick, bent over and scratched a circle in the ground. "We are here. If you go in that direction—not a long march," he pointed a bit to the right of the sun, "you will come to a shallow river." The stick scratched a slow loop in the dirt. "Within the loop in the river is a large and flat field. Just grass and small bushes. Your flying machine can land there."

He pushed the stick into the ground.

"You are sure of the direction?" He did not speak but

pulled back a bit, eyes widening. "Sorry. Never tell a chef how to cook. That's where the ship will land. Now, in which direction is the spaceport?"

He stood up and pointed to the forest.

"That will do fine."

I scratched an arrow into the ground and another pointing to our chosen landing site—then tried to align them with the sun. With his guidance other lines were made, erased and moved. Until we had settled on what—I sincerely hoped—would be the exact course that should be flown. Next step—

"We better start moving the porcuswine to the landing site as soon as we can. This morning if possible. They are not going to like leaving their chestnut grove."

Nor were they. All of the boys in the encampment volunteered to help; I needed every one of them. Bil, one of Bram's trackers, came along to be sure we went in the right direction. When we reached the grazing pack I gathered the boys together and gave a quick lecture on swineherding.

"Use your sticks to guide them—don't push or hit them or you risk death-by-pincushion. Ignore the piglets—they will follow their dams. They are all very lazy and would much rather eat than walk. It's all right if they snatch a mouthful on the way—but don't let them stop or it will be very hard to get them moving again. Ready?"

A chorus of yeses and a few ragged cheers. I hoped they could keep the enthusiasm during our slow trek. I cut a stout stick, took a deep breath—and walked over to Gnasher, who was chomping happily in the shade.

"Sooo-ey, swine, swine, swine—"

He raised his head, fixed one nasty red eye on me—and

went back to eating. It took an awful lot of scratching under his spines, sweet words and gentle prodding to start him moving. My childhood skills from down on the farm had not been forgotten.

Slowly and lethargically the herd got under way. We kept them moving. First the boars, then the sows—with the squealing piglets rushing to keep up. The boys ran and whooped and had a fine time. With seemingly endless energy.

I must admit that my power soon began to wane. I swore an oath that when I finally saw the last spine rattle by, never—and I mean never—after the last twist of a corkscrew tail, that I would never, repeat never, see another porcuswine again.

Bil had gone ahead to scout direction—and was soon back with smiles and immensely cheering news.

"Just beyond these trees—the field and the river are there."

And indeed they were. The boars rumbled happily when they smelled the water and they moved a little faster in that direction. I set down heavily on the ground.

Done. I selected the first happy volunteers from among my helpers. Promised that they would be relieved well before dark. They were proud of the responsibility, not that there was much to do. The porcuswine could take very good care of themselves. The return trip went a lot faster. Food and drink were waiting for us. My porcine pack could be forgotten, for the moment at least. I washed the dust of the trail from my skin, drink deeply of the cool water. Waved happily to Angelina.

"You seem quite cheerful," she said.

"I should be. The porcuswine trek is over and they are safely grazing in the field where our spacer will land."

She frowned slightly. "That's fine, but—is Pinky safe and well?"

"Very much so. She sends her love." She ignored my levity.

"Hans . . . he really was badly treated. It's a wonder he survived."

"But he's all right now."

"Very much so. He wants to see you . . ."

"A mutual feeling."

"We've washed and dressed his wounds and cleaned him, found some soft leather clothes for him. I'm sure he will be eager to talk to you."

"I'm more eager to listen. Before I meet with the gruesome Greenies again I need to know more about their social makeup. How are they controlled? Who issues orders? What is their one-to-one physical setup?"

We found Hans sitting at ease, leaning against the trunk of a thick tree. Chewing strenuously on some dried fruit, with a gourd of water at his side. When he saw us he started to stand, but Angelina stopped him.

"Don't undo all our good work. We'll join you," she said, sitting down in the soft grass. I sat beside her.

"I must thank you for saving my life. The new estro didn't care if I lived or died. A big change from Doria. She was smart enough to see that I stayed alive."

"A woman boss?" Angelina said. "We've only seen men."

"There aren't many, but sex doesn't matter among the estroj."

"Are they the leaders?" I asked.

"I guess you could call them that. That's because they are smartest. There is a natural rank division among most of those green bastards, just varying degrees of stupidity. Some don't even have the brains to survive. The ones that do are the workers, who are kicked into line, forced to work, by the slightly more intelligent. They are bossed by the thugs with clubs— and so on right up to the estroj. They have punishment sticks too, called frapiloj. Thin, strong—some even with metal tips or barbs. Hit or be hitten—a sick society ruled by casual violence."

"Are the estroj particularly intelligent?"

"Not really. I guess they have what we would call normal intelligence anyplace else. And there aren't many of them."

"And this woman, Doria, was one of them?"

Hans nodded and shifted his wad of dried fruit to chew on the other side of his jaw.

"Yes. Basically, she was as brutal as the rest, beat me often. But she saw to it that I always had enough to eat—and was guarded from the workers. When they saw my skin they flew into a rage. They all did—no matter how smart or stupid they were. Doria knew that and saw that I was protected from random violence. I was too vital to their sick economy. Particularly when she found that I could repair those ramshackle looms. All but the absolute dumbest could be trained to operate them. But they had no idea how they worked. If something broke, or a thread snapped, they would just sit and stare at it."

He leaned back heavily, breathing hard. Darkened by those years of misery.

"Well, you're away from them now. And you will soon be able to leave this planet—and put this all behind you."

He actually smiled. "For which I will never be able to thank you enough."

"My pleasure. Happy to help. But a few more questions. When I broke into the weaving mill it was after dark. Only a few of the guards saw me—before they were rendered unconscious. How would my green disguise work in daylight?"

"Horribly well! Even now I find it hard to look at you."

"But would I be stopped, questioned?"

"Never. Those creatures are like an immense herd of incredibly stupid animals. I am sure most of them don't even have names. As long as you stumble about, drool a little, don't call attention to yourself—you will be invisible."

Better and better.

"But what if I look like I have authority, say I order one of them about?"

"You will be instantly accepted as superior. You can't believe how rare the slightest trace of intelligence is. You will see hundreds—perhaps thousands of them before you meet one that can speak a few words, or understands orders."

Angelina touched Hans's forehead: it was damp with sweat. "Enough talking for now. You must take a rest Hans. We'll have plenty of time to talk later."

He nodded and slumped back against the tree as we left.

"I'd like to talk to you," she said, in a voice that must be obeyed. She led me past the tents to a quiet glade where we could be very much alone.

"I think you got Hans out of their hands just in time. He could not take much more of that kind of treatment. Some of his wounds had gone septic—I had to use my last antibio pen on him."

"Won't be long before we're back in the ship and get you more. And clean clothes, showers, yummy dehydrated meals . . ."

"Don't change the subject. You know what I want to talk about."

"Do I?" With wide-eyed ignorance.

"Your coming visit to the buildings at the spaceport."

"Absolutely! I must find the comm machines, get a message out—"

"You know that I'm going in with you?"

"I know nothing of the kind. Dangerous, deadly, certainly no job for—"

"If you say for a woman I'll cut your heart out."

". . . no job for more than one person!" I quickly improvised.

"Nonsense. Two are better than one. And you heard Hans, women are equals. At least among the estroj. And who else could do as good a job at this kind of work than I do?"

This was unanswerable—because it was true.

"I'll get the skin cream," I said. One more success for the fairer sex. She patted my hand; never one to score points.

"When Hans wakes up I must ask him what that Doria person wore. Something baggy and shapeless I'm sure."

Then she furrowed her brow, looking worried.

"Do you think I look good in green?"

CHAPTER **23**

IT HAD BEEN A HECTIC couple of days. What with forced marches and swineherding I was beat. I dined well off some cold venison and yawned heavily.

"Get your head down for a bit," Angelina advised. "You're little good to anyone the way you are."

"Must have a meeting—council of war . . ."

"Later. Sleep first."

I did not have to be told twice. I stretched out, yawned widely, rolled over—and must have corked off at once. The next thing I knew Angelina was gently shaking my arm.

"I feel better for that," I said hoarsely with my dry mouth. "Water . . ."

"Here," she said, passing the waiting gourd. Cool and life-restoring. "Hans is waiting—and I've sent for Bram. Do you want anyone else?"

"Not really. All sides are represented now."

Bram was the last to arrive; he sat down quietly next to Hans.

"This meeting is called to order," I said. Rapping an invisible gavel on the ground. "Our mission is to penetrate the spaceport buildings and gain access to the communication room. Angelina and I—with suitably green skin—will be doing the job . . ."

"I want to help," Hans said. "I have been in there—I can show you the way . . ."

"I appreciate the offer," I said. Pretending not to notice the tremor to his voice; he was terrified yet had still volunteered. "But you have given us the vital information that we needed . . ."

"And we won't let you get into their loathsome green hands again," Angelina said, sternly and decisively. "It will be just the two us. End of discussion."

"Bram," I said. "It will be up to you to get us near the buildings. We certainly can't do it by crossing the landing areas in broad daylight. What is it like on the other side?"

He broke a stick in half and scribed a line in the ground. "There is a road through the forest that leads to their nearest settlement. It opens out when it gets to the spaceport. There are stables there for the horses, buildings for the workers and some storehouses."

"Are there many people there?" I asked.

"During the day, yes. Always some coming and going."

"Estroj too?" Angelina asked.

"Of course. More than the usual number. We have watched closely, but do not know why or what they are doing in the buildings."

"The estroj—how are they dressed? Differently from the others?"

"I do not know. We hide when we watch them—never very close."

"I can tell you," Hans said. "That is one of the ways to tell them apart from the mob. Their clothes, they're made from a better grade of cloth—with a finer weave. All of them carry frapiloj, the striking sticks. They wear leather shoes . . ."

"Made of leather stolen from us," Bram growled. "Not often, but they do try to raid our encampments. Take our tents if they can. It evens out a bit because we raid them as well. Steal their cloth—when we can."

"Most important," Angelina said, "how do the women dress?"

"Those that work in the weaving mill—something loose, shapeless—most of them wear the same clothes as the men. But some wear long dresses, almost to the ground."

"And Doria, your lady boss?" He furrowed his brow.

"Different sometimes. A leather skirt I remember— shorter than the weavers."

"Knee length?"

"No, longer than that—calf length. She also wore high leather boots with the skirt."

"Better and better," she said, smiling.

I was worried about what that smile meant.

There was little more that Hans could tell us, and the meeting broke up. Angelina went off to talk to the women, while Bram and I chewed over the logistics of this penetration attempt.

"Do you go in at dusk or at night?" he asked.

"Neither. Full daylight so we can see where we are going, when there are plenty of people around."

"You'll be seen . . . captured!"

"Seen, yes. But captured, I sincerely hope not. The whole point of this operation is to penetrate into the technical section of the building. As to how we do that . . . we'll just have to make it up as we go along."

"It will not be easy. You don't know what you will be getting into!"

"That's the fun of the thing! You wouldn't know, but we have done this sort of operation in the past—and quite successfully too."

He shook his head, obviously not believing a word I had said. My long career in crime would have to remain a closed book for now. Along with my even longer career with the Special Corps.

We parted and I went to see how Angelina was making out in the costume department. But was turned brusquely away. I would go talk to Hans—our resource source. The more we learned about the gruesome Greenies the more we would be able to play our penetration roles.

IT TOOK THE BEST PART of two days to outfit us to Hans's satisfaction. I wore a nondescript jacket and trousers, but cut from a better grade of cloth than the peasant burlap. There was a wide leather belt at my waist, along with soft leather shoes. I also had a number of small inconspicuous pockets for a few devices that were always about my person. Not to mention my gun, that was resting comfortably in its holster on the back of my belt. I tucked the long hardwood stick under my arm.

"Will this do?" I asked.

"Yes, good, very good," Hans finally said. "You can walk right among them looking like that."

He had greater praise for Angelina's clothes.

"Yes, my boss, Doria looked very much like you do. But not as good—or as . . ."

He looked uncomfortable.

"You mean not as sexy," she said, twirling her white wood frapilo, smiling. Was it possible that Hans was blushing?

"You'll knock them dead," I said.

"I hope to," she said, the chill back in her voice. "But only after we have completed our mission."

Then she smiled—as though this were a joke.

Only I knew differently. We would go in, do what had to be done, then get out again—and no one was going to stand in our way.

"Bram wants to leave at dawn tomorrow," I said. "He also wants to have one last meeting."

"Shall I come?" Hans asked.

"Thanks, but there is no need. You have done more than any of us to assure our chances of success when we go in there."

We found Bram waiting, deeply worried.

"I have been thinking about this whole matter and I am not happy," he said, scowling to prove it.

"Don't be," Angelina said brightly. "You get us there, close to the spaceport—at that road through the forest. We go in, do what we have to do, then come out."

"Then what?"

"We join you and we all vanish into the trees."

"No. Too dangerous." He meant it too.

"Why?"

"There are too many of them there among the outer buildings. If the alarm spreads they will be after you in the thousands—and there will be no way you can possibly survive."

"But what other choice do we have?" Angelina asked.

"You must return to your ship—because that way will be open."

"Open, possibly," I said. "But what about all those armed green thugs around the ship? There are a great deal more of them there now, your scouts said."

"Not a problem. Alun and a large number of his men will meet us there. We will overwhelm their fighters so you can enter your ship and escape."

I resisted dropping my jaw at this startling development. "But what about you—and all the other trackers?"

He smiled broadly and said, "Why, we shall come into the ship of space with you. I'm sure there will be room for us, now that your porcuswine are not aboard."

Angelina clapped her hands and laughed aloud.

"What an original and fine idea! Shall we do it, Jim?"

I looked for any holes in this audacious plan; could find none. So I clapped my hands as well.

AT FIRST LIGHT WE WERE already on the trail. Since we were penetrating deep into enemy country, trackers had left earlier to make sure our way was clear. We marched, without a break, until midday, when Bram called a halt.

"The road is not far ahead," he said. "We'll get as close to the spaceport as we can before making contact. After that you must go on alone since they will be on all sides of us."

We had to pass through abandoned fields, very dangerous since we could be easily seen. Most of the trackers left us before we reached the road, slipping away a few at a time. In the end only Bram was left to guide us the final distance, to a stand of thick shrubbery. Stopping us with a lifted hand—signaling us to lie flat.

People were passing close by, their voices could be clearly heard. Bram slipped silently through the high grass, vanishing from sight. Seconds ticked by.

"He's been gone for a long time," Angelina whispered. Shifting her weight a bit so her gun was close to hand. There was a slight movement among the leaves and he rejoined us.

"The road is almost empty now—so we can move forward. Follow me."

We joined him beneath a large and thick bush. The dirt track of the road was just before us. Bram parted the leaves for a quick look—then dropped back down. "Two horsemen coming. As soon as they pass you get out of here—follow after them."

With his hand he motioned us to stay flat. There was the slow clop of hoofbeats and a muted voice. Louder then, until they passed close by—their shadows darkening us for an instant.

"Now!" he hissed.

We pushed through the last thin barrier, stood and walked after the two horsemen. They had their backs turned and never saw us as their animals trotted on out of sight around a bend in the road.

"And about time too," Angelina said, brushing dust off her clothes. "I hope that will be our last woodland crawl for a long long time." She looked up, touched her hair. "Is that a twig, here in my hair?"

"A little one. There—all gone."

The road turned again and we saw the horsemen, now far ahead of us. But something else as well. A small group, four or five people, sitting beside the road. Then they saw us and grew silent.

"Do we do anything?" Angelina asked.

"Yes. Ignore them completely. Chat a bit."

"It's a warm day. With no sign of rain at all."

We passed close enough to see the coarse weave of their clothes—the vacant look of their filthy faces. They watched us pass in silence, gaping and slack jawed. Then we left them behind.

"Easy enough," Angelina said. "First test passed."

"Look ahead," I said. "Horsemen coming our way."

There were three of them, all men. They were talking to one another, but became silent when they saw us. None of them had frapiloj. But one of them pointed to Angelina and said something behind his hand. The others smiled.

"What do you fools find so funny?" I said loudly. Reached out and grabbed the bridle of the nearest horse.

CHAPTER 24

THE RIDER BEGAN TO SHAKE, working his mouth, stammered something.

Next move, Jim? I thought, but Angelina was quicker than I was.

"Get down from that horse," she ordered in a cold voice. "You too," she added pointing to the rider next to him and slapping her frapilo against his leg. A good move—or a move too far? My hand moved closer to my gun, but both men scrambled to the ground.

"Now get out of our sight," I snapped.

They did. Running and stumbling down the road, the other rider galloped away, following, then passing the running men. Moments later they were all out of sight around a bend in the road. Angelina nodded with satisfaction.

"Well, Hans did tell us that if you acted like estroj, you were!" she said. "Anyway, I was getting tired of walking, so it seemed worth the try. And I also saw where your gun hand was."

We mounted and trotted on, smiling with smug satisfaction at being such bullying brutes. Which only works in a world of bullying brutes.

We let the horses have their heads, trotting slowly towards our destiny. I hoped our next encounters would be as successful. We passed a large group of men carrying what looked like a long pole down the middle of the road.

"Move aside!" I snarled. And of course they did, stumbling and half-dropping their burden. We rode by, not bothering to even look at their plight. It was very easy to slide into the bullying mode. Angelina was obviously thinking the same thing.

"I wonder what will happen when we meet someone who outbullies us?" she said, ruminatively.

I had no easy answer. We trotted forward, slower now since the road, bit by bit, was filling up with more and more people.

"Buildings ahead," she said pointing over their massed heads at the rough wooden structures by the road. As we got closer we could see the shapes of the spaceport buildings looming up behind them.

"Now," I said, thwacking my frapilo against my leg, "we'll soon find out how far up the chain of bullying command we are."

Our horses were moving slower and slower as the crowd grew thicker, until we were almost at a standstill.

"This is no good," Angelina said, pulling on her reins as her horse tried to rear up, frightened of the pushing people.

"Best to dismount," I said. "We're beginning to draw attention."

As soon as we were on the ground the massed figures closed in. There was only one way out of this. "Lead your horse!" I called to Angelina, lashing out at the backs of the nearest of the marching morons. There were no protests as they pushed others to get away. Angry—and claustrophobic—I used my frapilo to clear a path for my horse—and saw that Angelina was close behind. Then we were free of the crowd and on the trampled grass beside the road.

"This is a thoroughly disgusting planet—and the sooner we leave it the happier I will be," Angelina said, breathing deeply.

"No arguments from me. As soon as we finish our job in the spaceport."

Behind us the milling crowd kept moving, following those ahead of them towards a fenced area ahead that led off the road. Guards made sure they all went slowly in the same direction. Clubbing back into the mob the ones who strayed. Milling about like ants they eventually were all going together towards a long, low structure by the road. We stayed on the outskirts of the mob, then had to leave the roadside verge to pass behind the focus of all the activity.

It was feeding time for the animals. Which explained the walking, stumbling, surging mob scene behind us.

"This is not human," Angelina said, slowly shaking her head. "People shouldn't have to live like this . . ."

"The best you can say is—at least they are alive."

"If you can call that living."

They were rooting in their clothes now. Apparently everyone carried an eating bowl. There were heavy cauldrons on the low tables. Servers with ladles poured a stew or porridge of some kind into the waiting bowls that surged by. Attendants took away the swiftly emptied vats while full ones were brought forward from the nearby buildings. We led our horses around this hectic scene—much cheered to finally make our way clear at last—and remounted. Behind us those who had filled bowls squatted in the ground, digging into the food with their fingers, gulping it down. Here, guards with clubs wielded them freely against those who didn't bend over the nearby stream to rinse out their bowls and push them, still wet, back into their clothes.

I looked at Angelina and, for perhaps the only time in my life, I found that there was nothing I could say. The scene we had just witnessed was inhuman—yet terribly human as well. It was just raw survival at the most bestial level.

"We still have the job to do that we came here for," Angelina said, breaking the silence.

"We do indeed. Let's get rid of the horses and do it."

Once we had left the feeding frenzy behind us the scene became relatively peaceful. There were still plenty of people about, apparently involved in different activities among the many smaller buildings. However we had absolutely no desire to discover what they were doing.

"There," Angelina said, standing in her stirrups to see better. "Aren't there horses around that far building?"

"There are indeed. Let us drop these nags and find what passes for civilization around here."

It appeared there were a few slightly brighter individuals in charge of the stable. They took our horses reins without a word and led them away, shouting to their shambling assistants.

"Take to water . . ."

"Give way."

"Not that way!" Some pushes and kicks kept the stable organized to a rough extent. I tucked my frapilo under my arm, sneered what I hoped was a superior sneer as we strolled towards the solid, civilized-looking buildings of the spaceport.

Angelina had her weapon over her shoulder as we marched resolutely towards our destiny.

The sturdier buildings formed a small enclave that was set apart and separated from the surrounding wooden structures by a wire fence. There was no gate, just a wide opening in the fence where it was close to the road. This was manned by a group of guards, armed with clubs; obviously there to keep most of the citizenry at bay. We slowed down and I pointed at nothing in particular.

"Let's stop for a moment and see the drill they use at that entrance."

Angelina nodded following my pointing finger. "No activity right now."

Then there was a flurry of motion when two proles in the passing mobs ventured too close. The clubs whistled and they screeched and scuttled away.

"There," Angelina said. "Two people coming out of the largest building."

They were talking as they walked towards the gap in the fence—and did not slow when they came close. While the club-wielders pushed each other aside so as not to block their exit. As the men came out we saw that they were both carrying frapiloj.

"What comes out . . ." I said.

"Goes back in."

We waited until they had passed before we turned and retraced their path.

The guards merely glanced at us, then moved aside. We walked steadily past them and over to the main building entrance, opened the doors and went in.

We were inside a spacious central hall with a high, vaulted ceiling. It had been decorated with bucolic murals, horse-drawn plows, grazing cattle and such. But time had not been good to it. The paint had flaked away in part, other portions were darkened and marred by water leaks. A circular flight of stairs rose up on one side and there were closed doors along the walls. There were quite a number of people about. All neatly dressed and striding purposely. There were none of the shambling outside hordes here.

"We're clearly in the right place," Angelina said. "Obviously built during the far pleasanter times. Even the cows look happy . . ."

"May I be of service?" a voice said. I looked down from the dome at the short man who stood before us. He was green of skin, neatly dressed and did not carry a frapilo.

"Who are you?" I asked in my most arrogant manner.

"N'thrax. On the management staff of this building."

"That is very nice to hear. But our business here is not any of your business."

He shuffled back a bit and looked unhappy. "But I am here to assist you, estro. Is there someone here you wanted to see?"

"Yes," Angelina said in the coldest of cold voices. "But he is as high a rank as you are low. Dismissed."

N'thrax gasped and backed away from us. Before turning and hurrying out of sight.

"Bullying comes too easily," she said grimly. "I'll be glad when we are well away from this place."

"Agreed. But let's keep moving."

"Upstairs—away from the entrance."

As we climbed the worn steps a man came down towards us—with a frapilo tucked under his arm. He only glanced at us as he went past.

"We're obviously in the right place—with none of the low-caste peasantry about," I said.

"Wonderful, but what do we do next?"

"Good question." We had reached the second floor. There were doors—all of them closed—along the outer wall. The only markings were numbers on each door.

"Pick a number," I said.

"Two-thirteen. It sounds lucky."

"Why not," I said and we started that way. It was a good choice because the door opened just before we reached it. Two guards came out. Low green foreheads, rougher clothing, wicked-looking clubs in their free hands. A man walked between them, clutched tightly by the arms.

What was very interesting about the man was that his skin was a pale pink.

"Now what do we have here?" I said, standing before them so they could not proceed. They stopped, gaping widely, looking from Angelina to me. I slapped my frapilo against my leg.

"Where are you taking this animal?" Angelina asked.

"To eat place . . ." one of them mumbled. "Tell go feed . . ."

"Not yet," I said. "Take back inside."

Without hesitation they turned and reentered the room.

"You want work from me?" The prisoner said angrily. "Two days now without . . ."

"Shut up," I said, looking around the room. Some machinery, what looked like a generator, lagged pipes dripping water.

But no other people.

"I'll see to the one on the right," I said.

Angelina nodded. "On my count of . . . one!"

We struck at the same time and the guards crumpled to the floor, their clubs dropping beside them.

Their released prisoner stumbled backwards, gaping at us. "What are you green bastards doing?"

"Freeing you. And we need some information, quickly. Your name?"

"Wolfi . . . but leave me alone—you're mad . . ."

"First off, we're not green," Angelina said, pulling her blouse out of her skirt to reveal some very attractive and pink flesh. "All will be explained later. Just remember that we are going to get you off this world—so help us."

"How many of you prisoners are in this building?"

"Three of us," he said. "But—"

"Questions—and answers—later," I said. "Who works in the communications room?"

"We all do—"

"Take us there now."

He looked at us, baffled and confused—and unbelieving.

"Think," Angelina said, and smiled. "Isn't anything better than the life you have been living here? Now show us the way."

"Of course. Hold on to my arms—they always do that."

We went, closing the door behind us.

"Turn left. Room two-thirty."

We tensed when we saw three other men coming towards us. But they were talking and paid us no notice.

"This one," the prisoner said.

I turned the knob—it was locked.

"It's always locked. You have to knock."

I did. Once—then again. This time I heard a muffled voice saying what sounded very much like go away. This was not good. Some more of the locals walked behind us and I felt a touch of sweat on my furrowed brow.

"You can't go in there," a voice said from behind me. I turned to see N'thrax, the spurned official we had met when we first entered the building.

"It is a matter of most importance that we enter this room at once," Angelina said.

But he was firm—though his voice was shaking. "You don't understand—Overlord is in there—he commands . . ."

"Of course," Angelina said calmly. "He is the one we came here to see. This is an *emergency.*"

Torn between conflicting orders, N'thrax had a terrible decision to make. "Open!" I snarled as I pushed my frapilo under his chin. He tried to draw away but I only pushed harder. In the end the terrified man hammered on the door.

A passerby turned to look, turned back and kept walking

when I gave him a most terrible glare. This stalemate could not last . . .

The door opened and the large and angry man stood there. And I knew him—though no longer pink of skin.

He was the official we had talked to from the ship before we had landed here.

"Emergency!" I said and pushed the captive hard against him. "The most terrible thing has happened!"

He started to resist—then stepped aside.

"What the hell are you talking about?"

"Here—listen to N'thrax." I dragged the quavering N'thrax in after us. "He was there and saw the killing—all the blood!"

Out of the corner of my eye I saw Angelina and our engineer, turning and locking the door. I wasn't feeling subtle or patient. My fist caught Overlord square on his big green jaw and he went down. N'thrax was cowering and beginning to scream, which Angelina silenced with a quick short blow. He joined his boss on the floor. I turned around and smiled.

The far wall was covered with communication equipment, gleaming screens and cameras, control panels and speakers. Lovely! I smiled at the technician—pink of skin and slack of jaw—who was kneeling before an open panel, soldering iron in hand. The only other person in the room.

"Welcome," I said. "To the first day of what will be a long and happy life."

"W-what . . . ?" he said.

"They are friends," Wolfi said. "I don't know how, but they said that we are all going off-planet."

"After I make a singularly important call," I said. "Which of these fine machines is your interstellar communicator?"

"Here, this one," he said pointing to a hulking apparatus.

"Can you can send a message?" I said, while beaming a wide and beatific smile.

"No I can't. It's been dismantled—the guts are gone."

My brief elation plunged downward into grim despair.

"It . . . can't be . . ."

"It always has been like that. The last thing these green devils want is off-planet contact. It's fine to keep the radio comms going—to lure more spacers here. You aren't really green are you?"

"No—skin dye," I muttered, depressed by my horrifying discovery.

"I suggest," Angelina said, ever practical, "that we forget all about communication at the present time. And get off this depressing planet just as soon as we possibly can."

I took a very deep breath—and gave myself a stiff mental brace. "You're right, of course. Next plan . . . get us all out of here."

I took a long moment to look around at the row of silent bodies on the floor—and the still dazed but now smiling former prisoners.

"You said there is one more of you here?"

"Yes, Giorgio. He's working on the steam generator. It's in the basement."

"Take me there—right now," Angelina said. "While Jim makes plans for our escape." She took the prisoner by the arm, called back over her shoulder as I opened my mouth to protest. "Don't argue. No time." Then they were out of the room and closing the door behind them.

"Right," I said, relocking the door. "Let's get to work . . . name?"

"Tomas."

"Tie these men up, Tomas. Use wire—you must have plenty. Then gag them so they can't scream. Do you have a blade?"

"In the toolbox there."

Overlord was muttering and starting to stir. I cut off the sleeve of his uniform and gagged him with it. Then wired his wrists together. He was writhing, eyes popping, chewing on the gag; I made it tighter. We had just wired up the last prisoner when there was a sharp rapping on the door. I jumped to open it and heard Angelina's voice.

"I have two more guards here who are helping me with the prisoners."

Forewarned, I let Angelina, the prisoners and guards go past me and closed the door behind them. Before the guards could raise their clubs they joined their mates, wired and gagged upon the floor.

"I had to enlist aid," Angelina said. "I was getting strange enough looks with a single pink prisoner. Not to say two."

"Well done. Always room for a few more on the floor."

"Next—?"

"A good question." I was suddenly very tired. I pulled out the radio operator's chair and dropped into it.

"We are safe for the moment—I hope. So let us take the time to plan our escape."

The three technicians were bubbling with excitement, as the possibility of leaving this planet began to sink in.

"We'll be stopped as soon as we try to take these pale-faces out of the building," Angelina said.

"My very thought."

"We have no more skin cream dye."

"We don't need it." I whistled and they turned. "We can't show your skin. So cut up these zonked out Greenies's clothes. Wrap up your heads—then your hands. You will look strange, but not pink. You'll carry clubs. There will be confusion but hopefully no attacks. Do it!"

I heaved myself out of the chair and admired the results. Then sat down again when I realized I was forgetting the most important part of the escape. The ship.

"Radio on," I said. "Captain Singh—are you there?"

"Of course." His voice spoke clearly inside my head. *"What's happening?"*

"We are about to join you. Five of us in all. We are in the building complex across the field from you. We'll be coming out of the front entrance of the larger building. Be ready to open the lower spacelock—both doors. Because when we get there we'll be in a hurry."

"I have you on the screen—a magnified image of the front entrance."

"Great. We'll be picking up more passengers on the way. Our paleface local friends who will, hopefully, take out all the green guards. Is the takeoff siren working?"

"Of course."

"Sound it before you open the lock to alert our allies."

"This is the most insane plan I have ever heard in my entire life. Over and out."

"It's nice to have encouragement . . ." I muttered. "Ready troops?"

The three masked and mittened engineers waved their clubs enthusiastically, mumbling through their masks. I pushed myself out of the chair.

"I'll go first. Club men will follow. Angelina will bring up the rear."

"Do it!" she said, thwacking the frapilo against her thigh.

We went. Out the door with military precision, marching in step.

I don't think we looked particularly menacing, but we did get a lot of gape-jawed attention.

Down the stairs and out through the double doors. Straight to the opening in the fence where I beat the milling guards aside with my frapilo. The surging masses parted as well and then we were short meters from the landing field—with our welcome spacer directly ahead in the landing pads.

And standing in our way were three resolute green trackers with drawn bows. Arrows aimed.

"Stop!" their leader shouted. "Forbidden to go on field."

A speedy resolution was needed and my gun was already in my hand.

"Run!" I shouted as I fired.

The quick explosions threw up great chunks of earth and concrete, knocked the trackers over. My shouting engineers clubbed them back to the ground as we passed.

We ran. Angelina, fleet as a deer, passed the running men and joined me in the lead.

"Great fun!" she laughed. "And look who's up ahead!"

More green-skinned hunters waving clubs and bows. But not for long. A shouting Bram was right behind them, leading his men in the charge. Clubbing our adversaries to the ground as they caught up with them. It was quickly done.

I took one glimpse behind us—at the roaring mass of the enemy in close pursuit—and was imbued with new strength.

"To the ship!"

Which we were drawing close to—the welcoming space-lock now gaping wide—and my legs getting very tired indeed. The siren was wailing, our pursuers howling, our men cheering. Quite an interesting and unusual scene.

Up the ramp we poured, stumbling and falling, helping one another to our feet to stagger on. Once inside I leaned against the bulkhead, gasping for breath, as the ramp slowly ground back into the ship. Just before the outer door swung shut I saw a microsecond surge of flame and smoke from our landing jets: just enough to dissuade our followers.

Our pursuers screamed even louder as they turned and ran back towards safety. The outer lock ground shut, as did the inner one. I slumped down and sat with my back to the bulkhead.

"Now that was fun," Angelina said, laughing, eyes sparkling.

I made no attempt to agree.

CHAPTER 25

"B*OSS TO BRIDGE SOONEST—BOSS to bridge,*" the wall speaker rasped.

I crawled to my feet, supported by the wall as I did. Supported also by the sturdy Angelina. Who was scarcely breathing hard.

"Just—ha-ha—a little out of shape." I laughed hollowly. She wisely did not answer. "Bram, best come with us. Help us locate our landing spot. Plus you will have your first elevator ride!" And I will avoid the stairs.

"Tell me where we are going—and quickly," the captain said in welcome. "I don't want any more trouble here. Nor do I want to fry the locals when we take off."

"We're about twenty klicks from the landing site. My colleague will show you the way. Bram?" I pointed to the viewscreens that now gave a 360-degree image of the field.

He looked around slowly, orienting himself, taking his

time. I ignored the rushing green hordes that were closing in and did not hurry him. He carefully pointed.

"There. Go towards that group of trees with the low hill beyond."

The engines roared and the deck pressed up against our feet.

The forest moved by below us and, very soon, the loop in the river came into sight. The image grew as we approached.

"There," I said, "land in the center of the field—well away from the river. The boys have herded the porcuswine together, over by the water."

It was a smooth landing, with only the slightest jar as we settled down. I turned and looked at Bram—who was clutching hard to the console, staring fixedly at the scene below.

"I could not believe—a thing such as this . . ." He choked out the words, overcome by the ship, the flight. Suddenly catapulted from the iron age into the advanced age of science. Angelina was looking at him as well, understanding what he was feeling. She put her arm around him.

"This is your future, Bram. You are now part of it—you will see all of its wonders." He smiled, and nodded.

"There is much to be learned," he said quietly, then left the bridge.

The lower airlock was already open and on the viewscreen we saw the cheering passengers streaming out onto the field, heading towards the milling herd. The porcuswine heard them, saw them and stormed past the boys for a grunting, shouting, scratching happy reunion.

"Shall we join them?" Angelina asked as she took my hand.

"We shall indeed. But I hope that you will first join me in a toast to victory. Of a kind."

"Of course. And we did get those poor engineers out of loathsome captivity, Hans as well. That's something to be proud of."

After our days of roughing it the bar was a dream of luxury; soft chairs, softer music, rehabilitating drinks. We clinked glasses.

"I've missed the joys of civilization during our Neolithic adventures," I said, and looked up as the captain came in.

"Happy to join you," he said, taking a glass. "I'm off duty. Thought I would find you here. Thanks." He drank deep and dropped into a chair. "There is much that we must talk about."

"Indeed. But can't it wait until later?"

"It will have to. I hate to disturb this moment of leisure, but many outside are clamoring for your attention. Stramm is keeping them at bay—since he is concerned about who he lets into the ship."

"Understandable." I creaked when I stood up.

"I'll join you later," Angelina said. "I won't feel clean until I have scrubbed off this awful green color."

"You want to go out there?" Stramm said accusingly, when I came up. He was looking at the screen above the lock controls that showed the scene directly outside. Bram was there, talking with two of his trackers. A scowling Elmo was sitting on the grass, chewing on a straw and looking most aggrieved.

"If it is permitted, I do," I answered.

"No one gets back inside until I say so. The maintenance is running weeks behind so I can't babysit strangers."

"Agreed. But we may have to get out of here in a hurry. The grotty Greenies will be here in force as soon as they get organized. They will not be happy."

"Before we take off again I need reaction mass and drinking water. I will want some muscle to run the hoses to that river."

"I'll send some to you. Anything else?"

"Not at the moment . . ."

Ever so reluctantly he let me out—and closed the inner lock as soon as I was on the ramp.

"Cousin Jim, we got a shore big heap of things to settle—"

"Later," I said. "Right now we need you and half a dozen more volunteers to help Stramm run out some water hose. Soonest." I brushed past him.

I had seen the horses as they appeared on the far side of the field. A goodly number of them pulling heavily loaded travois. Then more and more people appeared.

"We must leave this place at once," Bram said. "It is very hard to say good-bye to our new friends from the stars. Yet we know that the green trackers will be leading their people here in great numbers, after all the trouble we have caused. We must go away, far and fast."

"But we were the ones who attacked them, not you—and freed their prisoners."

"They see no difference. Any pale skin will now be pursued, killed."

"That's not fair!" I said.

"It is our existence, we know no other. But now we have hope, from our new friends from the stars. Leave this unhappy world. I hope that you will remember these forests and those who live here."

"Of course I will! But can't you come with us?"

There was a deep sadness in the shake of his head.

"Would that I could! How I long to see the wonders of the many new worlds out there. But my place is here, on this troubled planet. With my people. But do not forget us—our new friends from the stars."

"We will do more than just remember. I vow this. I will return—bringing with me those who will stop this racial war of hatred. I cannot say when this will happen, but I will be back."

He nodded—smiling at me through an immense sadness. Turned and went over to join the others. They were already moving out of this field by the river and disappearing back into the forest. Moving on in their endless flight from a ruthless and merciless enemy.

"Coming through!" a voice shouted. I stepped aside as the troop of farmers rushed by with coils of hose on their shoulders. A moment later I heard plaintive squeals from the distance—plus the occasional grunt of protest. The boars led the way with the pack trotting steadily behind. The farmers were shouting and laughing as they kept the porcuswine moving. Up the ramp and into the ship.

Behind them the field was empty. The sky darkened as storm clouds appeared, a sudden shower beat down on the field. I walked back into the shelter of the ship, my thoughts as black as the sky. The speaker above me crackled.

"Boss to bridge soonest."

I went. Glad to escape my growing depression. What had we accomplished on our perilous visit to this planet? Got into trouble—and then out of it. Disturbed a wasp's nest of hatred and anger. In an effort to bring some peace we had brought more conflict instead. It was some small satisfaction that we had released four men from captivity. But the rest of the planet was the original stewing, hate-filled world that it had been before we arrived.

Angry now, I grabbed myself by the metaphorical neck and gave a good shake.

"No Jim! You are a power for good in the universe today. Not now, but one day you will bring both aide and succor to this troubled world."

"Talking to ourselves, are we?" Angelina said. "Sign of advance old age."

"No. I was just swearing an oath to return to this awful planet with its suffering people. We must—and we will— change that."

She smiled and blew me a kiss. "From anyone else that would be feckless bragging. But from Jim diGriz it is a powerful certainty. I'm off to the party."

"What party?"

"The one we are throwing for those poor men we rescued. Figured we all needed a bit of cheering up."

We went our various ways; I to the bridge. I wondered what was the next crisis awaiting me there. It was there all right—and a big one indeed.

"We have enough gravitons for one medium-sized Bloat. Or two short ones," the captain said with unrestrained gloom. "Either way it is a matter of chance were we end up. Pot luck."

"Not too encouraging. Are there any other factors that we have to take into consideration?"

"Direction," he said, turning to a star-filled screen and pointing at the brightest area, with the thickest array of suns. "The galactic center. I have been turning our course that way whenever possible. The more suns, the more possible worlds for us to contact."

I was looking at the outside images on the panoramic viewscreens as we talked. The rainsquall had swept by, leaving a rainbow arcing across the now blue sky. Our new friends and their horses long gone. Just a few men were in sight below, standing by the hose that reached out into the river.

"The farther the better," I said.

"What?"

"When you gamble you have to play for keeps. Decide on a strategy, then do it. Make the biggest Bloat you can. Go for broke."

I hope that I sounded more positive then I felt. Faint heart ne'r won fair lady. Or something like that.

"We'll have to leave some gravitons in reserve. To approach any planets in the area."

I did not like the casual use of *any*. On the screens the hose handlers were slowly walking back to the ship, the hose undoubtedly throbbing with water. The rainbow had faded away with the storm. Nothing else moved . . .

Or did it? Was that a flicker of motion on the far side of the field, where the trees came down to the riverbank? The scene enlarged as I spun the focus. Nothing. I was just seeing things. A mirage of stress and fatigue.

"I can't set the final course until we get into orbit," the

captain muttered as he hammered away at his keyboard. "As soon as the water tanks are filled I want to take off."

"Nothing better. We have all had enough of this perilous planet . . ."

"Stramm," he said, keying on the intercom. "What's your water status?"

"Passenger tanks full. Topping up rest of reaction mass."

A flicker of motion caught my eye at the forest's edge. There *was* something out there.

"Captain, if you look towards the trees . . ."

My voice died as, with a single motion, the woods erupted.

Men running, hundreds—no, thousands! Coming from all sides.

The captain banged hard on the alarms, which wailed piercingly inside the ship and out.

"This is an emergency. We will be taking off as soon as the port is closed. Emergency takeoff. You men outside to the ship!"

They were running for their lives now, as more and more green-skinned figures poured out onto the field—from all sides. The leading attackers hesitated, but were clubbed forward by the men behind them.

"Stramm! Pumps off—and cut that hose!"

The last man fell into the ship as the ramp was retracted. The sirens still wailed. The captain beat his fist against the console—staring at the red light that meant the airlock was still open.

"They're inhuman fiends," he shouted. "Beating their own people to approach the ship. Knowing they'll be cinders if we fire the takeoff tubes. Hoping that will stop us."

Beaters and beaten still surged towards us. Heading towards instant incineration.

The red light turned green.

"TAKEOFF!" the captain roared—pounding down on the switch.

An instant later a distant rumble grew and grew to a mighty roar. The deck trembled then punched up. Flame and smoke obscured the viewscreens. The alarm sirens died away.

As soon as we were in orbit the captain reran the screens in slow motion. Smoke and flame roared out, diminished and died down.

"Freeze that!" I said.

No grass could be seen in the field—it was covered by the running, pushing, falling figures of the attackers. The ship's jets flamed down towards them. I leaned over and touched the screen.

"Congratulations on a well-timed takeoff, Captain."

"The front of the attacking mob was just meters from the blast."

"You saved their lives."

CHAPTER **26**

THE TORTURED PLANET OF SALVATION dwindled behind us as the first Bloat began. After our strenuous adventures on that unhappy world, our voyage now on the spacegoing swinesty was like unto a holiday cruise. As the sore muscles and bruises faded into memories I found that the easy pace of existence suited me fine. I watched an ancient film or two, read some books from the multimillion-volume database and looked forward happily to an afternoon tipple in the bar.

The released prisoners blossomed under the maternal attention of Miz Julia and her mates. They applied themselves with great relish to the reconstituted and frozen food—a banquet after the slop their green captors had served up. I smiled on them benignly: at least some good had come out of our desperate visit. I renewed my oath at the next cocktail hour, raised my glass and swore to someday, somehow, bring peace to that sorely troubled world.

"I'll drink to that," Angelina said, and we clinked glasses. "And doom and destruction upon that villain Rifuti."

In the rush of events I had completely forgotten the criminal captain. She had not. Nor would he escape. Justice would be done: in person if needs be.

The intercom had been turned low, and could just be heard behind the soft melody of the Mozart sonata.

"Boss to bridge."

"Coming with me?"

"Later. This is bath day for Pinky. She does enjoy her scented scrub."

"Rather you than me," I said with some feeling. At the top of the list of things I preferred not to do was to shower the spines of Pinky porcuswine. A meeting on the bridge was a far more attractive proposition.

"Moment of decision for our next Bloat," the captain said, pointing at the black viewscreen. "There is just that single star ahead." I leaned close and saw the tiny glowing spot. "Do we Bloat again in that direction?"

"Nothing else around?" I asked hopefully.

"No. Nothing we can reach using the gravitons we have left. Even this will deplete most of our reserves."

Decision time.

"Do we have a choice?"

"Not really."

"Then let's do it."

He nodded grimly. And turned to the Bloater Drive.

I turned to the bar. A quick energizer was very much in order. Angelina was already there, putting a last gloss on Pinky's spines with a polishing cloth. A plaintive grunt announced that porcuswine were always ready for a quick munchy. I put out a bowl of pirri pretzels so we could join her.

"Libation?" I asked.

"Why not." She shared some munchies with Pinky while I poured.

I brooded over my drink and she quickly caught my mood. "Worried?"

"Not really. Just concerned. We are on our final Bloat. About two days more and we'll know just how unlucky we are . . ."

"Or lucky—there are two sides to every coin."

"True. Maybe I'm just suffering from the Greenie blues. But—"

"Aren't we all. No pleasure planet that."

After this I tried to keep my worries to myself. All would be revealed soonest in any case. It was a relief when the captain's voice on the intercom said:

"Bloat will end in two hours."

Angelina went with me to the bridge. Soon after we arrived we were joined by Stramm. "We'll know soon enough now."

A master of the obvious, our engineer. It didn't merit a response.

For good or bad, the shivering pop of the Bloater field collapsing was welcome.

As the glowing star appeared in the center of the screen, the radio crackled into life.

"Welcome to the star system of Alpha Adonis . . ."

"We've done it!" Stramm said.

"This is a starwatch robotic beacon."

Gloom descended while the recording continued.

"There are three planets in this system, and an asteroid belt. There are no settlements on any of these planets . . ."

"Command order to beacon," the captain said into his mike. "Does this beacon contain communication capability?"

"Planetary coordinates follow . . . skrrk . . . This beacon's communications consist of radio only. Nearest full communication facilities are at star system one dash thirty . . ."

The captain clicked the connection off and turned to look at us.

"Now what?" he said with a great weariness.

His answer was only silence. Angelina was the one who finally broke the spell.

"Turn it on again. Let us hear about those three planets."

Stripped of all excess robotic verbiage the answer was simple.

"One gas giant," the captain said. "Has an impressive ring, but no moons. Two planets in the habitable zone. One has an atmosphere—a bit less than one G—and sounds hot but inhabitable. The other one has a livable atmosphere but . . ."

I added the clincher—"But it is a big and heavy world, with a gravity of almost three Gs. And oxygen tension almost a third less than normal."

The silence was palpable, depression dark in the air. Where did we go from here? Only Stramm showed signs of life, tapping his jaw and muttering to himself. Then, without a word, he turned to the control board and began to punch in numbers. Equations raced down the screen. After more jaw prodding he entered more figures, nodded—and turned to face us.

"There is one possibility," he said.

"To do what?" I asked.

"To escape this star system."

"How?" the captain snapped.

"First, by landing on the heavy planet. The human body can work at that gravity, if only for a short time."

"Doing what?" Angelina asked, speaking for us all.

"Unloading the graviton collector onto the planet's surface. Once it began operating in a three-G environment it would take"—he turned back to his computations, then pointed to screen—"exactly three months to collect enough gravitons to make a long enough Bloat to, hopefully, another star system."

There was a cogitating silence as each of us considered this uncomfortable solution.

"It can't be done," Angelina said firmly. "We couldn't stay alive long under that gravity."

"We wouldn't have to," was Stramm's surprising answer. "We land, push out the graviton collector, then take off. The only problem, a minor one, is that we might have to load more reaction mass to take off from that gravity. Then we go into orbit . . ."

"Not possible," was the captain's firm answer. "Not enough food and water aboard to last us for three months in orbit. This ship was not designed for long periods in flight."

It was time for me to add a note of hope to this thoroughly depressing conversation. "We don't have to stay in orbit," I said, and beamed a smile on all. "Why don't we spend the time on the companion planet? Warm, habitable—but not inhabited as yet. We will be the founding fathers—and mother of course," I added tipping my head in Angelina's direction.

"A wonderful idea," she said. "I didn't realize it until now, but I have always wanted to found a planet. And what is this planet's name?"

The captain consulted the readout on the screen.

"No name, just an identification number. One, x-ray, seven . . ."

She shook her head. "That won't do. We must have a name."

"Why don't you name it?" I said.

The captain nodded agreement. "Capital idea. You will be the first to set foot on this new world."

She laughed. "Then I'll make claim to it as well!"

Gloom-and-doom Stramm wasn't pleased with this moment of good cheer. "We don't know yet if we will be able to remain there. Shouldn't we make a survey first?"

The cold voice of reason put a damper on our earlier enthusiasm.

"I have a suggestion," I said suggestively. "Before we make any decisions shouldn't we consult all the others? Everyone on this ship should be told what is involved—with their lives and their future."

"A fine idea," the captain said. "Do our agrarian passengers have a leader?"

"They do," I said. "Regrettably it is my long-lost relative, Elmo. I also suggest we have a representative of the freed prisoners. When I was talking to them I discovered that Tomas is really Captain Tomas Schleuck, the commander of one of the captured vessels."

"That is an excellent idea," Captain Singh said, obviously a steadfast member of the Captain's Union. "I am going to transcribe the specs for both planets. I suggest a public meeting in two hours in the dining room. Do we agree?"

"Motion carried," Angelina said. "Make the announcement and we'll see you there." She looked at me and pointed at the door. "Don't you think it's time for a light refresher?" she asked. I didn't have to be asked twice.

Back in the bar I poured, then dropped into the chair.

Dropped into a deep gloom as well.

"Look at Pinky," Angelina said. "That pearl among swine can read our emotions quite well." I looked up and caught the last sight of burnished black quills scuttling out the door. Angelina looked at me and shook her head. "Is this the fearless and stainless Rat who brooks no bonds?"

"Nor bounds no brooks. But a slightly rusty one right now . . ."

"Nonsense. I have a feeling that that last depressing planet is still getting you down. Don't let it."

"I won't!" I cried. Leaping to my feet. Then refreshed our drinks since I was already standing. "I cleanse my head and make plans to rescue us from this spacegoing *Flying Dutchman*. Information—then action."

Imbued with my newfound energy I accessed the records and printed out the specs of our planetary home to be: I hoped.

Angelina and I passed the sheets back and forth.

"Nice and warm," I said.

"Some would say hot and humid."

"But bearable. More important the survey found no pathogens in the atmosphere or in the ground. At least none that would affect our metabolisms. There is no mention of visual contact with any life forms."

Angelina raised her eyebrows. "But no samples."

"Forbidden. The robotic surveyors can look but not touch. Let's take a look at the scans that they sent back!"

There was a single large continent set in a planet-wide ocean. The point of view dropped down and stopped above a wide, sandy beach at the shore. It tracked along it for some time, following the empty beach and the breaking waves. Nothing. It then tracked inland above what appeared to be a planet-wide verdant forest.

"Nothing in the ocean—or on the beach. We'll just have to land and investigate." I clicked off the screen.

"Time to go to the meeting," Angelina said and ordered the scattered printout sheets into a neat bundle.

The room was packed: the first time that all the passengers had been assembled at one time. A table had been set upon a raised platform at the far end of the hall. We joined the engineer, and the two captains, who were already there.

"Thanks for having me here," Tomas said quietly when I sat down.

"It's your right. As senior officer of the recently freed prisoners of war."

"Which freedom will never be forgotten."

Captain Singh rapped his knuckles on the table. "This meeting will now come to order." He tapped the file of papers before him to straighten the edges, then spoke.

"Sire diGriz, the owner of this vessel, has asked me to call this extraordinary meeting to discuss our present situation. When I am finished we will have an open discussion."

He read out the details of the two planets we planned to visit. There were a lot of gaping jaws and glazed eyes among these swineherd agrarians—and I could easily understand why. We were a long, long way from the simple pleasures of porcuswine herding now. When he had finished there were a few questions about climate and ecology—food sources in particular. Then Elmo, who had done a lot of head scratching and jaw rubbing, raised a tentative hand.

"The way I see it, it looks like we have only a couple of choices—is that right, Captain?"

"It is."

"First we have to put down on this big world where we all gonna feel heavier, right?" Reassured, he went on. "If things is heavier our animals gonna be even heavier. And them boars is pretty heavy now!" There were shouted cries of agreement: the captain rapped loudly on the table. Thus encouraged, Elmo went on.

"Now you take one of them boars—they are big critters. Take Gnasher—he must be all of a tonne. How much is he gonna weigh?"

"I would say in the vicinity of three tonnes."

"Three . . . why that's a pretty heavy vicinity!"

He ducked his head and smiled broadly as his peers laughed loudly at his simple jest. The captain rapped loudly again. Elmo rattled on wearily, boring us all. I did not have the captain's patience and eventually I had to interrupt his pastoral chuntering.

"Point of order, Captain. Can we save ourselves from more of this comment now—and ask you to tell us what choices we have?"

"That is simple. We have two . . ."

Stillness descended.

"The first one I have just outlined to you. Land on this high-G world and leave the graviton collector there for a three-month period. While it is working we land on the habitable planet and . . . survive." He was working hard to keep the doubt from his voice.

"Or what?" Elmo broke in and was shhhh-ed to silence.

"Or we take the other choice—the longest possible Bloat towards the galaxy center, where there are the greatest agglomeration of stars. With settled planets. We use all our gravitons on this Bloat. And stop when they run out."

Tomas's voice broke the silence that followed.

"What are the odds that we will be in the vicinity of suns and planets?"

The captain straightened up.

"They are very slim indeed. At a rough guess—I would say perhaps a hundred to one."

"Then we have no choice at all," Tomas said. "All in favor of the plan to accumulate gravitons respond by saying aye."

Little by little the ayes were reluctantly muttered until the response was very positive.

Even Elmo must have realized that there was absolutely no choice after all.

CHAPTER 27

"THIS MUST BE PLANNED AS carefully as a military operation,"
I said. Looking around at my troops. Tomas had joined us on
the bridge—a logical addition to the team. "Engineer Stramm,
how big is this device that we have to unload?"

"Including the graviton container—I would say no bigger
than the captain's chair." We all turned and stared at the chair.

"That small?"

"Of course, it is electronic after all. And it operates at the
molecular level."

"How much does it weigh?" Tomas asked.

"I would guess about twenty kilos. I'll weigh it for an exact figure."

"How much will it weigh when it is full of gravitons?" I
asked, smug in my technical expertise.

"Exactly the same, of course," he snapped, mighty in his

knowledge. "Since gravitons have no mass." Implying that only a total fool wouldn't know that. I hit back with another hard one.

"But the machine will still weigh sixty kilos on the planet. Not easy to lift."

"No problem," Stramm said—was that a curl to his lip? "I'll put wheels on it."

I visualized the lower airlock . . . and the next problem. "So you put wheels on it and we roll it down to the open lock and onto the ramp. Which, as I remember, tilts down from top to bottom. How do we stop it from running away?"

"The ramps tilts about fifteen degrees. I'll arrange some pulleys to make a relieving tackle. With a monofilament cable. Breaking strength over a thousand kilos."

I had one more question before I retired from the field. "Reaction mass! You are going to need an awful lot to land— then take off fighting a three-G gravity."

"We have more than enough. The porcuswine have topped up the tank."

There were was one final question from Tomas.

"There isn't enough oxygen in the atmosphere to keep us alive . . ."

"We have oxygen breathing apparatus. You'll have to wear them," Stramm said.

"Then we are ready for the landing. I'm volunteering my-self and my men to handle the operation," Tomas said, and smiled. "I imagine you will prefer their technical background— rather than that of the farmers."

"No question!" I said. "I shiver at the thought . . ."

Captain Singh raised another and most important point. "At the end of three months, when we return, how do we find the machine?"

"I'll put a transponder on it." Smugly. This was Stramm's final technical victory.

"We'll go and get the collector ready now," Tomas said. "I'll give the engineer a hand."

After they left, Captain Singh made a tick on a list. I thought of another problem.

"Aren't you worried about an air leak from the lower lock outer door? We had to burn the seals away after we first landed on that fractious planet."

"No. Stramm put a new gasket on the outer door during our stay in the spaceport—so we can keep atmospheric integrity in the ship. We're on course now to this heavy world . . ."

"That's it! Heavyworld—we needed a name for it."

"We'll be in orbit around Heavyworld in a few hours."

Something was nagging at the edges of my brain. Something important. We landed. Then what . . . ?

We would all weigh three times as much after we were on the planet. Passengers would be on the acceleration couches for the landing. They would have to stay on them afterward. Uncomfortable but necessary. But the animals! I had a terrifying vision of what would happen . . .

"After we land . . . what about the porcuswine? The boars will weigh three tonnes! If they try to walk—broken legs—gnashing tusks—no way!" I turned to the intercom.

"Elmo to bridge soonest. Elmo to bridge . . ."

He went pale when I told him the problem he would face.

"My goodness . . . that's shore no good, no good at all.

Them sows, they'll be no problem. They'll lie down, right lazy. The piglets, the small ones, they'll nurse . . ."

"But the boars—"

"Yep, the boars . . ." He echoed hollowly, face even paler.

I dredged through forgotten memories of my dismal past life down on the farm, groped around among the shards. Vague memories of ill porcuswine—that was it!

"Swine fever—we had a plague of it once!"

"Them days happily long gone, Cousin Jim. Inoculation at birth done wiped it out and—"

"Shut up," I suggested. "I remember now, we had to inject them in the snout, where there were no quills. The sows were bad enough, but—"

"Them boars, they shore didn't take kindly to that, let me tell you! Had to knock them out first."

"How?"

"Well, you know. Use the tranker."

"What's that?"

"Little teeny machine. Shore don't know how it works, but works fine each time. Just hold it near the back of the neck an' press the itty-bitty button. Bam! Some sort of radiation or something and that old boar just lays down and starts snoring!"

"And you have this tranker with you?" Gritting my teeth and resisting the urge to strangle him.

"Dunno . . ." My fingers arched, reaching for his neck.

"Suppose so. Should be in the swine-med box. If'n we didn't toss it away . . ."

I seized his arm and rushed him, complaining reedily, down to the animal deck, past the drowsing sows—to the storeroom beyond. Tore open the swine-med box . . . looked in . . .

"I'm not shore, but that little dingus does looks like it."

I reverently took out the shining metal device and seized it by the handle.

"Yep, that's it, all righty!"

Fought hard against the urge to try it out on his neck . . .

I escaped the porcine grunts and swinish squeals for the peace of the engine room. The laborers appeared to be finishing up their work on the graviton collector. Mounted now on sturdy wheels, it looked very much like a rolling file cabinet lashed to a sturdy block and tackle. With a metal lunchbox strapped on.

"Hit it." Stramm said and Tomas pressed the button on the small radio he carried. A light flashed on the lunchbox and it bleeped.

"Transponder works fine," Tomas said.

"Ready to go whenever the captain wants to," Stramm said. "After we truck this down to the airlock and secure it outside."

I climbed the stairs to the bridge and reported to the captain.

"Collector is ready to roll. The passengers will be on the acceleration couches when the order is given. Elmo and his farmers are bedded down on the sty deck. He said he'll need about an hour to secure the animals."

"And you?"

"I'll be with the collector crew on the lower deck. We have mattresses there for the landing. The sooner the job is done, the sooner we can take off again."

I did not add that Angelina, reluctantly acknowledging that she had no role in the operation, would take to her acceleration couch.

"Fine. Tell them to start securing the animals. We'll make the landing when they're done."

Stunning the boars went far more smoothly than expected. Gnasher looked at me and grunted a swinish hello, then thudded to the deck when Elmo reached out and activated the tranker at the back of his giant neck. He simply collapsed— and snored. Ignored by the others—who quickly joined him with their grating wheezing.

I joined the volunteers on the lower deck, where they lay on mattresses just outside the inner lock door. The collector was locked against the bulkhead. The cable secured to it, the block and tackle attached to a cleat on the floor. A half-dozen oxygen tanks were mounted on the wall above. I told my radio to turn on.

"Everyone is ready, Captain."

The wall speakers crackled to life.

"Starting final approach. Acceleration couches now. Landing deceleration begins."

The landing seemed to go on for a very long time. When the jets finally cut out we knew that we were down on Heavyplanet. Only it did not feel like that—the three gravities felt like the acceleration was going on and on.

"Here we go," Tomas said, struggling to his feet and staggering over to the lock activation switch, pushed it. He swayed, almost fell, then hit the ramp control as, with great groans of protest, the inner door opened wide. Tomas, pressed hard against the bulkhead, slid suddenly down onto his knees, gasping for breath. I staggered to the bulkhead, pulled free an oxygen tank and passed it to him. Grabbed one for myself since breathing took a distinct effort.

When the inner door was open we all struggled into the lock chamber. The easiest way was to roll off the mattresses and move forward on all fours. Once inside we put on the oxygen tanks and masks, rolled the now ponderous machine into the airlock with us. The inner door ground slowly shut.

"Opening outer lock door now," Tomas said as he hit the switch. The seal popped—as did our ears—as the pressure equalized in the lock chamber. The slowly opening door revealed a gray wasteland of desolate and rocky ground set against an ominous black sky. A chill wind blew dust in around us.

"All right, let's go to work," Tomas said. "Wolfi and I first. If we can't finish the job the next two men take over." He released the shackles on the machine and it started to move— but was snubbed by the block and tackle. Then it rolled slowly down the ramp as the cable payed out. At the foot of the ramp they stopped when they reached the ground.

"Leave the cable attached . . ." Tomas gasped. "Use it when we . . . come back . . . to pull it . . . into the ship."

"Don't try to stand up," he said, his voice muted by the oxygen mask. "Stay on all fours—divide your weight."

Leaning forward, working together, they rolled the reluctant mass away from the ship. It was exhausting work, straining their strength to the limit. They had progressed about three meters when Tomas struggled to raise his hand.

"Next . . . team . . . now . . ."

I crawled forward on all fours and took over. Pushing the collector across the ground with the cable paying out behind us.

I don't think I have worked that hard in my entire life—and

sincerely hope that I won't have to ever again. We pushed the awful weight against the immense grip of gravity, then stopped. Others took over. We crawled, like infants on all fours, strained at the machine, moved it a few reluctant centimeters . . .

"Captain here . . ." The voice echoed in my head and it took long blank moments for me to realize it was my radio.

"Yes," I gasped out.

"Stramm says you have gone far enough—takeoff blast won't reach that far."

Speaking was hard but I finally made the others understand. "Done . . . back to ship . . ."

It was just survival that kept us going. If you didn't keep moving—on bloodied knees and hands—you were going to die. No one else could possibly help you.

Kept going through a red haze of pain, felt something pushed against my hand. The cleat on the cable's end. I blinked at it, not understanding.

"Pass it back . . ." Tomas gasped. "Last man . . . leave it out of blast range!"

I pushed it back to the man crawling behind me, then went on.

I felt the cold roughness of the ramp beneath my hands. Left smears of blood on the metal as I forced my way up it and into the ship. Could only collapse helplessly onto a mattress. Gasping hoarsely for breath.

Then, from a great distance I heard a voice. Tomas's?

"Close lock . . . counted . . . all back inside . . ."

"Radio on—" I rasped hoarsely. "Close the lock . . ."

I must have lost consciousness about then. Was scarcely aware of a greater weight on my chest. It must have been takeoff.

When I opened my eyes again I became aware of feeling almost weightless, of breathing easily, tearing off my oxygen mask and moving without effort. I sat up slowly, dizzy at the effort, saw Tomas looking at me. Smiling.

"We did it, didn't we?"

I could only nod in mute agreement.

CHAPTER **28**

THERE WERE TOO MANY PEOPLE around us, too many congratulations. Well-intentioned slaps on the back that hurt—as did every muscle in my body. It was Angelina who rescued me, led me, supported my stumbling progress to—wisely— the bar, not my bed. Collapsed on the lounger, feet up, hand and knees balmed and bandaged, I raised the chilled glass shakily and drank.

"A decided improvement," I said. Hoarsely. My throat still raw from the oxygen.

"You were wonderful—you and the others. The captain caught the whole thing with the hull cameras. At times we were sure it couldn't be done . . . then we saw the blood on the ramp . . ."

I put my finger to her lips. "What's done is done. The collector is now collecting at a greatly increased rate. The captain explained it all to me—lectured really. It seems that the collection rate goes up by the square of the gravity. So instead of grabbing three times as many positrons, our busy machine is storing nine times as many as normal . . ."

"More Manhattanteeny?" she asked, topping up my glass as I held it—shakily—out to her. End of physics lecture.

"Do you know when we will land on the next planet?"

"Captain said tomorrow morning is target time. He wants a full day to run tests before he opens the airlock."

"After our recent planetary experiences, who can blame him."

Planet time was just a few hours after ship's time. After a few more cocktails—and a painkiller—I slept the sleep of the just. Awoke at dawn feeling sore but almost human. After breakfast it was back to the acceleration couches for the landing. I must admit that I dozed off until the captain's voice drilled into my consciousness.

"Boss to bridge. Captain Schleuck to bridge."

I stretched and yawned. "Coming with me?"

"Not this time. Pinky isn't too perky—and Elmo promised to have the porkermedbot take a quick examination."

"A fine machine—that even he can't foul up. If he remembers to press the ON button." I joined the others on the bridge.

"I've been running an orbiting survey of the planet, and sent a surveybot to analyze the air and sample the biosphere," the captain said when I had joined the party. Stramm was already there and Tomas arrived soon after me.

Data and figures were scrolling across the screen. "Gravity is ninety percent of normal—we'll all enjoy that. Oxygen percentage just about normal." He pointed to a row of figures, all flashing green.

"No pathogens in the atmosphere. Plenty of pollen floating about, The same is true of the soil. No pathogens. Lots of vegetable matter."

He leaned back in his chair and steepled his fingers.

"I would say that this planet is ready for further onsite inspection and I volunteer for the job. I haven't been off the ship in living memory—"

"No way!" I said. As firmly as I could. "You are the indispensable man on this space safari. Besides, we did promise Angelina the pleasure of naming this new world."

"You did remember," she said as she came onto the bridge. "And of course Jim will insist on joining the primary recon. Which is fine—as long as I step down first. Agreed?"

There were no dissenting votes. There dare not be.

The image of a tiny blue planet was on the screen. The captain pointed to two white dots off to one side. "It has two moons, so there should be measurable tides." He zoomed in and the planet rotated slowly as he tapped the controls.

"A water world for the most part—but there is one large landmass, with a chain of islands nearby. They are steep-sided, obviously the summits of a mountain. No flat areas for us to land on them. But I did find what could be a possible landing site on the continent."

The image rotated, stopped—and zoomed in. Down through a thin cloud layer, to the landmass below. Stopped above tree-top level.

"There appears to be a planet-wide jungle, with the

occasional small clearing, wide beaches all around it—but here is what I found along the coast."

Our viewpoint lifted, drifted to one side. A large bay opened up, bordered by a wide green arc.

"This is the place," the captain said. "I checked the geo-radar. About a meter of soil above solid bedrock. This portion of the landmass—bordering the bay and the bay itself—seems to have been lower at one time, then was inundated by the sea. It must have risen again, in recent geological history. Grass, or something that acts like grass, recolonized the land. But the trees aren't present. The surface appears to be quite smooth."

"Looks ideal," Tomas said, adjusting the controls for a closer look. "Grass on soil over solid bedrock. In all my years in command of a spacer I have never seen a better landing site."

"Then the ayes have it," I said. "Are we landing there?"

"Possibly," the captain muttered. "Tomas and I want to do another detailed survey. We'll be landing in about an hour if the location is still the best."

"Fine. Angelina and I will get the basic gear ready for a first recon."

After we finished our drinks the basic gear proved very basic. Good walking boots. Two cameras. A pack with sampling gear. And our never-parted-with weapons.

"A brave new world," Angelina said. "I'm looking forward to visiting it."

"And naming it!"

"Of course."

The landing was smooth, the passengers excited, the porcuswine squealing for fresh pastures. As were we all. We waited by the lower airlock as the inner door swung open. I averted my eyes from the now-dark smears on the ramp; the bandages on my knees reminder enough.

Once the inner lock was sealed the outer one opened. We sniffed the fresh-smelling and hot, damp air and stepped out onto the ramp and down to the green, flat mass on the ground below.

"Hot," Angelina gasped. "Like walking into a sauna . . ."

"That's it!" I said.

"What?"

"You have just named the planet. Sauna."

"You're right—it fits. Sauna it is."

I bent down and looked at the ground cover of Sauna. Not grass, but a spongy mass of stems and tiny leaves. Thin stems on top—with thicker ones below. It stretched uniformly to the narrow beach with the blue ocean beyond.

"Report." The captain's voice echoed in my head.

"All fine so far—and the planet will now be known as Sauna."

"Fine. We'll need ocean water samples. But be careful. It's warm. The ocean seems to be a uniform forty degrees near the shore."

"Will do."

I turned to Angelina who was staring at the not too distant green wall of the jungle. "I wonder what is going on in there?"

"We'll soon find out—but the captain wants some water samples first."

We walked towards the ocean and the wide beach. Small waves breaking and rippling up the golden sand. We went on towards a shallow tide pool there. At its edge I put down my pack and dug out a sampling vial.

"I don't like the look of that water," Angelina said.

"Like why not—wildlife?"

"Not that. Just come over here."

I did. The water had a yellow tinge in the shallow edge of the pool. And it was seething slowly. Tiny bubbles that appeared to rise from the sand and break when they reached the surface.

"It looks like it's boiling," she said. "Be careful."

I was. I put the sampling vial down and dug out a pair of plastic gloves. Put them on before I dipped the vial in and took a sample. "Looks harmless enough," I said as I sealed the vial.

"Look at your gloves now."

I did. They had lost their transparency where they had been immersed in the water, and were now a murky white. I dropped the sample into the bag. Then pulled the gloves off—not letting the stained plastic touch my skin—and dropped them onto the sand.

"The first interplanetary litterbug," I said. Neither of us smiled.

"Let's see what the trees have to offer," she said. "I've had quite enough of the ocean."

As we walked towards it we began to appreciate the enormous scale of the jungle. Massive trees rose up—reaching thirty, forty meters above the ground. Instead of leaves they were covered with green, spiny growths. Thick spikes at the branches, then growing out to form tiny and tinier spines. Like living barbed wire.

Below and between the trees there was a prolificacy of green plants, both big and small. Some had large flattened leaves. There were golden globes hanging from some of the boughs—and flowers with all the colors of the spectrum.

"Looks impenetrable," Angelina said, stopping before the green wall of growth.

I pulled on plastic gloves again and took a long pair of tweezers from my pack, then prodded one of the vicious-looking green thorns. It was squishy, and bent easily.

"They're very soft," I said, and pushed my arm in through the tangled growth to seize a golden globular fruit. It burst when I touched it and warm liquid dripped from my fingers. I held a sampling container under it until it was full.

Then the alarm siren sounded from the ship. Angelina and I turned as one—her gun drawn and ready. I was slower, since I had to peel the gloves off first. The siren died and there was the sound of distant shouting from the ship. An instant later a large black form thundered down the gangway and out onto the green.

"Looks like Gnasher wants a bit more tusk and trotter room," I said as our guns vanished.

"I don't blame him. Must have been the smell of fresh air."

He was trotting resolutely about, sniffing the air and grunting happily. He turned his back on the ocean and trotted towards the green wall of the jungle.

"Shouldn't we try to stop him?" Angelina asked. "The plants . . . we don't know anything about them."

"He does. A porcuswine's sense of smell is second to none."

Gnasher snatched a mouthful of the green ground cover as he walked, tearing up a great swathe of greenery and chomping happily on it as he walked.

It was very different when he reached the edge of the jungle. He stopped suddenly—grumbling loudly. Then he poked his massive head in among the greenery.

Pulled it quickly out squealing in anger. Turned away, still grumbling. Then began to root again in the ground cover.

"That message is clear enough," I said as I bent and pulled up a length of vegetation. "This stuff is palatable enough, but stay clear of the jungle."

We collected more samples, sweating and hot, and brought them back to the ship. Elmo and some of his mates were waiting on the ramp. The inner port was now closed.

"He ain't hurt none, is he? Went right through the gate, knocked Lil' Abner down and nearly trampled him . . ."

"He's doing fine. He's staying away from the forest but is making a feast of the ground cover."

I held my sample up, prodded the black lumps hanging from it. "He's chomping his way through these tuberous growths—really enjoys them."

"It's safe for the herd then?"

"If he doesn't keel over soon I imagine it is."

When the inner lock opened the porcuswine had made Elmo's mind up for him. We stayed behind the door as the herd thundered by. Followed closely by the farmers: not thundering. The chill air that washed over us was a benediction.

"Best take these samples to the captain," I said without much enthusiasm.

"Stopping on the way for a chilled drink at the bar," the ever-practical Angelina said.

We brought the drinks jug to the bridge with us. So we could loll in cool comfort while Stramm and the captain labored over the analysis. The machines were fast, the readouts excruciatingly detailed.

"We will be able to stay here until we have to go after the gravitons," the captain said, holding up the printouts. "A most interesting planet." I pointed and he filled a glass for himself before he dropped into his chair.

"While the analyzer was analyzing the computer came up with a related reference." He flipped through the sheets.

"Here it is. An exobiochemist from galaxy-famed MIT— Murkee Institute of Technology. A Professor Doctor Merkler. He writes about a planet that sounds very much like this one . . .

"Many times, early in planetary development a planet will pass through a stage when, while still molten, lightweight metals and other elements rise to the surface. Occasionally large deposits of sulfur dominate available elements as the planet cools and solidifies. Exhaled steam and other gases form the oceans and atmosphere. In a young planet—early in its development like this one—sulfur is dissolved in the oceans. So much that, in essence, they consist of sulfuric acid with a pH of three. There are immense exposed quantities of sulfur under the sea. Very inimical for life. But the landmass is different. When the water evaporates from the ocean it is free of sulphur. Through the aeons the vegetable life has grown and proliferated. In the race for survival different plants have developed many poisonous compounds."

Angelina nodded. "Crusher must have smelt or tasted them—and avoided them. But these growths we brought back are different." She held up one of the tuberous black vegetables.

I nodded agreement. "It makes sense. Landmasses are still in transition here in this early geologic era. When the sea recedes—as it has here on our landing site—the soil left behind is heavy with sulphur compounds. Over a great period of time the ground-covering plant has mutated and survived in the sulfurous environment. It propagates vegetatively by means of these tubers. It doesn't produce seeds. Instead these tubers store food. Then it develops eyes—like a potato—from which new plants grow. It is these stored starches that the animals now enjoy."

"Could we eat them as well?" Angelina asked.

"Undoubtedly. And I volunteer Elmo to be the guinea pig," I helpfully suggested.

Angelina ignored me and poured another round of drinks.

I asked the important question.

"Can we stay here safely for three months?"

"Assuredly so," the captain said. "There will be acid-free surface water that will be potable, though we may have to distill it first. These ground tubers may be edible, which will save on our frozen food supply—"

"And will undoubtedly taste better," Angelina said. "Let's do it!"

THEY WERE LAZY DAYS. THE tubers of the abundant ground cover—quickly named terpomoj—proved to be nutritious and tasty. Miz Julia and her coworkers soon began to serve them in many tasty ways; seasoned and fried, mashed, cold in salads and adding flavor to the frozen meat stew. We prospered.

Although it was still a sauna during the day, the atmosphere was most comfortable once the sun had set. Tables were set up and we dined alfresco under the light of the moons. Tents were erected to protect us from the many showers and we lived outdoors more and more. The swine grew fat and happy—even Pinky despite Angelina's attempts to keep her figure under control. The absence of animals of any kind— including insects—made for an easy existence.

The weeks, then the months, sped by and it was almost a surprise when the captain called a meeting.

"We'll be leaving soon, so it is time to make our plans for departure."

Reality returned. We had to end our holiday and prepare for takeoff. Sporting our new tans and very improved figures, the ugly reality of Heavyworld loomed in the near future.

CHAPTER 29

IT WAS THAT MAGIC TIME; the imminent arrival of the afternoon cocktail hour. I intended to forget about the presence of Heavyworld—growing ever closer. And the labors we would soon have to do there. For the moment, at least, blessed forgetfulness. I was just polishing some glasses in the bar, humming as I scanned the labels on the tiered bottles, when Angelina came in.

"A truly perfectly timed arrival, welcome."

"Not quite perfect," she said softly. I raised my eyebrows.

"You have a visitor who would like to talk to you before you hit the sauce."

"Anyone! As long as it's not Elmo."

"It's Elmo."

I sighed a shuddering sigh. Bite the bullet. Get it over with. Look forward to the drowning of sorrows. Later.

"Yes, ahah . . . of course . . . lead him forward."

"Already here, Cousin Jim." Appearing like a bad memory in the doorway. "First off, want to tell you, we all appreciate what you and them other fellers did on Heavyworld. It was like, you know, kind of great. If you know what I mean . . ."

Black memories swept over me, silenced me.

"We all want to thank you—for what you did that day," Angelina said, with great warmth in her words.

"You said it, Miz Angelina. What I woulda said iffen I had the words. And me and the boys been talking, and we figured a way so that you wouldn't have to do it again."

The meaning of his garbled syntax cut through my growing depression.

"That's right. We been talking and got the boys from the Brutal Barbell Club to volunteer—an' they were right willin' to, let me tell you!"

What was he on about? Never use one word when ten will do better. A growl rumbled deep in my throat.

"Have them come in," Angelina said. Was she involved in some complex agrarian plot? Before I could speak the boys filed silently into the bar. My jaw wanted to drop.

Shuffling, embarrassed, wide of neck, thick of thigh— each of them over two meters of bulging muscle.

"They world champions at the weight-lifting championships!" Elmo said paternistically. "They want to bring that there machine back—instead of you and them scrawny little fellers."

Light streamed into my forebrain. Of course! No intelligence required for the retrieval job. Just brawn, which was here in swollen abundance.

"Yes!" I said in instant reply. "Speaking for the other scrawny little fellers—the job is yours!"

They beamed and blushed, ripples of happiness spread from biceps to triceps to pecs. They shuffled hurriedly out and the spirit of largesse possessed me.

"Join us in a drink, Cousin Elmo. I'll crack out a bottle of the best."

And I did—for this was indeed a most wonderful day.

I was still smiling happily when the captain called a meeting on the bridge. When I entered I saw that Heavyworld's menacing presence filled the viewscreen. The captain, Stramm and Tomas stared at it in gloomy unhappiness.

"I bring good news to eliminate the aura of doom that presses on all here." They looked dubiously at me, obviously thinking I had lost most of my marbles. "We have some sturdy volunteers on this ship who will crawl out in our place to retrieve the collector."

Despair turned to joy when I had explained.

"I must supervise them," Tomas said.

"By all means," I agreed. "From a prone position on a soft mattress."

Our second visit to Heavyworld was a major improvement over the first one. As we dropped into orbit the boars snored happily, the sows lay down gruntingly. The largest yearlings joined their elders in electronic-induced sleep—no broken legs this time. I lay on the acceleration couch and blessed the overweight musclemen who would make this visit a success. With the large viewscreen on the wall before us we had a ringside view of the action.

As soon as the landing jets cut out, and the 3Gs jumped on us, I saw Tomas struggle to a sitting position.

"No grandstanding," he ordered as the airlock door

ground open. "I know you guys can probably do it—but don't try to stand up."

They nodded in agreement.

"If you are on all fours you have half the weight on any one limb. Shuffle. That's why you have pads on your knees and hands. OK—let's move into the airlock."

They grunted as they pushed up onto their elbows—then onto their knees. But they did it. Moving a lot more smoothly than we had. Tomas followed slowly afterward, collapsing, gasping for breath, onto the padding inside the airlock.

The heavy mob waited patiently until the inner door closed and the outer one—creaking loudly—slowly ground open.

"First team forward—" Tomas had to pause until the coughing fit ended. "You see the cable end out there—with the loop on the end?"

Slow nods.

"Get over to it. Drag it back inside here."

They moved out. Slowly and patiently. And steadily. I remembered our shaking and painful progress. Not these musclemen. This was a situation where brains did not matter at all. When they were halfway to the cable Tomas called out.

"Second man wait there. First man retrieve the cable and drag it back to your second man."

Without hesitation the leader crawled slowly and steadily on.

Stopped when he reached it—breathing hard. Stayed immobile until he got his breath back. Reached out shakily to grab the loop. Then, with muscle-bulging effort, clipped it to the hook affixed to his belt. Crawled in a half-circle and started back.

I found myself sitting up, sweating with the effort, knowing what he was feeling. Lay back down with a gasp. With a great effort Angelina brought her hand over and held mine. I smiled back at her.

"Better him . . . than you . . ." she gasped.

I gave her a feeble nod in return.

These musclemen were the greatest. Slowly and steadily, with no fuss, they passed on the cable, dragged it back after them. The second team met them at the foot of the ramp, kept the cable moving steadily—until they dropped it over the hook on the block and tackle.

The first team leader struggled to raise his fist erect and shake it.

"Done . . . !" he said, smiling through the sweat that was pouring down his face.

The rest was routine. Winch in the collector and lock it into place. Heavy work, but swiftly done. With all the equipment secured for takeoff we were soon back in orbit and away from the crushing gravity.

When I felt up to it I made my way to the engine room. Where Stramm was pouring the last of the gravitons into the hopper on the Bloater Drive. At least I presumed that was what he was doing. Since gravitons are massless, weightless and invisible it was hard to be sure.

But they were the key element that was going to power the Bloat that would get us out of here.

We sincerely hoped . . .

There was no wood to knock on in the spacer so I crossed my fingers instead. Crossed my eyes as well, in an appeal to the invisible gods of superstition.

Stramm closed and sealed the cover on the graviton tank, looked at the gauge.

"Full of positrons and rarin' to go for a super-size Bloat!" I said.

"Maybe," he said, tapping the gauge and looking at the readout again. "Maybe we should have left it on Heavyworld longer . . ."

"It's full! Brimming with gravitons. More than enough to Bloat us back to the civilized side of the galaxy. To write a happy ending to the endless voyage of this spatial *Flying Dutchman!*"

His only answer was a weary shrug. Which I ignored. We went up to the bridge in silence.

The two captains were at the Bloat controls, running equations across the screen. Angelina was sitting by the plotting table, with the recumbent Pinky at her feet, snoring swinishly.

"She checked out fine on the porkermedbot. Just a touch of dyspepsia. From overeating." This required no response.

"We've settled on a course," the captain said, swinging about in his chair. "A bright star that appears to be halfway back to the nearest cluster of central stars. We should reach there in two long Bloats. With a course correction after the first. Any questions?"

Silence was his only answer. This was it. Our only chance. Make or break.

"Do it," Angelina said. Speaking for us all.

He activated the Bloat.

"The bar is now open and you are all invited," Angelina said. "Including the captain who is now officially off duty. Drinks—and snacks for all."

At these words Pinky's eyes flew open and she gave an

anticipatory grunt. Climbed to her feet and shook herself with a great rustling of spines.

THE SHIP WAS IN A relaxed and festive mood. The planet of gruesome Greenies was lost behind us in the depths of space. The strains and sprains of Heavyworld long healed and the perspiration of Sauna long dried. Great gravitons sped us Bloatingly towards our destination. We rested in the hands of fate. What would be, would be. We would find out soon enough.

A series of festive evenings were enjoyed by all. The Barbell Boys gave a demonstration of weight lifting and martial arts that was most impressive. Elmo led a combo of rustic musicians, who tortured our ears with musical combs and one-string and box banjos. Remembering my brief career as a stage magician, I gave a display of prestidigitory arts that drew great applause. Joy prevailed.

Until our first Bloat ended. We assembled on the bridge for this seminal event.

Waited and fidgeted until the Bloat popped and we emerged into normal space. Our target star was bright and central on the screen.

"A good Bloat," the captain said. "Now let's look at its spectrum." The figures rolled across the screen.

"Hot. Large. Can't be sure at this distance, but the perturbations indicate some occulting."

"Meaning?" Angelina asked.

"Satellite planets. Big ones. We'll know better after the next Bloat when we are much closer."

"How long?" I said.

"Two days. No more."

The parties were over. It was a time for introspection—and hope. It had been a long, long voyage. The end was well overdue.

Knowing the overwhelming anticipation of all aboard, including the porcuswine who had been penned too long, the engineer had rigged a large screen at one end of the dining room. For us. The swine would have to do without. A pickup and projector relayed the scene from the bridge, with the viewscreen enlarged and central.

As the final countdown approached, Angelina and I went to the bridge and joined a privileged view at the scene of the action.

The countdown this time seemed endless—but it finally did crawl to an end. The Bloat collapsed with a final *ping* and the viewscreen filled with blazing light for an instant before the filters clicked on.

Glaringly bright. There was a warning buzzer as the spectral analysis raced across the lower part of the screen. The captain recoiled, seizing the armrests on his chair.

"The spectrum—that can mean only one thing . . . this star is ready to go nova!"

There was crackle from the speakers as the radio turned on to receive an incoming broadcast.

"Welcome to Castor Epsilon. Even though this star is ready to go nova!"

CHAPTER 30

I'LL GIVE MY SHIPMATES THIS—they didn't panic. Even though there are few times in your lifetime when you have been told— twice—that the closest star to you is about to turn into an exploding nova.

The captain spoke—calmly!—into the mike.

"Radio contact. Identify yourself."

"Welcome newly arrived spacer—welcome to star system Castor Epsilon. Spectral analysis reveals that this star will go nova—any millennium now. So forget your troubles and let your stay here be a wonderful one! Welcome to Bronco Pete's Trading Post, a friendly satellite paradise!"

At this point the TV screen burst into life with the beaming face of a robotic Bronco Pete. Tanned, toothy, wearing a wide-brimmed hat with a high pointed top: I assumed that his head fitted up into the hat. The captain was not amused.

"Stop this recording. I want a human operator."

"So do I! Alas, the last human left over three hundred years ago. But our robot service is one of the best! Try our yummy steaks, aged over a thousand years at a temperature one degree above absolute zero. Stay in our hotel with the best room service in the known galaxy, featuring girls that . . ."

"Shut up!" the captain snarled. "Provide listing of services available."

". . . grrrrk. Available are Aardvark Steaks, Asteroid Tables, Apprehensive Counseling . . ."

"Stop. List communication facilities."

"Communications. Astral Database. FTL Comms . . ."

"Stop. Make available FTL Comms."

We looked on in silence. Dumbstruck. Was this true? Had the *Flying Dutchman* finally reached safe harbor? Was our voyage to nowhere finally reaching its end?

"Bronco Pete bids you welcome to the finest communication facility in this sector of space. Our Buckboard Roboboat is now on its way to greet you. To bring you and your dear companions here to enjoy our galaxy-wide acclaimed services. Payments of all kinds accepted, after bank clearance. Transport now latching to your upper spacelock as soon as portal dimensions are adjusted. There—attached! Please open outer door to enjoy the most exciting consumer experience of your life!"

We could hear the cheering from the farmers—and squealing porcuswine—from the decks below.

Stramm spoke in a calm voice, "Ask him if they have a graviton supply here . . ."

"I heard that, honored guests—and yes indeed—we do have the best gravitons in the known universe and at rock-bottom prices!"

Our cheers echoed the bucolic cries and grunts from our passengers below.

"Gravitons!" the captain said, relaxing back in his chair.

"Communications!" I chortled and punched the air.

"Steaks—fresh food!" Angelina reminded us. "Oh what a party we are going to have."

The three of us rose as one and headed towards the door.

"Stramm," the captain called back over his shoulder, "prepare to receive gravitons. Tomas, please explain to our passengers what we are doing."

"And tell them about the party," Angelina added as we reached the stairs.

We waited impatiently at the airlock as the outer hatch slowly opened. The airlock pressure indicator flashed red—then turned green as the pressure equalized with that of the docked craft. Its locks were open as well and enthusiastic music greeted us as we entered. Greetings as well from a hostessbot who waved us to cushioned seats.

"Welcome to Bronco Pete's—who now asks you to enjoy a free drink of your choice. First one is on the house! After that all future imbibements will be paid for with a credit card, cash or interstellar gift vouchers. So, name your potion!"

It was a brief trip and a happy one. I think we were all a little dazed by the quick transition from the depth of despair to the pinnacle of elation. It still had not sunk in that our endless voyage had ended at last.

We entered Bronco Pete's to a blare of bugles from a one-robot marching band. Who stayed right behind as we started down the gaily-decorated entrance hall. The music was overwhelming. It only stopped when the captain—wise in the ways of the commercial spaceways—slipped a coin into the cancel slot that was the robot's belly button.

The captain peeled off at the door marked GRAVITONS-R-US, while Angelina headed for BRONCO PETE'S SUPER SUPERMARKET. I made a beeline to COMMUNICATIONS.

"I am here to help!" the comm robot said, standing, vibrating with eagerness before a towering control panel.

I took out my memory file card, "Contact Inskipp," I said to it, and passed it over. The all-too-familiar number appeared on the call screen.

"That will be three thousand credits, plus galactic sales tax."

Eager robotic fingers seized my credit card and pushed it into the PAY slot. The machine made a throaty eructation and spat the card out onto the floor.

"There is no money in this account," the now surly robot said.

"Make that a collect call."

"Treble charges plus satellite sales tax."

"Do it—they can afford it."

"Booth three. Have a nice day—or night—whichever your choice may be."

Inskipp appeared on the screen. Already in full snarl.

"Do you know how long I have been trying to contact you, diGriz? There is a catastrophic emergency brewing up in . . ."

"My bad news is worse than yours. Let me tell you about some planets I have recently visited—and the deadly situations they harbor . . ."

Give him that—he managed to listen in silence to my tales of woe.

". . . of the lot Salvation is the worst. That deadly green mutation has made life a dismal hell for their own people—as well as the descendants of the original settlers."

"The Special Corps is already on top of it. Our OOGA branch."

"Ooga?"

"Office of Green Affairs. We'll add your planet to the list." He turned away from the screen and mumbled to an unseen companion, turned back. "General Caruthers, commander of OOGA, is with me now. He'll be on the ship that we are sending to bring you in. He'll explain then."

"Fine. But before my next assignment you'll have to transfer one million credits to my account—for incidental expenses."

He snarled—but nodded reluctant agreement. "Do you want it deposited to your credit card account or one of the secret ones we are not supposed to know about?"

"Your choice." As the call disconnected I made a mental note to have my banker son James do some swift account juggling.

It had been a long day and I had much to think about.

"Where is the bar?" I asked. The comm robot pressed a button.

"A guidebot is waiting for you without, honored sir," he smarmed, as he handed me back my rejected—and now topped up—credit card.

I could have done without the frontier theme, all logs and stuffed cows, in the saloon. At least I could bribe the Country and Rock–crushing band into silence.

I sipped from a cold one, puffed alight a thousand-year-old cigar, and counted off what had to be done—and now could be done.

The good ship *Porcuswine Express,* its tank topped up with bargain gravitons, could now complete its journey to Mechanistria. Without me.

Then, as soon as he arrived on this rustic satellite, I would brief General Caruthers, commander of OOGA, on the green tragedy of that unhappy world.

After completing whatever dismal duty Inskipp had in mind for me, Angelina and I would return at last to our holiday world for a well-deserved—and hard-earned!—holiday. I puffed and drank, very much at ease with the world.

Along the way Tomas and his escapee companions would return to their home worlds.

The good captain Singh would—if he wanted the job!—continue as master and owner of the spacer. With no regrets I would turn my back on the spacegoing sty and all who sailed on her.

"I thought I might find you here," Angelina said.

"I had no doubt you would. Drink?"

"Of course." She dropped into a chair, calling out *Sit,* as she did so. Behind her the overladen porterbot dropped with a clank to the floor.

"You'll never guess who I have been taking to," I said. As her drink, cool and frosted, rose up from the middle of the table.

"Inskipp. And he has a job for you that is already terribly long overdue."

"Oh reader of minds—it is true." I looked at the mighty

burden of packages she had bought. "But let us first celebrate! This is going to be the mother of all parties."

"Indeed it will."

I REMEMBER THE OPENING OF the evening's festivities, the many toasts, the magnificent meal, the many toasts, singing strange songs along with an off-key chorus, the many toasts . . . But the ending of the party is, for some reason, quite blurred.

When I struggled awake—lip smacking with a bone dry mouth—I had just enough energy in one feeble finger to press the dispenser button on the headboard of the bed. Managed to catch the Back From the Brink pill before it rolled onto the floor. Washed it down with a liter of water. Lay there until the vibrations stopped. Opened one undoubtedly bloodshot eye as Angelina appeared in the doorway.

"Quite a party," she said. "Enjoyed by all. Including the porcuswine—who managed to munch their way through a ton of mangle-wurzels. Coffee?"

"Yes nurse . . ." I rasped hoarsely as I struggled to sit up.

"The captain would like to see you on the bridge. As soon as you are fit."

"More coffee first, if you please."

As soon as it looked as though I would live, Angelina relayed another invitation. This one much more dubious than the last.

"I have been talking with the ladies—who would like to see us both."

"No men?" Hopefully.

"Well, just a few of them."

I didn't have to guess who would be heading the male posse. "After I meet with the captain." Putting off the inevitable as long as possible.

Tomas was already on the bridge when I got there.

"Glass of wine?" the captain asked; he and Tomas had filled glasses before them: a dust-covered bottle of red wine was open and breathing on the plotting table. "There are some excellent, well-aged wines in the satellite cellar here."

I sipped, savored, drank more. Just being sociable, of course.

"I've updated my charts from the satellite's memory bank," the captain said. "We can get to Mechanistria in five, six Bloats at the most. When we arrive this charter ends. What do you plan to do with this vessel then?"

I could think of a few snappy answers that could not be spoken in public. I took another drink; excellent wine. Noting my hesitation, he went on.

"I—and Captain Schleuck here—have a proposal to make."

"But before we do that," Tomas said. "We have to see to the other escaped prisoners, who are planning to return to their home planets."

"My organization will take care of their transportation."

Inskipp had grumbled over the cost, but in the end had agreed.

"I won't be with them," Tomas said. "I don't propose to return home. I've contacted my union there and they have already transferred my accrued back pay, sick leave and pension funds."

"And I have a bit laid by from my ship broker days," Captain

Singh added. "We would like to buy this ship from you. We rather like the old tub—as does Stramm who is ready to sign on as well."

"We are going to do scenic old-time tours of pastoral planets in a rustic spacer," Tomas added. "The retirees and veteran cruise passengers will love it."

"You're on!" I said, raising my glass. "To a happy future for the Bloat Family Tours!"

"And one thing more," I said. After we had clinked glasses and drank deep. "The ship is now yours. Prepare the documents of ownership and I will sign."

"But payment . . ."

"None. It's all yours now. I will get the money back, from my employers, whom I know will be thrilled at the thought." Or not, as the case may be. I felt no nostalgia, no regrets.

Just a sensation of immense, overwhelming . . . relief.

CHAPTER 31

DECORATIVE BUNTING FESTOONED THE WALLS; the tables were
heavily laden with cookies and jugs of hard cider. I nibbled
the one, eschewed the other. After the captain's wine I was on
the wagon for life. Or at least the rest of the day. I looked
around at the bucolic audience and tried to smile; did not quite
succeed. The dreaded Elmo rose to a spattering of applause.

"Ladies and folks, honored guests. Got a few words to
say . . ."

They weren't a few. Numberless would be a more accu-
rate description. My fragile constitution forgotten, I looked
longingly at the hard cider—and restrained myself. A spreading numbness set in and, after a century or two, I heard the
welcome words . . .

"To get to the business of the day, as the feller said. Miz
Julia has got something important to tell you."

She rose, blushing, nervously smoothing down her apron.

"I just want to say how much we have to thank Angelina and Jim for. So—thank you ever so much!" We nodded and smiled at the fervent round of applause. It died away when Miz Julia gestured for silence.

"It ain't much I know, but our knitting ladies have done this for you, Angelina."

She waved one of the knitting ladies forward, who produced a fine, multicolored sweater that she gave to Angelina. More applause—then I realized I was fated to be next when she glanced my way.

Through a gray haze I tried to do and say all the right things as the hideous knitted thing was passed over. For the first time—and undoubtedly the last—I was happy when Elmo rose to speak again.

"And we have a little something extra as the feller said. One of the boys—Little Billy—does what he calls scrumpshap"—*scrimshaw* a dozen voices hissed—"or whatever. Go on Little Billy, show us what you done."

Little Billy was one of the hulking weight lifters who had retrieved the collector from Heavyworld. Speechless, he shuffled forward, holding out a box. Managed to squeeze out a few words. "Carved from a boar's tusk, that's what."

It was a work of art. A fluid image of a porcuswine boar. Delicately done with each quill carefully delineated. My thanks were legitimate, his handshake crushing and numbing at the same time.

After all this heady excitement I did have a small cider. And fled as soon as possible.

Angelina joined me later in the bar. Where I was packing up the bottles.

"I shall miss them," she said sadly. "Pinky most of all. But you know what they say: get a piglet today, and have a sow tomorrow." I clunked another bottle into the box and she looked up. "Packing?"

"Moving. Into the satellite hotel. Captain Singh wants to leave as soon as possible—as I am sure do our passengers as well. Mechanistria will look very welcome after some of the planets we have been on. Peace, security, TV—all the wonders of civilization."

"And the porcuswine. How they must yearn for green pastures and open skies."

"As do we all."

And that was it. After we packed the last bag she left me to supervise the porterbots in our move to the hotel while she went and said her last last good-byes. To Pinky as well, I am sure. I made a final call from our hotel suite to captain and crew.

"And don't forget to send me a brochure of your first cruise . . ."

When the call had ended and the screen went black I emitted a deep and heartfelt sigh. After Angelina returned we went to the satellite lounge, with its immense viewport, and watched our home for so many months as it drifted free. It moved slowly into the distance, turning as it did.

Long seconds later it was illuminated by a pink glow. There was a familiar, distant Bloat pop. When the glow faded the *Porcuswine Express* had gone.

"I shall miss them all," Angelina said. "Pinky in particular."

There was the distant chime of a bell, followed by quick trumpet call from the wall speaker. "*Welcome newly arrived customers, welcome,"* a synthesized woman's voice cooed. *"The Cactus Lounge is now open for lunch—or dinner—whatever the case may be. Snacks or a whole roast cow—the choice is yours. Plus the finest beverages in the known universe . . ."*

"Silence," I ordered.

"It has been a long time since breakfast," Angelina said, turning away from the viewport. "Shall we?"

IF ANGELINA MISSED HER SHIPBOARD friends she never mentioned it. She frequented the Filly's Beauty Lounge for facials, rubdowns, tail-braiding, hairdos and all the other arcane rituals that women and fillies enjoy. I worked out in the gym, swam many laps in the pool—and did not miss my late incarceration in the spacesty in the slightest. May it have many a successful voyage in its new role as a cruise ship.

Better them than me.

Dinner was by candlelight, charmed by soft music from the Bronco-Busters Rodeo Band. Transformed in the evening to Martha's Musical Maidens. In addition to changing sex, the robots now played sentimental violin music.

"I think this is wonderful," Angelina said as we glided across the dance floor.

"Quite a change from down on the farm," I added as we executed a fancy bit of footwork.

But by the time the Special Corps spacer arrived I had had about enough of the robotic pleasures and looked forward to the great outdoors again. But without the green men around to spoil it all.

"Message from newly arrived vessel for Sire diGriz," the

speaker said. A moment later the smarmy robot voice was replaced by a crisp military one.

"General Caruthers here."

"Welcome aboard, General. Will you join us in suite One Prime One?"

"On the way."

The general was not one to lay about; the entrance bell chimed soon after.

"Open," Angelina said as she stepped forward. "Please come in, General."

She opened the door and the general came in . . .

A fake—a trap!

The general was GREEN!

Even as this realization churned across my brain I was leaping forward.

Fingers extended and pointed in the deadly larynx-destroyer blow. Which caused instant death.

Striking at that loathsome green throat . . .

Angelina's neatly extended foot caught me on the ankle— sending me sprawling on the rug. The general stepped back, eluding my snapping fingers. Angelina stood on my hand.

"Of course I'm green," he snarled. "Why else do you think I head OOGA?"

The red haze faded and I dropped, muttering, back into my chair. Nursing my crunched hand.

Angelina calmed things down. Relieving the general of his case and returning with champagne and glasses on a tray.

"That was not quite the reception General Caruthers deserved, Jim," she said as she passed him a glass of bubbly.

I muttered an apology—and took my glass with my good hand.

"I can understand your feelings," the general said. "Now perhaps you can understand the reaction of the Greens when they see a pink face. Pure hatred."

"But you seem immune to those feelings," Angelina said.

"That is the whole point of the Office of Green Affairs. The incident that caused the green changes, while not common, has happened a number of times in the past. One model of an early spacer atomic engine did emit, under unfortunate circumstances, gamma radiation. A sublethal dose of gamma irradiation causes Chloasma—from the Greek *chloazein,* to be green. The green skin associated with this condition, Chloasma, occurs due to an increase in melanin, of melanocytes and melanosomes. Usually, the condition is caused by UVB exposure that causes the green skin phenomenon. Unfortunately, due to the unusual effect of the gamma radiation, there is the added consequence that means they will have green skin with early maturity, increased fertility and lowered intelligence. Since gamma radiation can penetrate deeply it also damages the neuromelanin, which is active in the synthesis of monoamine neurotransmitters. This resulted in what you have seen. Hatred as well as a combination of heightened fertility with concomitant lowering of intelligence. But the condition is treatable."

"How?" I asked. Cooler and calmer; the champagne helped.

"The loss of these neurotransmitters is commonly found in advanced Alzheimer's disease, which is why these unfortunates suffered the loss of intelligence and the increased aggression when the very sensitive neuromelamine-producing cells were killed off by the gamma radiation. So, by injecting into the brain stem cells that have been engineered to turn into neurotransmitter cells, it is possible to restore brain function but leave the harmless green skin intact. The heightened fertility is simply due to the loss of intelligence. Too dumb to think but not too dumb to . . . well, you know what. Once you restore normal intelligence and introduce birth control measures fertility returns to normal.

"OOGA are peacekeepers. All of us, of course, are green. So there is not the instant hatred that a pink skin would elicit when landing on a newly discovered Green planet. In fact, we are warmly welcomed for the aid that we bring."

He drained his glass and put it on the table. Took what looked like a pencil from his pocket and placed it beside the glass. Then I realized that it was a recorder—the eraser on the end the microphone-eye.

"On," he said. "Now, I want you to tell me everything you know about this planet. The groups, subgroups, social organization, relations with nongreens—everything."

It took a very long time, for the general was a painstaking researcher. The champagne was long gone and I was growing hoarse, before he sat back in his chair.

"I think it is time we took a break. And I have orders for you."

"I'll get your case," Angelina said.

The general took some papers from the case, then passed an envelope to Angelina. "Can you identify this man?" he asked.

She frowned as she slipped out a photograph—then gasped aloud.

"It's Rifuti!"

"Good," he said, taking back the photo and putting it away. "We wanted to be absolutely sure. You reported that he was guilty of spacer sabotage. The Special Corps takes a very dim view of this crime. More so when Inskipp saw your name on the report. He was found, arrested, tried—and sentenced to ten years labor. He is in chains aboard my ship. He will serve his time wearing green makeup and helping us in our many tasks."

"I wish him all luck," she said. "Particularly after his prison term is increased after we report more criminal violations."

We smiled warmly at the pleasant thought.

"For you," he said, extracting an envelope. I had to sign four different receipts before he passed it over.

I pushed my thumb against the seal. It bleeped after it had read my print—then hissed open.

"If you don't mind," I said, pulling out the sheets of paper.

"By all means," he said. "I'm afraid my throat is a bit dry . . ."

"Of course," Angelina said, going for a fresh jeroboam.

It was a quick read. I read it slowly a second time, then settled back into my chair. Angelina gave me an inquiring glance.

"Interesting," I said. "Undoubtedly dangerous."

"But we've been there before," she said, smiling. "But I'm sure that it beats early retirement."

"Oh, it certainly does that!"

Just how dangerous we were soon to find out.

SOME TIME—A GOODLY TIME—LATER

WE WERE TRAVELING ON A stripped-down no-frills Special Corps troop transport. We were probably going to have been put in steerage class, but Angelina had a friendly talk with the captain before we unpacked our bags. An unlucky officer volunteered his cabin and vanished belowdecks. I was perfectly happy piling up rack time in the cabin since I had a lot of sleep to catch up on. Plus I needed time for the worst of my bruises to heal. Our last assignment had been a little strenuous—to say the least. I relaxed seriously—while Angelina became the toast of the officers' mess. She beat them on the pool table and took their money at poker. They loved it and came back for more. I joined her there after a postprandial siesta.

I still hesitated—if ever so slightly—at being among all the smiling green faces. But it was good acclimatization for the planet.

"I talked to the captain," I told Angelina. "We are due to land tomorrow morning. At six bells in the morning watch."

"What do you think that means?"

"Haven't the foggiest. I think he has been reading too many historical novels."

"Be nice to breathe fresh air again." She held her hand up and looked at her fingernails. "I think I had better do my nails."

She waved good-bye at the troops, while I ordered a ship's rum—a beverage I was increasingly quite drawn to. As I sipped I was joined by a green-skinned officer.

"I'm Major Bond. Jim Bond."

"We share a first name."

"I'm to be your guide. I'll have a squad with me."

"Guides . . . or bodyguards?"

"A little of both. There are still a few Pinkies on the Green parts of the planet. So we have to be careful. Emotions run deep."

"Sit. Rum?"

"Yes indeed. I'm still off duty."

"Have you been to Salvation before?"

"This is my second tour. It will be a fine planet once the new mutation proportion increases."

"Good luck. Have you ever had anything to do with the . . . Pinkies there?"

"I was liaison officer with one of the larger septs. Nice people. It is all pretty much at peace now. They are more than happy to stay away from the Greens. We have established separation zones to make sure they don't meet. Some fences, but mostly electronic detectors to assure that it stays that way."

"I'm looking for one group—one hunter in particular."

"Go to the Bureau of Pink Indigenous Affairs. They have complete records of all the groups. I don't deal with them anymore. I'm with FAN now—Food and Nutrition. We establish eating stations and train people to go there at the correct time. Instead of the old fight and feed way."

"That's a big job."

"It's a big planet. Population is now steady at a little over four million. That will go down steadily as the birth control management kicks in. Each year it will be a little better. Particularly after the average IQ rises."

"Years . . ." I sipped my rum and suddenly realized the magnitude of the Green operation. "Must cost an awful lot in the long run."

"Billions." He smiled. "But there are plenty of planets in the galactic league. They each contribute a few million a year for the Corps—so we are well endowed."

The spaceport was the same one we had first landed on so long ago. We sat in the rec room during the landing as the image below grew on the screen.

"There is the old port—the same buildings are there," Angelina said.

"But the abandoned spacers have been removed. And a modern port built on the other side. Three, no four, deepspacers there. One of them a dreadnaught class."

We landed on the pad close to the others. Gantries and ramps closed in as the locks opened one by one. We watched all the activity on what had once been a baited trap for passing spacers. A strange officer—green of course—entered the room, looking around. Came over and saluted when he saw us.

"Captain Stroud. I have transportation waiting. I was told that you are going to BOPIA?"

"That's the place."

"Please come with me."

I noticed that the waiting ground car had polarized windows that were mirrors from the outside. "Incognito?" I asked.

"A precaution," the captain said. "The first new generation has yet to be born. The sight of a pink face could cause a riot in the streets among the masses. Some of the brighter of the estroj, who are now working with us, manage to control their reactions to pink skin, though it requires intensive therapy and hypnotic indoctrination. It isn't until the third generation of gene therapy that the automatic hatred dies away."

"You have an awful long and hard job of work to do," Angelina said.

"It is worth it," he said grimly, pointing to the shuffling people beyond the barrier fence. "Without the help from OOGA, centuries ago, I would have grown up like them on my home planet. A short, wretched, stupid, hate-filled life. I am only repaying the service done to my own world."

We parked in the courtyard of a large, four-storied building.

"These are the offices of the Bureau of Pink Indigenous Affairs," the captain said when we had emerged from the ground car. "It is a major operation, as you can see. These nongreen people have been just as deprived as mine by the centuries of hatred. Providing medical aid, education, farming advice is most important to us."

"Speaking for all us Pinkies—I thank you," I said.

"Let me take you to the records section. Do you remember the names of the tribal leaders—and where they traveled?"

"Show me a map—I'll point out the places we visited. And the boss hunter was named Bram."

"I know him well!" Stroud said. "My first assignment was with his people. Let me check with our resident-commissioner there. How soon do you want to leave?"

"Now—or sooner," Angelina said.

Captain Stroud was efficiency itself. He checked records, made some calls—then showed us to the parking area where our transportation waited. A hulking brute of a vehicle; with wheels in front and tractor treads to the rear.

"All purpose," he said as he started the engine. "There are no roads yet where we are going."

It was an enjoyable ride through familiar country. We soon came to the pasture by the river where the porcuswine had been quartered. Splashed across the shallow river and into the low hills beyond. Then a green meadow opened before us with the familiar tents beyond. Smoke trails rose up into the windless sky.

Laughing children ran out to greet us as we braked to a stop. They swarmed around our vehicle—their elders close behind. I stood up and looked over their heads—to see a familiar figure emerging from one of the tents. I waved and shouted—and he hurried forward.

"How are you keeping, Bram?" I asked as he seized my arms.

"You said that you would be back," he said. "All the changes—the Green army that landed, the peace that followed—that was your doing?"

"We did promise you," Angelina said.

"You did. And I thank you from deep down in my heart. All the gratitude in the universe of stars is not enough—"

"Let's celebrate," I said, passing him down a box. "There are some interesting drinks in here that I think you will enjoy."

It was a celebration. A homecoming and a feast. The sun shone, the grilled venison was delicious, the laughter loud and long. Only the coming of darkness put a damper on the festivities.

"You will stay with us this night," Bram said.

"Of course," Angelina said. "And Jim has something he wants to give you."

I rooted in our bags until I found it and passed it over. A large, gold envelope.

"Open it," Angelina said. He held it up to the dying light and frowned and moved his lips, then said, "In the writing it says Bram. That is my name. I am learning to read, you see."

I opened the envelope for him, and in the last of the light, read

LIFETIME GALACTIC PASS. GOOD IN ANY SPACER
GOING TO ANY PLANET
Billing Instructions Inside.

He took it carefully, brushed his fingers across the raised lettering.

"What it says—that is true?"

"True as I was when I told you that someday you would visit the stars. Now you can do just that—"

"And visit you and Angelina?"

"We hope that will be your first stop," she said, taking his hands in hers. "Just let us know."

We left early next morning. I don't believe in wearing out a welcome.

"They are nice people," Captain Stroud said, splashing the halftrack across a watercourse and grinding up the bank on the far side. "That pass that you gave Bram—I never heard of anything like that before."

"Nor did we—until we came up with the idea."

"Wonderful!"

Not to a certain Inskipp, I thought. Because he was going to be billed for all the costs.

As we ground into the parking compound, Stroud said, "Are you going back again in the spacer?"

"That's what the captain said. A quick turnaround."

"I have talked to the staff here and they would be greatly pleased if they could meet you, to show you some of the operation here. Since you are the ones who are responsible for bringing this planet out of the dark ages of death and despair. They would like to thank you for this. For the countless Greens to come who will no longer have to live lives of total degradation . . ."

"Of course we will come," Angelina said. "It will be a great privilege."

This was the largest building in the compound—obviously the headquarters. No Pinkies here. Green skins and green uniforms were the norm. We passed a communications section where the troops—male and female—worked away at their screens. Scarcely glancing up as we went by. A number of them had red shoulder boards on their uniforms. One of these glanced up at us—kept looking for long seconds—before his attention went back to his keyboard.

And I recognized him—I think. One green face looked like any other. It still disturbed me.

"We have organized a small meeting," the captain said. "The senior staff would like to meet you."

"No problem."

They were gathered in a function hall—tables with glasses and bottles held out some promise. But before we could reach it a gray-haired officer, red boards on his shoulders, stopped before me.

This time I did recognize him.

"You are Overlord," I said. He nodded solemn agreement.

"I was. We met last under far different circumstances."

"We did indeed."

"I now work with the kind people who came here to help us. That is your doing, I suppose?"

"I'm happy to say that it was."

"I thought so. Now you must excuse me for there is much work to be done."

He turned and was gone. Angelina wasn't pleased.

"Isn't that the thug who wanted us killed?"

"The same. Reformed now."

"We hope . . ."

After many greetings, and some resolutely nonalcoholic drink, we left. Down another long hall.

"One more meeting," our guide said. "Our commanding officer would like to see you."

"A pleasure," I muttered.

The hall was empty except for a single uniformed man standing by a set of doors. He had red shoulder boards. When we drew close he turned quickly and threw open the doors.

A wave of men rushed out in silence—waving familiar clubs.

Overlord led them. Grimacing in hatred as he swung his club down.

I raised my arm—by reflex—and roared with pain as it struck.

Without turning I knew just what was happening behind me.

"Not in the heart," I shouted, staggered by the blow.

Overlord struck down again—then screamed as the bullet tore into his arm. Screamed again and fell as Angelina's carefully placed bullets hit him in both legs.

Her next three shots hit the legs of the next attackers, more bullets exploded in the ceiling above the crowd of attacking men. Chunks of plaster and a cloud of dust rained down on them. They stumbled over each other, fell. Dropped their clubs as they ran to escape the deadly fire. Moments later they were gone and just the wounded men lay huddled on the floor.

"You shouldn't have saved his worthless life," she said, her smoking gun muzzle questing and ready.

"Thank you," I said, rubbing my numb and painful arm.

WE ACCEPTED THE MANY AND fervent apologies. A doctor bandaged my arm, but only after administering a welcome painkiller. We were happy to see the armed guards who saw us safely back to our transport.

"I can understand Overlord's motives," I said. "Until I came along he ran this world as his own property."

"King of the dung heap," Angelina said, death still in her eyes.

"Yes. But it was his dung heap."

She took my good arm, and finally smiled.

"It's time to go home—don't you think?"

"Past time! Sunshine and peace, relaxation and all the civilized pleasures."

We laughed together and the future was bright and happy.

Until next time my subconscious whispered.

I ignored it . . .